PAPER-THIN ALIBI

P9-CLR-248

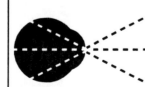 This Large Print Book carries the
Seal of Approval of N.A.V.H.

PAPER-THIN ALIBI

MARY ELLEN HUGHES

WHEELER PUBLISHING
A part of Gale, Cengage Learning

GALE
CENGAGE Learning

Detroit • New York • San Francisco • New Haven, Conn • Waterville, Maine • London

GALE
CENGAGE Learning

Wheeler Publishing Large Print Cozy Mystery.
The text of this Large Print edition is unabridged.
Other aspects of the book may vary from the original edition.
Set in 16 pt. Plantin.
Printed on permanent paper.

LIBRARY OF CONGRESS CATALOGING-IN-PUBLICATION DATA

Hughes, Mary Ellen.
  Paper-thin alibi / by Mary Ellen Hughes.
    p. cm. — (Wheeler Publishing large print cozy mystery.)
  "A Craft Corner mystery."
  ISBN-13: 978-1-59722-839-8 (pbk. : alk. paper)
  ISBN-10: 1-59722-839-7 (pbk. : alk. paper)
  1. Craft festivals—Fiction. 2. Poisoning—Fiction. 3. Large type books. I. Title.
  PS3558.U3745P37 2008
  813'.54—dc22   2008031745

Published in 2008 by arrangement with The Berkley Publishing Group, a member of Penguin Group (USA) Inc.

LT-M

Printed in the United States of America
1 2 3 4 5 6 7 12 11 10 09 08

For Suzanne and Stephen
No mystery why

ACKNOWLEDGMENTS

I am very grateful to Karlene Hicks, without whose talent and expertise Jo's gift boxes would never have taken shape. Heidi Abend gets my special thanks as well for her encouragement and support along with giving me a peek into her very creative mind. Dr. D. P. Lyle helped greatly and generously with the medical questions I needed answers to, as did John Baker concerning photography. If I didn't get things right, it's my own fault entirely.

Once again, my editor, Sandy Harding, used her amazing skills to keep these many thousands of words on track, as well as to bolster and encourage me generously. To my agent, Jacky Sach, who started the ball rolling. I'm very grateful to you both.

Of course many thanks to Janet Benrey, Ray Flynt, Debbi Mack, Trish Marshall, Sherriel Mattingly, Marcia Talley, and Lyn Taylor, who kept me on my toes as usual with their "on-target" critiques. I could never slip anything past any of them, though I'll probably keep on trying.

As for Terry, "thank you" is totally inadequate for the many ways he's helped. But — there you are.

CHAPTER 1

Jo was making good time, driving smoothly through light traffic along Route 30, just outside Abbotsville, Maryland, when a black SUV suddenly swerved in front of her. She hit the brake and immediately heard her boxes of jewelry shift behind her. Swallowing several explosive comments that sprang to mind, in consideration for her friend Carrie sitting next to her, Jo braced for the sound of spillage in the back seat, but heard, to her relief, only internal rattles.

"All I need is a car accident along the way because of an idiot like that," she grumbled as she resumed speed. She threw a quick glance behind her, but saw that the precious cargo, though shifted, appeared intact. "There all my handcrafted jewelry would be, spread across the highway, tires mashing them right and left."

"Not to mention us," Carrie pointed out mildly, adding a sudden, *"Ah-choo!"*

"Bless you. *We* have seat belts and air bags to protect us. My jewelry has only flimsy boxes. Allergies pretty bad today, huh?"

"Uh-huh." Carrie wiped her nose with a tissue and rubbed at her itchy eyes.

"What is it this time of year?"

"Tree pollen. In April the trees around here are pumping out their progeny like there's no tomorrow. This morning our car was covered with the yellow stuff. Just looking at it made my eyes tear up."

"Maybe it's time for shots?"

"Nuh-uh. No shots. Maybe a trip to the doctor's, for a prescription. I hate to, though. Our deductible is high and it'll cost us."

"Think about all those cases of tissues you won't have to buy. Or," Jo said, knowing Carrie's weak spot, "consider the delectable meals you'll feel more like cooking for Dan and the kids because you had a decent night's sleep." Carrie might skimp on care for herself, but she'd think twice about shortchanging her family. Carrie's response was another sneeze.

An overhead sign told Jo her exit was coming up, so she turned her focus back to the road and, unlike "idiot-driver," carefully checked the adjoining lanes and put on her turn signal before moving her Toyota into the right lane. Exiting the highway, she headed up Bell's Mill Road toward the Hammond County Fairgrounds. The Michicomi Craft Festival had set up there, one of several three-day stops in its annual cross-country tour, and Jo had managed to snag a booth to show her jewelry, a feat that pleased her immensely after sending in color slides of her work to the judges and waiting anxiously to hear their ruling.

Michicomi, she knew, was particular about which crafters were allowed to participate. Those who made it in were professionals — potters, leather workers, artists of all kinds. The prices on their wares corresponded to their skill level, but the crowds who flocked to the festivals were usually happy to pay them, as well as the price of the ticket that allowed them the privilege of doing so. Jo was excited to be a part of it all.

But she would need plenty of browsers to buy from her booth. Participating in Michicomi was a significant investment, a huge chunk from her tiny budget. The cost of renting a booth ran into the hundreds. Jo would need to sell a hefty amount of jewelry to cover that, as well as the costs of her supplies, and come out ahead.

"Thank goodness the weather's looking

good for the next few days," she said as she pulled through the gateway to the fair-grounds. The road leading in was paved only with crushed gravel, and the parking areas, as far as she could see, were mostly dirt with a sparse covering of tamped down weeds. "Imagine the sea of mud this would churn into with heavy rain."

"I don't have to imagine it," Carrie said, pulling out another tissue. "I saw it last August when we brought the kids here for the county fair."

"Really? That was just before I moved to Abbotsville. A mess, huh?" Jo saw a sign directing her to vendor parking, and drove on.

Carrie groaned, remembering that county fair outing. "There had been thunderstorms for several nights before. Let's just say they could have used some shuttle buses to get people around — pulled by water buffalo. Anyone selling hip boots that weekend would have made a killing. *Ah-choo!*"

"Gesundheit. Well, here we are!" Jo said, coming up to groupings of windowless, rectangular buildings, with several plastic tented stands set up near them. She pulled her Toyota into an empty space between two cars that were hitched to small trailers, the license plates indicating one had driven from Vermont and the other from Georgia. Rows of similar trailers, along with campers and vans, stretched out on either side, each with different colored plates. Transporting one's creations to a festival like this often involved much effort. Jo was grateful the festival had come within commuting distance of her adopted town, and that her wares — necklaces, bracelets, earrings, and pins — were compact.

"Thanks so much for helping me set up, Carrie, especially since you're not feeling that great."

Carrie flapped a hand dismissively. "We're all so excited you got into Michicomi. Most of your Craft Corner customers have never seen your jewelry designs."

"That's true." Jo had needed to temporarily suspend her beloved jewelry making with the busyness of setting up Jo's Craft Corner, a venture that sprang from Carrie's suggestion. Jo had needed to pull her life together after her husband Mike's fatal accident at their New York artist's loft. Carrie, a long-time friend who had settled in Abbotsville with her husband, Dan, saw an opportunity there for Jo to use her artist's background to make a living on her own, something her jewelry work, much as Jo loved it, wouldn't do.

So Jo had invested Mike's meager life insurance into the shop and shifted her life from big city to small town. The adjustment hadn't always been smooth but had proven satisfying, especially because of the new friends she had made, who had been extremely supportive at critical times.

Many of these friends had participated in her craft workshops, where Jo demonstrated the ins and outs of crafts like scrapbooking, wreath making, and beading. But few were familiar with the fine jewelry Jo could put together. This would be her first chance to display it all, and it would be like introducing her new friends to a beloved relative, an important part of her life they had heard about but never met. She was happily looking forward to it.

"Okay," Jo said, pulling out the letter of acceptance she'd received from the Michicomi organizers, along with her identification badge. "My booth is number 188 in building 10. I hope Dan found it all right this morning when he came to set up the display cases. Building 10 is that one over there."

Carrie studied it thoughtfully. "I think that might be where the hog pens were during the county fair."

Jo rolled her eyes. "Let's hope it's been

thoroughly deodorized since then, particularly the area around booth 188. Grab a box from the back, and let's find out."

Jo and Carrie reached into the disarranged boxes in her back seat and loaded up with as much as they could carry. As Jo led the way along the row of parked cars, she noticed a black SUV. Surely it couldn't be the one that had raised her blood pressure out on Route 30? Then the car's vanity license plate caught her eye: LW-GEMS.

LW? With New York plates? Could that be . . . ? No, no way, she thought again, shaking the whole idea off and continuing on to the building. She stopped to have her credentials checked by the security guard stationed near the entrance, then pushed along with Carrie through the clear plastic curtain that served as a door in the open-air, unheated structure. The place was a beehive of activity as other vendors worked at setting up their wares in the few remaining hours before the festival opened. They walked past one man carefully hanging panes of stained glass from hooks, and a middle-aged couple arranging their shelves with hand-tooled leather bags and wallets. Jo breathed deeply of their rich scent, and if she'd had a spare hand would have loved to touch as well. A collection of beautiful

15

handmade sweaters and vests caused Carrie to slow, while passing a booth of unique metal sculptures brought sad-sweet flashes of Mike to Jo's mind.

Jo checked overhead numbers as they progressed and saw they were getting close. She came to a booth filled with colorfully painted wooden toys with a "187" above it, and just beyond was hers: number 188.

"Here we are!"

Jo had contracted, because of cost considerations, for the smallest-size booth available — ten feet wide and eight feet deep. She'd then asked Carrie's husband, Dan, a professional home remodeler, to build display cases for that space. There they were, deftly fitted into place.

"Wow, Dan did a great job!" she said, setting her load down carefully on a Plexiglas surface. Made in sections that fit together in an L shape, the cases, she saw, provided the greatest amount of display area while allowing her customers to step out of the crowded aisle and partially into the booth to examine and try on their selections. "I'm so glad Dan suggested this arrangement. I owe him big time."

"Dan feels we still owe you, you know," Carrie said, sliding her own box next to Jo's, "as do I. If it weren't for you, who knows how his business would have survived that Parker Holt situation in January."

Carrie and Dan had been in real danger of losing their income when a client of Dan's was murdered and Dan's reputation — and worse — was jeopardized. They, on the other hand, had helped Jo so much after Mike's death, first in just getting her through it, then by helping her set up her new situation in Abbotsville, that she felt the scale tilted sharply in their favor.

"We won't get into that argument again about who owes whom," Jo said. "We're friends, and friends try to help each other. Let's just bring in the rest of the stuff so I can get into the fun of arranging it all. And so you can go check out that knitting booth."

"I did happen to notice some beautiful sweaters," Carrie said, grinning. Knitting was her specialty, and she generously applied her time and skills handling that section of Jo's Craft Corner. "I'd love to ask how one particular piece was done. But first things first."

Since Jo's booth turned out to be at the far end of the building, next to that end's curtained doorway, they exited there and walked back to Jo's car via the alleyway between buildings; the virtually unobstructed route proved much faster than the building's busy aisle. Two more trips transferred the rest of the cargo, and when she'd set down her final load, Carrie stood back to take it all in.

"When ever did you manage to make all this?"

"Some are things I made in New York and withdrew from consignments before coming here. But I've been working hard since I first applied for Michicomi."

"Please tell me you managed to sleep occasionally."

"Don't worry. I haven't run myself ragged — yet. But you know how I love working at my jewelry. What better way to relax than by doing what you love?"

"Hmm." Carrie gave her a skeptical look. As the mother of a teen and preteen, Carrie recognized sidestepping explanations when she heard them. "Well, you certainly haven't been over to our place much lately. The kids have missed you."

Jo was godmother to Carrie's fifteen-year-old, Charlie, and therefore had a soft spot for him. But she was inordinately fond of eleven-year-old Amanda as well.

"I've missed them too, and I promise to make up for all the lost time. If Charlie comes tomorrow to help me out, I'll at least

18

see him then. Is that still going to work out?"

"Absolutely. And I'll handle the craft shop, of course, while you're tied up here. Amanda will come there after school, and Ina Mae promised to pitch in now and then during the busier times."

"You guys are so great," Jo said, struggling with the lump that threatened to form in her throat. Jo remembered how retired schoolteacher and perennial dynamo Ina Mae Kepner had shown up unannounced at the shop to help out when Carrie had been briefly unable to work several weeks ago. Jo always felt she and Mike had some good friends up in New York, but nothing topped the people she'd encountered in Abbotsville. Most of them, anyway.

"Speaking of the shop," Carrie said, glancing at her watch, "Dan should be coming by soon to pick me up and take me there. He went to meet with a prospective client not too far from here after he set up your display cases, so this worked out great. I said I'd meet him at the ticket stand. And I think I have just enough time to stop at that knitting booth. Unless, that is, you need me to help set things up?" Carrie pulled out a Kleenex and rubbed at her nose, looking questioningly at Jo over the scrunched up tissue.

"Go," Jo urged. "I have a plan in my head for where I want everything to be, so it's best I do it alone. Really. And when you get to the shop, call the doctor's office for an appointment. Okay?"

Carrie smiled. "Maybe." She took off, and Jo saw her stopping to chat with the proprietor of the knitting booth, both reaching up to the sweater Carrie had spotted earlier.

Jo turned to her own concerns. Where to start? she wondered as she gazed at the pile. She decided to first arrange her meticulously labeled boxes in the order that she would empty them, then got to work, putting silver with silver, gold with gold. Her most expensive pieces went inside Plexiglas-covered viewing cases, and her less costly ones on top where customers could touch and try on.

It was time-consuming and tedious, but Jo still took special pleasure in it. Handling each carefully wrought item meant briefly revisiting the creativity that had gone into it and the joy she had felt as it progressed. The time flew by, and so absorbed was she that Jo barely noticed the controlled pandemonium going on about her. Until, as she crouched over a final box, searching for the twin of an opal earring that had gotten separated from its mate, a piercing voice floated over her front display case.

"Well, well, if it isn't Jo McAllister. I thought you were dead."

Jo froze, not wanting to believe that voice belonged to who she thought it did. Then the vanity plates she had seen on the black SUV came to mind. Had the erratic driver on Route 30 been blonde? Jo suppressed a heart-sinking wince and slowly rose.

"Linda Weeks," she said as she turned and faced her visitor. "What a surprise. It's been a while."

"Yes indeed. I hadn't heard a thing about you so I naturally assumed you had perished as well in that explosion."

"At our loft? No, I had been away at a gallery when it happened." Jo maintained a stony smile. "There was a hugely comforting turnout for Mike's funeral, though. I guess you didn't hear about it in time to come."

"No. And what a shame. It would have been wonderful to see some of the old gang."

Jo managed not to choke. She didn't believe for a minute that Linda had thought Jo had perished or hadn't got the word about Mike's funeral arrangements. More likely she simply didn't have the strength of character to show up and face Jo, as well as the many good people erroneously referred to by Linda as her old gang.

"Well, what brings you to these parts?" Jo asked, hoping against hope that Linda was just passing through, maybe taking in the cherry blossoms in D.C. But her worst fears were confirmed when Linda's smile turned sharklike.

"Why, I've been a regular at Michicomi for ages now. They're fairly consistent, you know, about only allowing the best. And you can imagine how my jaw dropped when I looked over from my own booth and saw *you* here. It's amazing, isn't it? After all those years in the Big Apple, sharing suppliers and buyers, not to mention design ideas — then going our separate ways only to end up right across the aisle from each other for the next three days."

Jo could agree on that point at least, as her wooden smile turned to granite.

"Amazing."

CHAPTER 2

Fortunately for Jo, the arrival of a delivery-man drew Linda back to her own stall, where she remained to unpack the large box that had just arrived. Jo watched for a few moments, still unable to believe her incredibly bad luck. Of all the booths she could have been assigned, here she was within spitting distance — a phrase that made Jo salivate — of possibly the last person in the world she'd ever hoped to encounter again.

Linda was looking good, though, Jo had to give her that. She wore a youthfully styled jacket and pants that made her look in her midtwenties rather than what Jo knew to be close to her own age of thirty-six. Her hair was still blonde, having been lightened from her natural brunette shortly after Jo first met her, and was tossed in a casual style that was quite flattering. Her makeup was understated, but like every other aspect of Linda's appearance had probably been studiously chosen and meticulously applied.

Jo intensely disliked the woman, but couldn't deny her skill in personal presentation. As far as jewelry design, however, she honestly was amazed at Linda's claim to regular participation at Michicomi, aware as she was of Linda's shortcomings in that department. Was Michicomi less selective than she'd been led to believe? Or was something else involved there?

Jo turned away, not willing to go down that road. There was no point wasting any more time on the woman. Linda's appearance at Michicomi was a definite downer, but Jo couldn't let it affect her own Michicomi experience. She had invested too much in it. Besides, she had a lot still to do on her booth before Russ showed up to take her to dinner.

That thought brought up a smile and she felt her good spirits return. Jo had begun seeing Russ Morgan, a lieutenant in Abbotsville's small police force, a few weeks ago, a fact that continued to surprise her, considering how they had met — over a dead body — and how rocky their early encounters had been. Russ and Jo had butted heads on several occasions, but over it all had hung a definite spark. Jo had tried to deny it for a long time, unwilling to allow herself to move in that direction while still feeling Mike's loss keenly, but the attraction finally grew too strong to ignore.

"How're you doing here?" A voice, this time male and much friendlier, interrupted Jo a second time. She looked up to see a pleasant-faced, white-haired man in a loose brown cardigan sweater over slouchy pants. He held out his hand. "Gabriel Stubbins. Most folks just call me Gabe."

"Hi, Gabe," Jo shook his hand. "Jo Mc-Allister."

"Mine's the wooden toy setup over there." Gabe jerked his head toward the adjoining booth. "Been coming to these festivals close on to twenty years. This your first?"

"It's my first time at Michicomi, though I've been to one or two smaller shows in the Northeast."

"Thought I hadn't seen you before. You get to know people after a while. Some of us become pretty good friends." He grinned. "We're a lot like circus folk."

Jo hadn't thought of it that way but realized that it must be true, with all the traveling required for the more regular vendors. "I'm sure that makes a difference, when you're away from home a lot."

"Sure does. A few of us bring along the family, but for the rest, we *become* family,

25

at least for two, three days. Makes the off hours a lot easier. Where're you from?"

Jo had to think about that a moment. Abbotsville? Where she still occasionally needed directions to find her way around? New York? Where she and Mike had lived and worked during their all-too-few years of marriage? One of the many places she had lived growing up, as her dad's job moved them about? Gabe, however, wasn't asking for her life history.

"Abbotsville," she said decidedly. "It's a small town just down —"

"Down Route 30, isn't it? Been there once or twice. Very nice little place. I'm from Pennsylvania myself. Bought a little farm near Harrisburg that the wife runs, mostly." He smiled. "But I'll tell you more about that when you have time. I see you've got a few things to do. Just wanted to say 'Hi, neighbor.' If you need help, just give a holler."

"Thanks, Gabe." Jo watched her new acquaintance wander off, stopping to greet other vendors at several booths along the way. She noticed, though, that he had skipped Linda's booth. Interesting, since they both mentioned being in Michicomi shows often.

Jo turned back to her jewelry, eventually

26

getting the last of it arranged as she wanted. She started to move out into the aisle for a final check, then remembered the colorful tissue paper flowers she'd made and had carefully packed into their own container. She scrambled through the boxes to find them, then looked about her to choose the perfect spots to set them. Overhead, she decided. Hanging from the overhead beam that held her booth number, the flowers would both brighten and frame her area, turning gracefully on their strings with the air currents. She pulled a folding chair over to stand on and hung away, then stepped out into the aisle to gauge the total effect.

Not bad, she thought, feeling quite pleased.

"Good luck getting any customers with that setup." Linda's voice interrupted Jo's reverie.

Jo clenched her jaw and turned to see Linda standing beneath a small computer monitor that she had set on an upper corner shelf of her booth. It ran a narrated video of Linda demonstrating her various jewelry-making techniques — with music in the background.

"That's very impressive," Jo said.

"Oh, it's just one of —" Linda stopped,

her attention caught by something to Jo's left.

Jo followed the gaze to see Russ Morgan making his way through the crowded aisle toward her. Out of uniform, he was dressed simply in a gray V-neck sweater and slacks, but his height and dark good looks made him stand out in the throng. Jo's heart did a little flip, particularly when he spotted her and smiled.

"Hi," he said, coming up and greeting her with a quick peck on the cheek. "Am I too early?"

"Not at all. Perfect timing. Do you mind helping me get these packing boxes out of here, though?"

"Well," Linda broke in, "you certainly didn't waste much time, did you?"

Jo felt her cheeks flame, which Russ thankfully couldn't see, having turned toward Linda.

She reached her hand out to him, smiling widely. "Linda Weeks. Jo and I know each other from way back."

Russ shook her hand. "Russ Morgan. Nice to meet you."

"Oh, *very* nice to meet you."

"Russ," Jo interrupted, "can you grab these bigger boxes over here? I think I can get the rest."

Russ turned back, giving Jo a quizzical look, but said, "Sure." He loaded up, and Jo grabbed her own batch and followed him after first spreading a large tarp over her merchandise, glad that she had been able to compact the empty boxes enough to avoid making a return trip under Linda's watchful gaze.

They pushed through the plastic-curtain door and headed down the alleyway to deposit their light but bulky loads in Jo's trunk and back seat. After a brief discussion, they agreed Jo would follow Russ to the restaurant, which would allow her to continue on directly home afterward. It had been a hectic few days for Jo, and she'd have to get an early start for the opening of the festival the next day. She was doubly grateful, therefore, to be able to enjoy a precious few moments with Russ over a quiet dinner.

Giorgio's was an easy fifteen-minute drive beyond the gates of the county fairgrounds. Once settled within its muted, Tuscan-like atmosphere, Jo and Russ chose and ordered their dinners, then leaned back comfortably in their chairs to sip at Pinot Noir and nibble crusty warm bread. Russ asked a few questions about Michicomi, and Jo filled him in with as much as she knew about it, including its reason for existence, which was to create a venue for artists and craftspeople like herself to reach a wider market.

"The fees we pay go largely to the overhead costs of running the festival, along with publicity and promotion. The organizers are careful about who they allow in to the shows, so that the public is guaranteed to find a high quality of merchandise. Which makes me wonder . . . well, never mind."

With the uncanny way he had of sometimes seeming to read her mind, Russ asked, "That woman I met, Linda Weeks. How do you know each other?"

Jo sighed, but held off responding when the waiter appeared, setting down their orders of chicken marsala and shrimp-stuffed ravioli. Her ravioli dish smelled wonderful, and she was reluctant to cut into her enjoyment of it with less-than-pleasant talk. But after savoring a bite or two, she launched into the history between Linda and herself.

"We knew each other up in New York," Jo said, dabbing at her mouth with her napkin. "We both made jewelry and placed it with many of the same consigners, so it was inevitable that we'd run into each other. At first she seemed perfectly nice, and we started sharing an occasional lunch. I introduced her to Mike and some of our friends.

"But Linda wasn't having as much success with her jewelry as I was, and I guess it started eating at her. She complained to me about being dropped by a certain gallery, and she seemed to want my opinion as to what she was doing wrong. But when I ventured suggestions, such as thinking of her potential customers and what they might want rather than satisfying her own creativity, or working on one or two technical problems I had noticed, she didn't take it well."

"The old 'let me complain, but don't offer any solutions' routine, huh?"

"Pretty much. So we drifted apart, which was okay with me until I started hearing about things she was saying about me — really negative things — to the people I was doing business with. Things like claiming I had copied her best ideas, or that I was showing signs of a major addiction problem!"

"Uh-oh."

"Right." Jo took a soothing sip of her wine. "I guess she decided that her best way up was by pulling me down."

"Did it work?"

"It started to. My business dropped off,

and I lost a couple of gallery placements with no explanation. I didn't know what to do to defend myself. I was furious, of course, largely from the helplessness I felt. Then I decided to just let it ride, do my work as I always had, and hope that people would eventually see the truth of things and that Linda would be seen for what she was."

"Probably the best mode of action. How did that go?"

"Very well, thank goodness, due quite a bit to my regular customers who asked for my jewelry. Over time I began to hear that Linda's business might be suffering, but I didn't ask any questions or, tempting though it was, take any satisfaction in it.

"The last time I saw her was at a large Christmas party. She tried to pretend we were still friends, but the best I could do was be civil." Jo decided not to mention how outrageously Linda had behaved later that night after a few drinks, catching Mike in an isolated area and flirting boldly enough that Mike told Jo he ended up having to strong-arm her off of him. That had been Linda's final, desperate effort to hurt Jo, and it might have worked if Mike had been less of the man he was.

Jo thought of Linda's flirtatious behavior with Russ earlier that evening with annoyance. It was going to be a long weekend, she realized. And not nearly what she had envisioned.

"Would you like to see the dessert menu?" a mustached waiter asked, pulling Jo from her musings. He held out a slim leather-covered menu invitingly.

Jo shook her head. "No, thank you, but I'd love some coffee."

Russ asked for the same, and after the waiter took off with their empty plates, reached out to cover Jo's hand with his own large one. He didn't say a word, but Jo felt the empathy in that gesture and cherished it. Russ's entry into her life had made such a huge difference, raising her happiness level enormously. She had never expected to feel this way again.

But that also worried her. Was she rushing into something too soon, being disloyal somehow to Mike? Linda's comment about how Jo hadn't wasted much time had stung for that very reason. Jo didn't think Mike would want her to spend her life mourning him. But was opening her heart to someone new somehow saying that she loved Mike less? And was she being unfair to Russ, leading him on while being so uncertain?

"Something wrong?" Russ asked.

"No," Jo said, changing her thoughtful

frown into a smile.

No, not wrong. Just terribly perplexing.

CHAPTER 3

Jo arrived at Michicomi for the start of the craft festival the next morning excited, but also nervous. The excitement came, of course, from the fantastic opportunity she had for showing her jewelry to a new customer base. But nervous questions wove their way through her mind. What if she had miscalculated the tastes of the people who would come to this show? What if they thought her designs were unoriginal, or perhaps *too* original, or worst of all, too expensive?

Topping those worries, though, was the thought of spending the next three days in such close proximity to Linda. Jo's only hope of getting through it was that they'd both be so busy that neither would have time to spare a thought on the other.

If the crowds were thin and they ended up staring across the aisle at each other for three days, who knew what might happen?

Jo suddenly pictured Linda pea-shooting seed pearls at her, then ducking as Jo lobbed half-pound pendants back in retaliation, and chuckled. Things surely wouldn't sink to that level. They were both mature adults, professionals who could put their personal grievances aside while on the job. Weren't they?

Jo pulled into a spot near where she had parked the day before, and climbed out. The early morning air was crisp, but the weather forecast had predicted warmer temperatures for later on. She picked up tempting aromas wafting from the food vendors' area — coffee and cinnamon rolls, which would likely change to smoky barbeque and hamburgers as lunchtime approached. She had brought along her own thermos of coffee to sip from in the early hours, but hoped to pick up a lunch treat when she had a chance.

"Morning!" A wild-haired, bearded man dressed in beaded smock, faded jeans, and boots called out as he headed away from his rust-spotted VW camper. Yesterday Gabe Stubbins had likened the craft vendors to circus folk, but what popped into Jo's mind as she returned this man's friendly greeting was aging hippie. And he was not the first she'd seen who would fit that description, though there was such a variety of people manning booths at the festival that Jo knew she'd rapidly run out of labels if she even tried to categorize them. The only universal label, she decided, would be friendly, and that was further confirmed as she made her way into building 10 and through the deluge of greetings and nods.

There was definitely an air of excited anticipation as people made last-minute adjustments to their booths and waited for the first festival attendees to arrive. As Jo came to Gabe's booth, he looked up from the brightly painted wooden merry-go-round he was examining and smiled broadly at her.

"Good luck to you!" he said.

"And to you," Jo answered, glancing over his colorful wares with pleasure. Was there someone she could buy one of these delightful toys for? she wondered. Carrie's children were way beyond them. And her little namesake, Jo Ramirez, was still struggling just to turn over. Maybe by Christmas, though . . . ?

Jo's pleasant thoughts vanished as she caught sight of Linda, who was carefully adjusting the sound on her computer video. Jo slipped quietly into her own booth, hoping to avoid detection for as long as possible. She dropped her coffee thermos in a back corner and got to work removing and folding the protective tarp, setting up her cash and credit drawer, and unlocking her display cases.

Thankfully, Linda remained preoccupied with her own concerns until the clock read nine and the sound of early-bird shoppers arriving reached Jo's ears. Before long people began trickling into building 10 from the entrance Jo had come through, the one closest to the main pathway. They moved up the aisle from booth to booth, and Jo waited, shifting from foot to foot, adjusting her showcase items by millimeters. It had been a long time since her jewelry had been put to the test.

"No need to worry," Linda called across to her, obviously picking up on Jo's butterflies. "There will always be people who get so carried away with the excitement of the show that they'll buy just about anything. Even Roy Perkins, who makes those God-awful ceramic trolls, unloads a lot of his stuff."

Jo nodded stiffly. "Good for him."

Two women, clearly mother and daughter with identical curly hairdos and matching rounded shapes, came up to Linda's booth, and Jo watched Linda turn on the charm. Happily she didn't have to watch very long, as a few people approached her own cases, and Jo found herself busily pointing out various pieces and explaining the materials she had used. She made one small sale — a pair of simple hoop earrings — and got one or two encouraging promises of coming back, "once we've seen everything."

Little by little the crowd grew, and Jo eventually found herself too busy to even think of reaching for her coffee thermos. The shoppers who came to her booth — mostly women — were unfailingly pleasant to deal with, many volunteering stories of family members for whom they wanted a gift or chatting about a particular occasion for which they needed a special necklace or bracelet. Even if they didn't buy, they complimented her work sincerely, and often carried away her business card for future reference. Jo's earlier fears began to subside.

Then, as she was writing up the sale of an amber-studded necklace for an elderly woman who had spoken at some length to Jo about the interesting pieces of jewelry her numerous late sisters had owned, Jo heard Linda calling to two women who were waiting patiently for Jo's attention after having closely examined several silver items.

"I'm having an opening-day sale on all my silver necklaces. Everything marked down

39

20 percent."

The two women immediately crossed over to Linda's booth. Jo stared at Linda, speechless, but Linda became instantly busy laying out several necklaces for the women to examine. Jo closed her mouth and completed her transaction with the amber customer, and thankfully became distracted by new browsers. The incident had nearly left her mind when it happened again. When Jo became occupied with one customer, Linda found a way of drawing other prospective customers over to her side of the aisle.

Jo soon realized that her own booth's situation had the advantage of being next to Gabe Stubbins's popular wooden toys. Women shoppers — mothers and grandmothers — tended to cross over to look at his booth, then remained on that side of the aisle as they moved along, stopping at her jewelry booth instead of Linda's. It was a very slight advantage, which would likely change as the day wore on and more shopper's entered from the other end of the building, which was closer to a food vendor's tent. Coming in that way, shoppers would likely keep to the right — Linda's side of the aisle.

Linda obviously couldn't think that far

ahead, though. All she saw were more people stopping at Jo's booth and she couldn't live with that. It was petty, and highly annoying, but outside of getting into an all-out tugging match over hapless customers, Jo didn't know what she could do about it.

"Oh, there she is!"

Jo knew that voice. She brightened and looked over to see Loralee Phillips making her way up the aisle, her large tote bag impeding her progress only slightly as she wound through the crowd. Loralee's bags were nearly as big as she was, which wasn't all that big as far as ladies went, but quite large bags. Jo wondered how she managed to carry them, filled as they always seemed to be with unexpectedly handy, but often heavy, items. Feeling peckish? Loralee could reach into her bag and offer you a fresh banana or granola bar. Have a sudden need for scissors, Band-Aids, or reading material? Loralee's bag could likely help you out.

"Isn't this wonderful!" Loralee came up to Jo's booth, taking in the jewelry display with shining eyes. "Oh, and look at the beautiful tissue paper flowers up there! You've made your booth the prettiest one here." She reached up to give Jo an affectionate hug. "This is so exciting! I could hardly wait to come see your things. I left Dulcie looking at pottery in building 8. She'll catch up in a minute."

Dulcie was Loralee's daughter who had recently moved — much to Loralee's joy — from faraway Seattle to Loralee's house with her husband and small children, while Loralee happily downsized into the newly built mother-in-law addition.

"And look who I ran into on the way over." Loralee grabbed the sleeve of a plump woman about Jo's age and pulled her closer. "Jo, do you know Meg Boyer?"

Jo admitted that she didn't, and Loralee introduced them. "Meg," she said, "has started working at Bert and Ruthie's Abbot's Kitchen, haven't you, Meg?"

"Then we'll probably see each other a lot," Jo said. "I'm always popping in there at lunchtime for one of Bert's sandwiches. Are you new to Abbotsville?"

"No." Meg pushed a limp strand of mousy brown hair from her face. "We've lived there at least five years, after we moved from the Midwest when my husband decided he could do better in Maryland. Kevin's in sales."

From the way she'd said it, Jo got the feeling Meg hadn't taken much part — or joy — in Kevin's decision, but she nodded

42

agreeably. Linda's voice interrupted them with a loud announcement that she was starting her demonstration on jewelry techniques. A large group of red-hatted women who had been heading for Jo's booth veered immediately toward hers.

"Oh, dear," Loralee said. Meg simply stared, open-mouthed.

"She's been doing things like that all morning," Jo explained.

"It doesn't seem quite nice, does it?" Loralee asked. "I mean, those women were clearly planning to come here. Shouldn't she have waited?"

Jo was trying to think of an answer when two women entered on the right through the nearby entrance. Seeing the crowd blocking access to Linda's booth, they crossed over to Jo's. Jo greeted them, then shrugged toward Loralee, saying, "It probably balances out."

Loralee shook her head, still amazed at Linda's action, but moved to give Jo's new customers space as well as examine a few things herself. "I want to find something for Dulcie for her birthday before she gets here," she explained, picking up and setting down various items, oohing and aahing as she did.

The other two women hadn't asked for

Jo's help yet, and Meg stepped closer to speak to Jo in a lowered voice.

"I know that woman," she said, tilting her head toward Linda.

"You do?"

"It took me a minute. Her hair's lighter than when I knew her. Linda Boeckman. I went to high school with her."

"Really? I know her as Linda Weeks, which must be her married name, though she's been divorced for a while."

Meg nodded. "I'm not surprised. She might have changed since I knew her, but it doesn't look like it. I'd be careful if I were you."

"How much is this bracelet?" one of the newly arrived women asked Jo.

Jo left Meg and stepped over to answer her customer. After she'd finished with her, her companion wanted attention. Then Loralee had made her choice for Dulcie — a delicate opal piece — and needed Jo to package it up quickly before Dulcie showed up. By this time Meg had moved on, saying she wanted to check out a quilt booth in the next building. But her words of warning lingered in Jo's mind. *Be careful.*

Jo looked over at Linda, still dealing with the red-hatted ladies, and nodded. She planned to be.

■ ■ ■ ■

"Hi, Aunt Jo."

Jo glanced up to see her relief man, Charlie, Carrie's fifteen-year-old, grinning at her across her counter. She checked her watch. It was, indeed, 5:30, a fact she'd have trouble believing if her aching muscles didn't confirm it.

"Charlie. You're a sight for these tired eyes."

"They been keeping you busy?"

"Oh, yes! Ina Mae Kepner stopped by and gave me a break around lunchtime, which was great. But I don't think I've sat down for more than a few seconds since then. How did you get here, by the way, and how long can you stay?"

"My friend Tony dropped me off," Charlie said, adding with a wistful look, "He got his license in January." Jo smiled, knowing how Charlie was champing at the bit to turn sixteen himself and gain driving privileges. "Anyway, Tony's gonna hang out with some buddies for a while, but he wants to swing by here again around 6:30 to pick me up."

"Okay, I'll watch my time. Things have calmed down quite a bit right now, probably because it's dinnertime, so you shouldn't have too much to do." Jo showed Charlie how to write up any sale he might make, with added tax, and how best to package the item for the customer.

"If anyone asks a question you can't answer, just say I'll be back in a few minutes. At this point, weary as I am, I'm not awfully concerned about losing any sales. Just mainly try to keep anyone from walking off with the merchandise. Shall I pick up something for you to eat?"

"No, that's all right. I grabbed a sandwich at home before I left. I wouldn't mind a Coke or something for the ride home, though."

"You got it." Jo picked up her purse and stepped out of the booth, thinking that her first stop would be at the nearest restroom. Manning a booth all day by one's self had its challenges.

A few minutes later Jo was munching on a delicious barbequed beef sandwich as she sat on a tree-shaded bench, her feet propped up on a convenient nearby rock. Sitting there, she became just one of the festival's crowd, and she felt the fatigue accumulated from constantly having to be "on" for the steady stream of shoppers slowly leave her. Jo watched the people passing by, and listened idly to the bits of conversations that floated her way, things like, "I wonder if I can bargain down the price on that table a little," and "Where's Harvey? He promised he'd meet us back here in half an hour."

Jo was licking the final bits of barbeque from her fingers when she caught a conversation of a different type: "Did you see that Weeks woman is back again?" Jo looked over to see a tall woman in an ankle-length skirt and a loosely belted top facing a balding, cowboy-booted man. The woman fiddled idly with her thick braid as she spoke.

"Yeah, I did," the man answered. "Amazing. I'm starting to wonder if those rumors are true." The cowboy's accent sounded to Jo's ears more Brooklyn than Austin, but her ears perked up at *what* he said rather than how he said it.

"I don't care who's sleeping with who," the woman said, "or what kind of favoritism it gets them. That kind of thing never lasts long. But Bill Ewing's gonna bust a blood vessel when he sees her, after what happened in Morgantown."

Others passed between Jo and the pair, covering over the rest of the words with their own chatter, and the two moved on, leaving Jo thirsting for more. Realizing, however, that the only thirst she could slake was the one in her throat, Jo stirred herself from her bench and went in search of two large Cokes, one for herself along with the one she'd promised Charlie. It was getting time to send him off.

Jo backed through the hanging plastic at the entrance closest to her booth, her hands gripping the two large drink cups, and called, "I'm back, Charlie. How did it . . . ?" Jo stopped as she saw the agonized look on Charlie's face.

"It just happened," he said, his hands gesturing helplessly. "I was at the other end over there, giving someone change, when I heard the splash."

"What is it?" Jo managed to croak as she stepped closer. A pool of brown liquid covered the top of her counter, oozing among a display of rings and pins and dripping through the seams of the Plexiglas into her collection of fine necklaces below.

"Coffee. There was this blonde woman — I think she worked in the booth across there —"

Linda Weeks! Jo turned to Linda's booth but saw only a frightened-looking teenage girl standing behind the counter. "Where is she?"

"She said something about getting paper towels and took off. She apologized a lot, but she didn't look all that sorry to me."

Jo closed her eyes. Linda had done this on purpose, of that she was sure. When she reopened them, she saw Charlie dabbing at the mess with one of Jo's polishing cloths. "Wait, Charlie, maybe I can get some towels."

"Will this help?" Gabe Stubbins appeared at her side holding out a bunch of flannel rags. Jo set down her drinks and took them gratefully. "I didn't see it happen," he said, "but I noticed her sliding over there. She must have waited for this young man to get distracted."

Jo felt pressure rising inside of her and struggled to control it.

"I'm so sorry, Aunt Jo. I should have watched out better."

"Charlie, this is absolutely not your fault. Believe me. No one could have prevented it. Here, help me move these things out of the mess, then I'll take care of the rest later. It's almost time for your ride to come."

"I can st—" Charlie began to offer, but Jo stopped him.

"It's okay, Charlie. Really. It's better that I take care of the jewelry cleaning myself."

Charlie, still looking wretched, helped her move the jewelry, and Jo continued to re-assure him while dealing with growing murderous thoughts toward Linda. She

49

then sent him on his way with a quick hug and watched as he headed off somewhat reluctantly before taking a quick glance at his watch and picking up speed. She turned back to her cleanup work.

"Oh, good, you got some rags. Well, I guess you won't be needing these, then."

Linda Weeks stood just inside the nearby entrance holding two paper towels and wearing the most odious look of "oops, my bad" Jo had ever seen. It tipped Jo over the edge. She had had it. The steam that had been building finally blew.

"Don't even try," Jo said, her tone low but rapidly rising. "Don't even pretend this was an accident, Linda. You've been working up to this all day, just waiting for your chance. I don't know why you think you have to behave like such a slimeball, but you do."

"Oh, really?" Linda dropped the smirk and her eyes flashed. "So suddenly you're Little Miss Perfect with the right to call names? I wonder what people would call you if they knew what you're really like — the ones who think you're such a *fabulous* designer, but don't know where you really get some of those designs."

"I suppose you'd like to claim I stole them from you?"

"You know what you've done. I don't have

to spell it out."

"Linda, if I were at all inclined to copy anyone's ideas, which I'm not, you would be the last person in the world I'd ever want to copy. How you made it as far as you have is beyond me. Your unbelievably low level of creativity is matched only by that of your ethics, and I regret every minute I wasted in New York trying to be nice to you."

Linda stood stonily staring at Jo, two small spots of red forming on her cheeks. Jo hoped that would be the end of it, that Linda would simply storm off in a huff. She was aware that nearby vendors had begun staring, taking in every word being spat out.

But Linda wasn't about to leave. That, of course, would have been too much to hope for. Someone like Linda always had to have the last word, and hers, it turned out, were particularly venomous.

"Well," she said, her eyes steely, "aren't we the two-faced one? Sweet as pie on the outside but full of all kinds of nastiness deep down. I guess I can finally understand why Mike committed suicide, now, can't I?"

She turned around and pushed through the plastic curtains before Jo could respond, though Jo, her mouth working soundlessly, couldn't have answered that comment if she'd tried.

CHAPTER 4

Jo dragged herself out of bed the next morning, dreading the day that lay ahead. How would she be able to function as she needed to with Linda so nearby? The answer, of course, was she would *have* to, though it wouldn't be easy, especially after the rotten night's sleep she'd just had, Linda's final barb pricking with every toss and turn. Bringing Mike's death into their argument had been a low blow, but throwing in the word "suicide" —

Jo stopped herself. There was no use going over it. It was typical Linda, and that was that. Jo rubbed at her tired eyes and grumpily suspected her nemesis had slept like a baby. The woman seemed to thrive on conflict and was likely bouncing with energy as she planned out fresh misery to inflict from across the aisle.

Jo downed her first cup of coffee, letting the caffeine do its work, then braced herself.

Darned if she was going to let Linda Weeks get to her anymore. She might not be able to control what Linda said or did, but Jo was certainly in charge of her own actions — and reactions. Not rising to the bait would be the best revenge. Plus it would save a lot of wasted energy, best spent on her own concerns and that of her jewelry booth, which, she reminded herself, still had a long way to go to earn back the cost of being at Michicomi.

Feeling better with a plan of action, or rather non-action, in hand, she added a bowl of energizing cereal to her breakfast, showered, then gathered her things before checking door and window locks on her modest two-bedroom rental house. As she breezed past her jewelry workshop in the small garage to jump into her Toyota, Jo felt her focus had moved from the negative of facing Linda Weeks to the positive of welcoming the fresh stream of Michicomi patrons who might come to her today for that special piece of jewelry.

Thirty minutes later, as Jo made her way through building 10 toward her booth, though, she noticed fewer friendly greetings and more than one uncomfortable look away. She was sure she knew why, and wished she could meet with each person who had overheard yesterday's exchange between Linda and her and explain exactly what had led up to it, but knew that would be both impractical and fruitless. Gabe Stubbins's welcoming smile as she approached, therefore, was wonderful to see. He beckoned her near to tell her — sotto voce, and with an impish wink — that she could count on him to ring the alarm bell from one of his wooden fire trucks if Linda came too near.

Jo laughed, and remarked, just as slyly, "Wouldn't it be great if those little fire hoses worked as well?" She continued on to her own booth, feeling cheerier.

A pink-wrapped package sat on top of the tarp covering her counter, and Jo picked it up, curious as to what it could be. A quick scan showed it to be addressed to Linda, however, not Jo, and that it had come from Kitty's Kandy, a gourmet candy shop with franchises scattered about Maryland. Jo looked over toward Linda's stall and saw the back of her blonde head as she worked at adjusting her computer monitor. An evil impulse pulled Jo's glance downward, toward her trash basket. *Dump it,* the fork-waving creature on her shoulder urged. *Pretend it never arrived.*

Jo shook her head, tempting though it was.

Still, she couldn't quite bear the thought of carrying it over to hand to Linda. Then a woman came up to Linda's booth and began engaging her in conversation, and Jo saw her opportunity. She quickly crossed the aisle with the package.

"This is yours," she said, setting it on an empty spot on Linda's countertop, and did a quick reverse back to her own booth.

"Well, well," Linda's voice sailed over, "looks like Jack Guilfoil remembered my sweet tooth."

Jack Guilfoil. That name rang a bell. Obviously Linda wanted her to know where the candy gift had come from. Then it clicked. Jack Guilfoil was one of the organizers of Michicomi. The brief conversation Jo had overheard during her dinner break the day before came to mind, with its hints of favoritism. Jo hadn't seen any sender's name on the box, but if Linda wanted to assume Guilfoil was who the box was from, that was up to her. Jo had her own business to attend to and she got down to it, readying her booth for customers, which was a good thing since before long the sound of approaching hordes reached her ears.

Jo had figured Saturday was likely to be busier than Friday, and she was quickly proven right. Building 10 was soon invaded by throngs of shoppers, exclaiming, touching, asking questions, and all thoughts of Linda disappeared from Jo's mind as she repeated several versions of:

"Yes, ma'am, those are indeed Swarovski crystals."

"No, these earrings are made with yellow sapphire, not amber."

"This choker? Only fifty-six dollars, and the beads in it are sterling silver. Something cheaper? How about . . ." and occasionally —

"Thank you, ma'am," as she rang up a sale. "Do come back if you decide you want the matching bracelet."

Jo was kept so busy that the time flew by. She could hardly believe it when a very familiar voice behind her commented, "Looks like business is brisk."

Jo glanced over her shoulder to see Ina Mae Kepner, white hair shining in the sunlight that beamed through the plastic doorway, the sleeves of her peach-colored warm-up pushed to the elbows, ready for action.

"Brisk enough," Jo answered, "that I haven't sat down since I arrived."

"Then for heaven's sake take a break now! I'll watch things."

Jo finished a transaction with the teen who

had just bought a pair of Jo's silver earrings, then turned back to Ina Mae.

"I'll be glad to run out for a minute, but I don't like leaving you on your own for too long." Jo looked over toward Linda's booth and Ina Mae nodded.

"I got the story from Carrie this morning. Don't worry, I didn't teach in the elementary schools for close to forty years without growing that necessary second pair of eyes in the back of my head. Nobody plays any tricks while I'm in charge." Ina Mae's face took on the stern look of a general preparing for battle — a *Viking* general — which made Jo laugh.

"Yes, ma'am, I believe that's true. Even so, I think I'll bring back lunch to eat here. Things have been busy enough that having two people here won't hurt."

"All you need to pick up are drinks. Loralee sent along her famous pasta salad with shrimp and snow peas" — Ina Mae held up the bag Jo hadn't noticed until then — "including, I believe, homemade bread. Better than hot dogs, or whatever you'll get here."

"Actually, the food's been pretty good. But nothing could be as good as what comes from Loralee's kitchen." Jo promised to bring back two large coffees, grabbed her

57

pocketbook, and set off, happy to get her first full look at the sky in four hours.

When she got back, Ina Mae was helping a customer choose between a turquoise and silver necklace and an elaborately beaded one in shades of blue. "From what you've told me," Ina Mae said in a tone that told Jo she had come close to the end of her patience, "I'd highly recommend the turquoise." She then gently but firmly withdrew the beaded necklace from the woman's fingers and set it out of reach.

"Yes, I think you're right," the woman said, and before she could add another qualifying thought Ina Mae was wrapping it up and totaling up the cost.

As the customer left the booth, pleased but blinking in a "what just happened there" way, Jo came around the counter with the tightly covered coffee cups.

"I think I just learned a new method in the art of salesmanship," she said.

Ina Mae smiled. "Some people need to be told what they want. I could see she'd be here for the next three hours if I'd let her." She took her coffee and reached back to get Loralee's plastic lunch dish.

As Jo helped scoop out the hearty salad onto two paper plates Loralee had sent along, Linda's voice sailed across the aisle,

58

announcing to no one in particular that after such an extremely busy morning she finally had a chance to open up the box of chocolates from Jack Guilfoil, and how wonderful he had remembered that she loved vanilla creams!

Ina Mae rolled her eyes at Jo. "She's also been letting me know about each and every significant sale she's made. Tried to steal one of my customers once, but I wouldn't let her."

"You slapped on a pair of sterling silver handcuffs?"

"Didn't need to use force." Ina Mae unwrapped two of Loralee's forks. "Ah, she sent along real ones. I can't abide those plastic utensils, can you? No, I simply conveyed to the customer with a firm look and one or two choice words that her best course of action was to remain right here."

Jo could only imagine the trepidation inspired in that hapless customer, who must have felt transported back to third grade — on test day — and might have bought almost anything at that point just to be allowed to leave.

Well, Jo thought with a grin, whatever worked.

Ina Mae opened Jo's two folding chairs and sat down on one to enjoy her lunch. Jo was carefully prying the lid off her coffee cup when she glanced over to see Linda standing beside her own counter. Something about her didn't look right. The pink wrapping that had been torn off the candy box lay on the countertop along with the box cover. Linda held the opened box in one hand, but her other hand clutched at her neck. Her face began to take on the color of the wrapping.

"Linda," Jo called, "are you okay?"

Linda turned toward Jo, her eyes bugging by this time. "I — can't —" she gasped, then sank downward, the chocolate candy spilling about her from their fluted paper cups.

A nearby shopper screamed. "She's having a heart attack!"

Others began shouting:

"Call an ambulance!"

"Call security!"

"She needs CPR! Can anyone do CPR?"

"No, it's a stroke! She needs aspirin. Who has aspirin!"

Everyone seemed to be shouting at once as people rushed to Linda's booth, crowding around her. "Give her space!" "We need a doctor!" "I think she's dying! Oh my God!"

The shock of it all had frozen Jo for an instant, but she snapped out of it and grabbed for her pocketbook. By the time she'd dug out her cell phone to call 9-1-1, though, she heard Ina Mae's voice already giving the information on her own phone.

Ina Mae closed her phone and told Jo, "They're on their way."

"Thank goodness." Jo looked back to the scene across the aisle. She couldn't see Linda anymore with so many others crowded about her, all shouting conflicting orders at once. After an agonizing length of time she heard, to her great relief, sirens in the distance. She realized the ambulance crew would need final direction and said, "I'll go show them where to come," then ran out and down the alleyway, glad to be doing something active. She saw the ambulance inching its way up the main thoroughfare through the parting crowd, and waved, calling, "This way! Over here!"

When they had pulled to a stop, a team of paramedics jumped out with their gear, and Jo led them back the way she had come, explaining over her shoulder, "I don't know what's wrong with her. She just suddenly collapsed."

The rescue team took over, sending people out of their way, and Jo too stayed back, out of the building but still able to glimpse some of what was going on, most of it a blur of activity and confusion. Gabe Stubbins appeared at her side, his shoulders hunched and hands in his pockets, as he too watched with concern.

"Your friend is taking care of your booth," he said. "I saw her moving things off the counter so nothing would get knocked off."

Jo nodded, feeling grateful to Ina Mae but at the same time guilty for caring about mere things when someone's life might be in danger. Much as Jo disliked Linda, she felt that simply as a human being she deserved total attention.

A stretcher was rolled in, and Jo heard pieces of radio communication as the rescue team prepared to transport Linda to the hospital. When they wheeled her out, oxygen mask in place and IV tubes attached, Linda's face looked pale against the dark blanket partially covering her.

What could have happened? Jo wondered as she stepped back along with the gathered crowd of curious onlookers. How could someone seem healthy and active one minute and collapse to the ground the next?

As these questions ran through her head, Jo saw one of the people who had first rushed to aid Linda step out of the building behind the rescue crew — a thin, middle-aged woman whom Jo remembered from the leather bags and wallets booth. The woman watched as the stretcher disappeared down the alleyway, her face screwed up tightly with concern. As she turned back toward the building her eyes suddenly locked on Jo, and her expression morphed into one of fury. Jo was dumbfounded, the anger projected from that look, causing her to recoil and bump into Gabe's shoulder.

Their gazes held for a few seconds until the woman continued on into the building. Jo remained in place, wondering what could have brought that on. She began to rub at her arms, surprised to realize she felt a slight chill. After being on the receiving end of such heat it seemed more reasonable that instead of goose bumps she should be rubbing at singed hairs.

CHAPTER 5

Feeling in need of TLC, Jo called Russ when she got home that evening. The craft show had gradually recovered from the crisis caused by Linda, with most of the vendors in building 10 returning to their business, though in somber moods. Ina Mae had lingered, claiming she had nothing whatsoever to do the rest of the day, and Jo, though sure that was a huge exaggeration, had been grateful.

The distraction of newly arrived customers who had no idea of what had occurred earlier and therefore were in full, carefree, fair mode, had helped. But during her quiet drive home, all the distressing thoughts Jo had pushed aside came creeping back, making her long for a few soothing words.

Russ, she knew, was on duty that night, and Jo hoped she'd catch him at a slow time. She was delighted, therefore, when, after waiting on hold for several minutes, she heard his voice, brisk and businesslike though it was.

"Morgan here."

"Hi, Morgan. McAllister here."

"Ah." His tone immediately softened. "That new guy at the desk is going to have to cue me in a lot better. How'd it go today?"

Jo sighed. "Got a minute?" When Russ acknowledged that he did, she spilled out the whole, disturbing story.

Russ, after offering a few consolatory phrases, zeroed in with his usual perceptiveness on the one thing that was bothering Jo the most, though she'd tried to minimize it — to herself as well as to him.

"The woman who gave you the evil eye, did she say anything to you?"

"No. We all simply went back to work. I didn't see her the rest of the day. Now that I think of it, I probably should have, since her booth is only two down from mine. I can't say for sure if she was there afterward or not."

"What about that candy? What happened to it?"

Jo had to think. "Most of it, I think, was spilled from the box, and probably got trampled from everyone that rushed to help. I remember a security guard showing up at

Linda's booth later on. He seemed to be packing her jewelry away and locking it up. I suppose he might have cleaned up the candy. I don't remember seeing the box or the pink wrapping anymore."

"Hmm."

"Why?"

"Nothing. Just wondered about it. So, did this very unfortunate event have an impact on sales the rest of the day?"

"Not terribly," Jo admitted, aware of her torn feelings about that. Why did she feel the need to somehow suffer because of Linda's illness? Would she be happier if in fact business had been awful? "Things eventually returned to normal, and Ina Mae and I made several very good sales."

"Great. Word must be spreading about the fantastic McAllister designs."

Jo smiled. "I don't know about that." She really didn't, but she liked hearing Russ say it.

"One of my officers said his wife bought something of yours yesterday. He seemed impressed enough with it to not even grumble about the cost."

Jo laughed. "She must have bought something with gold. Tell him if it makes him feel any better that the value will only go up."

"I will. But not when he's unwrapping his PB&J, the only lunch he can afford for a while."

"Oh, come now!" Jo said, still smiling. "I couldn't have made that big of a dent in their budget."

"Well, put it this way —" Russ stopped, then asked Jo to hold on. When he came back on the line he said, "Sorry, gotta go. Something's come up."

Jo hung up, disappointed to have their conversation end, but happy she'd at least had a few moments to talk with Russ. She went to bed that night feeling better than when she'd come home, and looking forward to her final day at Michicomi.

The next day, Sunday, Jo pulled up to the craft fair and was climbing out of her Toyota when Gabe Stubbins came up to her.

"I've been watching for you," he explained. "I wanted to tell you myself. There's been some bad news."

"What?" Jo closed her car door behind her. The look on Gabe's face told her this was serious.

"Linda Weeks died last night."

"Died! Oh, gosh." Jo leaned back against her car, staggered by the unexpected turn. She looked up at Gabe. "What was it? Her heart? A stroke?"

"I don't know. No one seems to have any details. I just thought you'd want to know before you came in."

Jo thought of the leatherworks woman who seemed to want to blame Jo for everything. But why? Could an argument like the one she'd had with Linda cause a fatal reaction? Jo couldn't believe it. But that didn't mean others might not.

"How are people taking it?" she asked Gabe.

"Stunned, mostly. Still coping with the news. You know how it goes, though. Scoundrels turn into saints on passing, so there's a lot of grief being expressed by people who could barely spare two words for her before."

Jo nodded. She'd have to deal with her own mixed feelings. She felt shocked and sad for Linda, but at the same time hypocritical for the sadness.

"Ready to go in?"

"Yes. I assume the festival continues as usual?"

Gabe nodded. "The show, as they say, must go on."

Gabe walked beside her through building 10, and Jo realized this respected, long-time Michicomi regular was in effect giving her his stamp of approval. Jo appreciated that, especially when they came to the leather-goods booth where the woman who had glared so fervently at her the day before worked busily at straightening handbags on a wall shelf.

" 'Morning, Amy," Gabe called, and she turned around with a smile, which faded as she spotted Jo beside Gabe. But Amy pulled herself together and returned his greeting cordially. Gabe escorted Jo to her booth, then said, "Don't worry. Everyone just needs a little time to get their heads together."

He turned back to his own booth, and Jo got down to work getting ready for business. She checked her clock: 9:45. The gates would open in fifteen minutes. She and Ina Mae had sold quite a few larger pieces the day before, and Jo needed to unpack replacements for them. She was crouching over her boxes on the floor when a man leaned over her counter and asked, "Mrs. McAllister?"

Jo looked up to see a mustached, pinstripe-suited man standing somewhat uneasily next to a taller, square-jawed man in a brown and tan uniform.

"Mrs. McAllister, I'm Julian Honeycutt, and this is Sheriff Franklin. He'd like to

69

speak with you. Would you please come to my office?"

"Oh! Right now?" Jo asked. "The festival is on the verge of opening up."

"I just have a few questions," the sheriff said, adding, "if you don't mind."

"No, of course not," Jo said, understanding the need but feeling, at the same time, pulled in two directions. She quickly re-locked her cases and stepped out of the booth to walk silently between the two men to the Michicomi main offices, two buildings down. Julian Honeycutt ushered Jo and Sheriff Franklin into a small room with a metal desk and two chairs, offered coffee, which they both declined, then excused himself.

"Mrs. McAllister," the sheriff began, pulling out a small notebook from his tan shirt pocket and slipping on a pair of half-moon reading glasses. He had very dark, thick eyebrows, Jo noticed, much darker than his hair, which had considerable gray running through it. His dark eyebrows furrowed together, either in concentration or displeasure, Jo couldn't tell which. "You are aware," he asked, "that Linda Weeks, the woman who had the booth directly across from yours, has died?"

"Yes, I heard it this morning. Just a few

minutes ago. I'm still quite shocked. She was much too young, and, as far as I could tell anyway, perfectly healthy."

Franklin looked at her over his glasses, an action that always made Jo feel uneasy from the air of skepticism it projected, though what there was to be skeptical about she had no idea.

"I understand you were acquainted with the deceased, before this craft fair. Can you tell me how?"

So the sheriff had been talking to others already, people who had probably reported on the acrimonious exchange between them. Not that it could have had anything to do with her death, Jo was convinced, but obviously he was leading up to that.

"Linda and I knew each other a couple years ago in New York, where we both placed our jewelry with many of the same consigners."

"You were friends?"

"We were friendly, at one time. That changed."

"Into enemies?"

"Enemies? No, I wouldn't use that strong of a word, Sheriff. We simply didn't get along. Look, I know you're probably aware that Linda and I had a big blowup, but it was hours before she fell ill. I really can't see that it had anything to do with her death."

"Mrs. McAllister, yesterday morning you gave Ms. Weeks a box of candy, is that correct?"

"I didn't *give* it to her. The box was on my counter but was addressed to her. I simply carried it over."

"Is that right?" Another over-the-glasses look. "You didn't buy the candy and bring it with you?"

"No, it was sitting there when I arrived. Why?"

"Well" — Franklin flipped a few pages of his notebook back — "witnesses saw you give it to her, and she seemed pleased to get it. I thought perhaps it was some sort of peace offering from you?"

"No, not at all. As I said, it was simply sitting on my counter, obviously delivered to the wrong booth. She seemed to think it was from Jack Guilfoil, but I didn't see that name, or any other besides Linda's, on the wrapping."

"I see." He referred back to his notebook. "So you weren't trying to patch things up between you?"

"No. Not at all."

"Then you still hold a lot of grievance against Ms. Weeks?"

"Up to the time she collapsed, she and I were not on good terms, no, though I *am* sorry this happened to her."

"You said you two had been friendly for a period in New York. Did that include meals together?"

Meals? Where was this going? "Yes, we met a few times for lunches."

"Only lunches?"

"I guess there were one or two dinners with others, plus a few larger get-togethers that had food. Why, Sheriff? What does that have to do —"

"So you've eaten with Ms. Weeks. You were aware of what she could and could not eat?"

"You mean, if she was dieting?" Jo asked, puzzled. "I don't know. I guess I remember once or twice she mentioned watching her weight, skipping desserts, that kind of thing. What —"

"I'm talking about her food allergies. You knew about them?"

"Allergies? No, I didn't know she had any allergies."

"She never mentioned that she could have severe reactions to certain foods?" The sheriff had pulled off his glasses by this time, and his eyes — which were very dark brown — watched her unblinkingly.

"No, she didn't," Jo said. "Don't tell me she was allergic to chocolate. But if she was, why would she —"

"She wasn't allergic to chocolate, Mrs. McAllister. She was allergic to peanuts. Highly allergic, it seems."

"But the candy was vanilla creams."

"You knew that?"

"Yes, because Linda said so." Jo finally realized, with shock, that she was being looked at with suspicion. "Linda said something about Jack Guilfoil remembering that vanilla creams were her favorite. Have you spoken with Jack Guilfoil about this?"

"Mr. Guilfoil is recovering from surgery in a Cleveland hospital at the moment, for a burst appendix that occurred two days ago."

"Oh. Then I suppose he didn't actually send the candy."

"Highly unlikely. Or that he was able to inject ground peanut paste into each of the vanilla creams in the box."

"Ground peanuts!" Jo stared at the sheriff, grappling with what that meant. He stared back at her, waiting. But waiting for what? Jo's mind raced. So Linda didn't die from a weak heart or a blood clot to the brain. She died from an allergic reaction to peanuts — an extreme reaction — which someone knew would happen, and caused to happen.

Someone who wanted Linda dead.

"Sheriff," Jo said, mustering up as much firmness to her voice as she could, "I disliked Linda but not enough to want her dead, believe me."

The sheriff remained silent a moment, then said, "I wonder if you can explain to me, then, why Ms. Weeks would say" — he searched through his notebook pages until he found what he wanted — "when she was still able to gasp out a few words, 'She poisoned me.' Ms. Weeks then, apparently, pointed toward you."

CHAPTER 6

Jo returned to building 10, shaken. Shoppers had flooded the place once more, and she hurried to finish the booth preparations that Julian Honeycutt and Sheriff Franklin had interrupted. She worked on automatic pilot, though, as her mind grappled with all that had bombarded it in the space of a few minutes: first that Linda had died; then that her death wasn't from natural causes as Jo had assumed, but from murder; then that she, Jo, was apparently a suspect!

How could this all have come about? It was too much. Jo looked over at Gabe's booth, longing for his calm and sensible input, but all she could see was the top of his gray head as he dealt with four or five enthusiastic toy customers at once. One or two drifted her way, and soon Jo became as busy as he, a situation that normally would have pleased her but that morning felt only burdensome.

Her professionalism, however, kicked in, and Jo managed to smile as she greeted and explained and rang up sales, while at the same time dealing with flashes of Linda as she gasped for air, her throat swelling closed from anaphylaxis. Questions sprang up like ragweed after a summer rain. With as severe an allergy as she had, wouldn't Linda have carried an EpiPen? Jo remembered a classmate in school who had swollen up from multiple bee stings and who thereafter toted the spring-loaded hypodermic, ready to inject what could be lifesaving epinephrine.

Why hadn't Linda ever mentioned such an allergy when they had known each other in New York? Wouldn't something like that normally come up? Obviously, Sheriff Franklin thought so.

And why had Linda seemingly accused Jo of poisoning her? That was the most infuriating question of all. It was as if even in dying Linda had to throw one final jab at Jo. The trouble was, that jab was a major one, tons worse than intentionally spilling coffee over jewelry or calling Mike's death a suicide. That jab could land Jo in prison. Jo found her earlier conflicted sadness over Linda's death replaced by a simmering anger. Linda had done it again. The woman caused endless trouble. Well, darned if Jo was going to let her get away with it!

Jo stopped herself on that thought. Let *Linda* get away with it? What was she thinking! Linda had been murdered. The person Jo needed to care about getting away with anything was whoever had put the ground peanuts into Linda's chocolates. If that person wasn't identified — and soon — Jo would remain suspect number one with her life turned upside down.

Her thoughts flew back to the conversation she had overheard Friday night while sitting on the bench during her dinner break. The two vendors discussing Linda had mentioned a Bill Ewing as having reason to have a grudge against her. Who was this man? Jo wondered, and how could she find out more about him? She glanced over once again toward Gabe, who was probably her best source of anything connected with Michicomi. She needed to talk to him as soon as she had the chance.

A couple of hours later, around the time Jo's empty stomach started sending distress signals, Jo was surprised to see Meg Boyer, the woman Loralee Phillips had introduced on the first day of the craft show, appear at her booth. With all the shoppers ebbing and flowing through her area, Jo might not have immediately recognized Meg except for the distinctive jacket she wore once again: a pale blue denim with a dancing Kokopelli figure embroidered on its breast pocket, a bit of whimsy that seemed somehow out of sync with the more subdued Meg.

Jo greeted her. "Come for another day of shopping?"

"Yes, but also to tell you that Ina Mae isn't able to come today."

Jo's empty stomach sank.

"Her next door neighbor," Meg went on to explain, "slipped on her deck this morning and cracked her shoulder, so Ina Mae took her to the emergency room. Ina Mae called Loralee to see if she could come in for her, and Loralee told her not to worry but then remembered she had a church committee meeting to go to. Loralee knew I was planning to come here anyway — there's a pottery-making demonstration I want to see at two — so she asked if I'd mind filling in for her. I said sure — that is, if it's okay with you."

Jo grinned at the slightly plump woman who had delivered this involved explanation in placid monotone and now awaited Jo's approval.

"It's more than okay with me," Jo said. "I had just reached the point of *really* needing a break, so I appreciate your stepping in for

Ina Mae — and Loralee — on such short notice." Jo then remembered Meg's words to her two days ago about having known Linda and asked if she'd heard what had happened.

Meg nodded. "It was on the news this morning. If it had happened in Abbotsville, I would have found out a lot sooner."

Jo agreed with that, having seen firsthand how quickly information could spread through the network of Abbotsville neighbors. "I'm sorry if it's at all upsetting. You said you'd known her in high school."

Meg shrugged. "I knew *of* Linda more than I knew her, and hadn't seen her since graduation. What did she die of? They didn't say on the news."

Jo gave Meg a basic rundown. She took it fairly calmly, but her eyebrows went up when she heard the cause of Linda's death.

"You hadn't heard about her allergy back in school?" Jo asked.

"No, but I can guess why. Back then Linda was working hard to be part of a group that was tops in everything — best dressed, student council, drama club leads — things like that. I don't think she'd be likely to bring up anything that would make her sound less than perfect."

Jo nodded. That might be exactly why

80

Linda had never mentioned it to her. It was a chink in her armor, an armor that needed to be kept highly polished in her efforts to dazzle. Career struggles and health problems did not fit into her image requirements. Too bad she hadn't also considered honesty and integrity as necessary to the fit.

Jo gave Meg a quick overview on handling the booth, then grabbed her pocketbook and promised not to be long. Instead of heading straight out of the building, though, she turned toward Gabe's toy booth.

"Like to take a lunch break with me?" she asked. "There's something I want to talk to you about."

Gabe looked up from the dollhouse he was examining. "Tell you what. You go ahead and grab something, and I'll meet you in ten minutes at the tea kiosk. I've already had a bowl of soup, but I wouldn't mind a cup of Patty's spicy tea."

"Sounds good." Jo checked her watch. "See you then."

In ten minutes she was standing near the edge of Patty's Tea Shack, nibbling at her chicken salad roll-up, while Gabe waited in line for the tea.

"How about I get two?" he'd offered, guaranteeing that Jo would love the chai. She'd agreed, and when he handed her the large foam cup and she inhaled some of the delicious-smelling steam that wafted toward her, she was glad she had.

"There's an empty bench over there," Jo said, pointing with her elbow to an area about twenty feet away, and led the way.

When they'd settled down, Gabe took a careful sip of his hot beverage and looked toward her. "Okay, fire away. What do you need to know?"

Glad to get straight to the point, Jo asked, "What do you know about Bill Ewing in relation to Linda?"

"Bill?" The gray eyebrows on Gabe's lined face went up. "You've been hearing things, huh?"

"Not much, just a hint that something major had happened between them in Morgantown."

"Well, normally I try to keep out of such things, but I suspect you have a good reason for asking. Is that so?"

Jo took a bracing sip of her chai, which she found delicious. In a cozier conversation she would have savored it, but for the moment a quick swallow had to do. "Apparently, one of Linda's dying breaths was used to indicate that I had poisoned her." She told Gabe about her interview with

Sheriff Franklin, and he shook his head sadly.

"Sounds like she put you in quite a spot," he said.

"That she did. But there's nothing says I have to stay there. I intend to find out who doctored up that candy and sent it to Linda. Bill Ewing may or may not be the one, but I have to start somewhere."

Gabe nodded, understanding. "Bill does photography," he began. "He sells framed black and white prints of things like bridges, snowy landscape scenes, things like that. He depends a lot, financially, on coming to these shows, but they're juried, as you know, and not everyone who applies gets into every show. Sometimes it's just a matter of trying to keep a balance — not too many of one type of thing — or of simply needing to make space for new people now and then.

"But Linda, once she started coming, was getting into each and every show. Rumors started flying about favoritism. That happens once in a while. People, even craft show organizers, are human, with all the usual human frailties. But Linda made the rumors particularly hard to shrug off." He took a sip of his chai. "You know what she was like. She had to be sure everyone was 100 percent aware of her success, pretending it was totally due to her outstanding skills, but at the same time dropping hints about her high connections.

"It drove Bill crazy, especially when she started putting down his work to others, which of course got back to him. Bill is not a calm, coolheaded person. If he were Irish like my dear wife," Gabe said with a small wink, "I'd blame it on that, but he's not. So he blustered and huffed and complained to the management, which got him nothing but what he considered empty assurances that there was no favoritism being shown.

"At Morgantown things came to a head. Bill had learned that he was turned down for participation at the Atlanta show — a major money-making stop — and that Linda was, once again, in. He stormed and fumed all day. Then, when he couldn't stand it any longer he stomped over to Linda's booth and made a big scene. He caused such a ruckus, part of it, I heard, brought on from her agitating him even more, that security had to pull him away, and he was disciplined by having to close up his booth a day early."

"And Linda suffered no consequences and continued to show up at every festival."

Gabe nodded.

"Would Sheriff Franklin have been informed of this, as he obviously was of my problem with Linda?"

Gabe squirmed. "He probably should have been, but I doubt he was. Bill, you see, is an old-timer here, and despite his prickliness, people like him, or at least feel some loyalty to him. They wouldn't want to get him in trouble."

"I, on the other hand, am a newcomer," Jo said.

"Unfortunately, true. But that doesn't, of course, mean that the sheriff won't eventually learn about what went on between Bill and Linda."

"But it might be greatly minimized as to its importance."

"It might be," Gabe acknowledged.

"Well, what do *you* think?" Jo asked. "Would Bill Ewing be angry enough with Linda to want to kill her?"

Gabe's face clouded. "That is a question I can't answer with 100 percent confidence, I'm afraid. I've been flummoxed too often by people to guess what they are capable of and what they're not. No one can see everything that's going on deep inside another person's head, can they? So, though I hope Bill would never think of committing a deed as terrible as murder, I can't guarantee that he hasn't."

85

Jo nodded, understanding. She too had been flummoxed in the past, and it had come close to having dire consequences for her. She hoped it hadn't destroyed her ability to trust altogether, but it had certainly made her more cautious.

"Well," she said, "then I guess I'll need to judge for myself." She pulled out and unfolded the map that listed Michicomi vendors by name and location. "Looks like Bill Ewing's in building 5." She checked her watch. "If I hurry, I'll have a few minutes to at least look him over."

Jo browsed through Bill Ewing's booth, which, unlike hers, had no obstructive front counters. Instead, an open area invited shoppers to stroll in and examine the many framed prints hung on back and side walls. Besides Jo, two other shoppers peered at his work, and Bill Ewing himself perched on a high stool beside a small table where Jo presumed he handled his sales.

A crew-cut, husky man in his middle years, he acknowledged rather than welcomed visitors to his booth with a brisk nod and answered questions about his photos when asked. But he obviously preferred to let his work speak for itself. Jo got the definite impression that given the choice, he would be out taking more photos instead of dealing with potential customers. His work impressed Jo, and if she'd actually been shopping and could afford them, one of his prints of a lighthouse at sunset would have greatly tempted her.

"Don't you have any pictures of animals?" a well-dressed woman asked. She clutched bags from several purchases and tiptoed along on what might have been three-inch Prada slides. "Baby seals or maybe kitties?"

The woman looked like she could afford to buy cart-loads of kitty pictures if she found them, but Ewing simply grumbled, "No animals."

"Oh," the woman said and tripped off. Jo watched her go with a small sigh, wishing she could guide the well-heeled woman toward her own booth to discuss any variety of custom-made, animal-themed jewelry. But she remained in place in her undercover role.

In a moment it seemed to pay off as another vendor, a sparkly T-shirted woman, wandered over to chat with Ewing. When Jo caught a low-voiced mention of Linda, she moved closer.

". . . heard the local sheriff's asking about anyone who had a beef with her."

"Yeah? My name come up?"

The woman barked out a laugh that ended in a phlegmy smoker's cough. "Can't say. *Someone* sure had it in for her, though."

Ewing simply grunted, then glanced over toward Jo, who immediately focused on a dramatic shot of the Chesapeake Bay Bridge. "Can you stay a few minutes?" he asked the cougher.

"Yeah, that's why I came. Figured it might be time."

Ewing bent down to a duffel bag at his feet and pulled out a small, black case. "You figured right," he said, and quickly took off.

As Jo turned to watch, the woman who was standing in for him smiled at her. "Diabetic," she said, apparently feeling Jo needed an explanation. "My gran had the same problem. Had to jab herself with needles every day. God, I'm glad I never came down with that, knock on wood. I can't stand needles, can you?"

Jo smiled and shook her head. So Bill Ewing was proficient with hypodermics, she thought as she looked toward where he had walked off. She doubted the fine needles used for insulin could handle peanut paste, but wondered about the coincidence. Thoughts of injections would occur quite naturally to a diabetic who handled such things every day, wouldn't they? Plus, he might know where to find the proper size needle. But would he have also known of Linda's allergy? That was still a major question.

CHAPTER 7

Jo hustled back to her booth to find Meg quietly manning it.

"Any problems?" Jo asked as she slipped behind the counter.

"No," Meg said. She scrunched her nose. "But I only sold one pair of earrings for you."

"That's fine. You also kept my merchandise from turning into free samples, so along with giving me a much-needed break, you were a major help. Thanks so much, Meg."

Meg gave a wan smile, causing Jo to realize that Meg's sales skills were probably about the same level as Bill Ewing's. "What kind of work do you do at the Abbot's Kitchen?" she asked. Ruthie Conway, one of the owners, had always handled the front counter in a way that made every customer feel like a longtime friend. Jo couldn't imagine Meg easily stepping into that spot.

"So far I've been helping Bert with the

food prep — chopping and mixing — and I clean up out front too."

Jo nodded. "As I mentioned before, I'll probably see you a lot then, since I pop over there often at lunchtime for sandwiches." She checked the time. "Oops! It's almost two. If you want to catch that pottery demo you'd better get going."

Meg picked up her things and after acknowledging more of Jo's sincere thanks with a nod, took off. Once Jo settled herself and had a chance to look around she realized from the suddenly diminished number of shoppers that the pottery demo must have been a major draw. She decided this would be a good chance to discuss Bill Ewing with Gabe a bit more. When she wandered over, though, Gabe was busy straightening several of the wooden toys that had been rearranged in the process of showing them to shoppers, so Jo paused at his front counter to let him finish. Gabe had just glanced over and noticed she was there when Jo was addressed from behind.

"Mrs. McAllister?"

Jo turned to see a young deputy sheriff, who touched his hat politely.

"Sheriff Franklin would like to see you for a minute."

Jo sighed and asked, "Now?" aware that

she had repeated her response to the sheriff's request of that morning and just as aware of the futility of it.

"I'll watch your booth," Gabe offered. "There won't be much happening for at least another half hour."

"Thanks, Gabe," Jo said. She tossed him a rueful look, then followed the deputy back to Julian Honeycutt's office, wondering what Sheriff Franklin needed to know that he hadn't asked about before.

The deputy ushered her in, and the sheriff half rose in what Jo supposed was a gesture of welcome, though she felt less than happy to have been invited. She sat down, and he immediately got down to business.

"Mrs. McAllister." He slipped on his half-moon glasses once more and Jo braced herself. "You said this morning that you had known Ms. Weeks when you both lived in New York City."

"Yes, that's right."

"I believe you indicated you had been friends for a while, but that friendship ended before you moved down here."

"I think I said we had been *friendly.*"

"There's a difference?"

"I believe so, yes. Linda and I had never reached the closeness, the sharing-confidences stage that friends have. We were more acquaintances with a few things in common."

"I see. So that *friendliness* ended, I assume, when you found out she was having an affair with your husband?"

"What!"

The sheriff simply looked at her, waiting. Jo was sure he expected her to blurt out confirmation of the absurd question he'd just thrown at her. Instead she counted to ten as she returned his stare, holding herself down until she could speak calmly.

"What in the world, Sheriff, makes you think Linda had an affair with my husband?"

"Are you saying she didn't?"

"Absolutely she didn't. I know that for a fact."

"Interesting, since she told others the affair was the reason for the problems between the two of you."

Jo grit her teeth and drew a deep breath, thinking how typical that was of Linda. She was sure Linda also claimed to have been a complete victim in the supposed affair, to have been totally unaware that Mike had been married to Jo at the time, and was cleverly seduced.

"Sheriff," Jo began, "Linda said a lot of things that were figments of her own, very creative imagination. This was just one more very hurtful lie of hers. I wouldn't put any credence to it."

"Then I presume you would also contend your husband didn't commit suicide when he realized he couldn't spend the rest of his life with her?"

Jo groaned, and shook her head in disbelief. How long, she wondered, was that woman going to continue to throw jabs at her? Wasn't death supposed to put an end to such things? At that thought Jo almost smiled, realizing that that question was the last thing she would voice to the man sitting behind the desk, watching her so carefully over the top of his glasses. She drew a breath, wondering what in the world she was going to say that would swing a predisposed opinion in her direction.

Jo's cell phone rang as she worked her way through the crowd toward building 10, and she checked it before answering, not in the mood for frivolous chat. The call, however, was from the one person she was willing to talk to. She pressed the answer button.

"Hi, Carrie."

"Hi." Carrie paused, probably reacting to the less than happy tone of Jo's greeting, then asked, "How's it going?"

Jo sighed, and looked about for a quieter place to talk. She spotted an empty kiosk that had closed up early as the final hours of the festival ran out, and headed for it. Leaning against its side and out of the flow of last-minute shoppers, she brought Carrie up to speed on the downward spiral of events that had occurred since they'd last talked. Carrie knew about Linda's death, but her reactions to what followed ranged from horrified gasps to sputters of outrage. These were exactly the gamut of emotions Jo had experienced and she was glad to have them confirmed as reasonable.

"Jo," Carrie said, "I think you should call Russ."

Jo straightened up from her lean. "Russ? Why?"

"For his help, of course. He can vouch for you to this sheriff, and anything Russ says will carry much more weight than what your friends would say."

"I don't know, Carrie. I'd hate to ask that of him." She really did, but for reasons that weren't totally clear to her at the moment.

"I don't think he'd feel imposed upon, if that's what you're thinking. At least get his advice. He'd want you to do that."

"I'll think about it. How are things at the shop?"

"Slow to moderate. Michicomi probably drew away most of our crafters. But I think we'll reap the rewards later as it inspires them to try new things."

"I hope so." Jo told Carrie about Meg Boyer having come by to help out in Ina Mae's place.

"Good for her," Carrie said. "She seems to be livening up a bit — taking that job at Bert and Ruth's, for one thing, after being pretty much of a recluse from the time she and her husband moved here. Some people wondered if she had a chronic illness of sorts, but I think it may have been a kind of depression. I'm glad to see her starting to come out of it."

"Was she unhappy over moving away from her hometown?" Jo remembered getting that feeling when Meg had indicated the move had been more her husband's choice than hers.

"I don't know," Carrie said. "And I feel bad for not trying harder to get to know her. *Ah-choo!*"

"Bless you. Did you call your doctor?"

"Not yet. Oh, someone's coming in." Jo heard the soft ding of her shop's bell. "I'd better go," Carrie said, "but I was calling to say Charlie and Dan will be there a little after six to help you dismantle your display cases."

"Great. And Carrie, call your doctor."

"I will if you'll call Russ."

"Take care of your customer, Carrie. See you later."

Jo had a flurry of decent last-minute sales, which was gratifying. It seemed as though the really serious shoppers had meticulously checked over the entire show for the last three days, comparing and mulling things over before making their final purchases. She recognized a couple of returning customers, women with whom she had spent a considerable amount of time discussing necklaces and pins. When they'd wandered off with vague promises of returning she hadn't really counted on seeing them again, but was pleasantly surprised when they reappeared, credit cards in hand.

She was happy, then, to see she had considerably less merchandise to take home than she had brought to the show, though she wasn't sure yet if she'd actually managed to earn back her expenses and make a profit. Less merchandise, however, at least meant less to pack, and she had made significant progress toward that effort by the time Carrie's husband and son arrived.

"Wow, you did great, Aunt Jo," Charlie

said, eyeing Jo's near-empty cases.

Jo laughed. "Not that great, Charlie. I was the one, not my customers, who emptied most of this out. Hi, Dan. I'll have the rest of these things out of the front case in a minute."

"Take your time." Dan rested a hand on his son's shoulder, a simple gesture that made Jo smile, pleased to see that small sign of the easy camaraderie that had developed between the two. It wasn't all that long ago that their father-son relationship had been highly strained, and both pairs of hands would have been shoved deep into their respective pockets, shoulders hunched.

Charlie shifted uneasily as he glanced over at Linda's closed-off booth, aware, so far, only of her death and not of any of the later-developing details Jo had shared with Carrie. If he had known it was murder, Jo was sure he'd be peppering her with questions, all squeamishness replaced with normal fifteen-year-old curiosity and excitement. She decided to let the squeamishness prevail for now in the interests of packing up quickly and heading home. She was looking forward to the solitude and peace she would find there.

When Jo gave the all-clear signal, the duo set about dismantling the cases that Dan had built for easy mobility, and one by one they carried them out to his truck while Jo loaded up her own car with the smaller boxes.

Michicomi itself was dismantling as well, and Jo, seeing vans and trailers being packed and readied to take off for parts unknown, realized that Linda's killer might also be slipping away, with only herself remaining within Sheriff Franklin's reach. On her return to her near-empty booth, therefore, Jo walked over to speak to Gabe.

"Would you mind giving me a way to reach you once you're gone?" she asked.

Gabe smiled. "I'm way ahead of you." He handed her a card with, Jo saw, a cell phone number, home phone, and e-mail address written on it. "My business cards have my website listed, but I thought you might want something that worked quicker."

"Yes, I do, and thank you. I hope I won't have to use this much, but I'm afraid unless someone walks into the sheriff's office soon and says, 'I did it,' that I may need to pick your brain some more about Michicomi people."

"Pick all you want. And I've already learned something you might be glad to hear."

"What's that?"

"Bill Ewing might be hanging around this area for a bit instead of heading home to Pennsylvania."

"Really? Why would he do that?"

"I heard he wants to take photos of several interesting old tobacco barns, for one thing, and he has a friend he can stay with."

"Well, that's interesting. Any idea where that friend is located?"

"Not yet, but I think I can find out. I'll let you know when I do."

"Thanks, Gabe." Jo pulled out her own card and scribbled her phone information on it.

Gabe's face grew serious. "Don't you be worrying too much about this whole business. It might seem bleak with the sheriff giving you the hard time he has. But you're part of the Michicomi family now, and I want you to know that I'm behind you 100 percent."

Jo swallowed hard. "That means a lot to me, Gabe," she said. She reached over to give him a hug, which he returned heartily. But as Jo looked beyond his shoulder, she saw Amy, the woman from the leatherworks booth, watching them through narrowed eyes.

Obviously, Jo realized with a sigh, not everyone in the Michicomi family felt quite as supportive.

Jo carried the last of her jewelry boxes into her house after Dan and Charlie had left her dismantled cases in the garage and taken off. Exhausted, she dropped onto her tattered living room sofa and leaned her head back against its cushion, eyes closed. She briefly thought of fixing herself something to eat, but after a mental inventory of her refrigerator decided what she wanted most for the moment was to rest and to think.

Carrie had urged her to talk to Russ, to enlist his aid for her shaky situation. It was a sensible suggestion, Jo knew, but her immediate and strong reaction had been to resist. Why? she wondered. Did she fear that accepting Russ's help would draw them closer together or make her indebted to him? Was that such a bad thing? Was Russ the kind of person who would take undue advantage? She didn't think so. He was certainly someone who would help if he could, with no strings attached. So why shouldn't she let him?

The situation with Sheriff Franklin was growing serious. People who had believed Linda's manufactured account of her relationship with Mike had obviously rushed to impress the story on the sheriff. Jo didn't know how much credence he put in those reports, but the questions he had thrown at her worried her. Couldn't Russ help balance Franklin's attitude?

Jo ran her fingers through her hair, scrubbing as she deliberated. Why not? Why not ask? She stopped scrubbing. No reason at all. It made sense and she would do it. She would call Russ tonight and ask for his help.

That decided, she felt better. Even energized. There must be something edible left in that kitchen of hers, she thought as she jumped up from the sofa. If her cupboard truly was bare, she'd call for a pizza, or maybe Chinese.

Jo scoured the shelves of her refrigerator, discovering a forgotten carryout chicken drumstick hiding behind an aging quart of milk. She pulled it out and had just bitten into it when the phone rang. Setting the drumstick down and licking her fingers clean, she reached for it, sincerely hoping the call wasn't coming from the Hammond County Sheriff's Department.

"Jo, it's Ina Mae."

Ina Mae's voice had a tone of urgency that put Jo on alert. Before she could form a question, though, Ina Mae hurried on.

"I'm at the hospital. Spent the whole day

here with my neighbor for her broken shoulder. There's a huge ruckus happening just now. I thought you should know."

"What?" Jo asked, bracing.

"It's Lieutenant Morgan, Jo. He's been shot. You might want to get down here."

CHAPTER 8

Jo grabbed her pocketbook and jumped into her Toyota, its motor still warm from her drive home. Ina Mae hadn't been able to give her any information beyond that terrible statement, and Jo struggled to keep her imagination from running wild while at the same time trying to drive safely. The urge to speed and to ignore stop signs was strong, and only images of wreckage kept her from yielding to it.

Ina Mae was watching for her in the hospital lobby when Jo came rushing in. The place was flooded with uniformed police as well as press people. Ina Mae pulled her away from the commotion.

"He's in surgery," she said.

Jo sucked in a relieved breath. At least he was alive. "How bad is it?" she asked, searching Ina Mae's face, which was grim but not desolate.

"All I've been able to learn is that his

condition is serious, which to me is encouraging since it could be much worse."

Jo was considering this when someone touched her elbow. She turned to see Mark Rosatti, one of Russ's sergeants, whom she'd met at a police banquet Russ had taken her to on an early date.

"I saw you come in," Mark said. "Russ will appreciate your being here."

"How is he?" Jo asked, trying to keep a tremor out of her voice. The sight of all the uniforms added a frightening intensity to the already alarming situation.

"I'm pretty sure he's going to be okay," Mark said. That "pretty sure" was nowhere near firm enough for Jo.

"What exactly happened?" Ina Mae asked.

"It was a domestic call. Suspect was drunk, upset that his girlfriend was going to leave him, and decided the best way to hold on to her was by knocking her around and holding a gun on her. Russ went there to try to diffuse the situation. Unfortunately the girlfriend panicked and tried to make a run for it. Shots were fired; she fell, and Russ, trying to get her to safety, caught one."

"Where?" Jo asked. "I mean, where was he hit?"

"His left shoulder. He was wearing a vest."

Jo breathed out. "So it's not life threatening?"

"Probably not."

"Probably?" Another word Jo didn't like.

The sergeant shifted his weight uneasily. "They didn't find an exit wound, which means there's a chance the bullet could have hit bone and veered off in another direction. *Which* direction would be critical."

"How long before they know?" Ina Mae asked.

Mark shook his head. "It could be hours." He turned to Jo. "I suggest you wait at home where you'll be more comfortable. Give me your number and I'll call as soon as there's news."

"I'd rather wait here," Jo said. She reached into her purse for a card and wrote her cell phone number on it.

He nodded, pocketing her card. "I'll see that they allow you in to see him when it's time."

"Thanks, Mark."

The sergeant took off, and Ina Mae, watching him, said, "He's right, you know. It could be a long wait."

"I want to be here, not half an hour away in case . . ." Jo stopped, not wanting to think the unthinkable. "I just want to be here."

"Then let's go down to the cafeteria. Have

106

you had any dinner yet?"

Jo thought of the chicken drumstick she had left sitting on her kitchen counter. The one bite she'd taken out of it didn't exactly qualify as dinner, but she didn't feel like adding more to it. "I don't think I can eat, but coffee might be a good idea." They were waiting for the elevator when Jo suddenly turned to Ina Mae. "You've been here all day. There's no need to stay longer with me. I'll be fine."

"Phhht." Ina Mae blew dismissively. "Virginia has to stay the night, and I was going to stop in on her a little later anyway."

The elevator arrived and Ina Mae stepped in along with Jo. "Virginia's husband," she said, explaining further, "has an eye condition and isn't supposed to drive. And their daughter lives way up in Cumberland and won't be here until tomorrow."

So Ina Mae had, of course, seen the need and filled in. What, Jo wondered, would the people of Abbotsville do without her? She smiled, then, at the thought that she too was officially an Abbotsvillian, and particularly grateful at the moment to be one.

Once in the cafeteria, sliding her tray past salads and sandwiches toward the cashier, Jo added a muffin at the last minute to her coffee purchase. Behind her, Ina Mae grunted approvingly but asked, "Sure you don't want to try some of this vegetable soup too?" Jo smiled and shook her head. After paying for both of them, she led the way to a quiet table near the back.

Thankfully, the commotion in the hospital lobby hadn't yet spread to the cafeteria. Jo unloaded her items, then sat, wrapping her hands around her mug to soak up some of its warmth.

"The hospital staff here is quite good," Ina Mae said as she sat down before her soup and tea. "You might not think that was the case in a small town like ours. But the hospital serves a fairly broad area beyond Abbotsville, and everything is top-notch."

Jo nodded. "I got that impression during my brief stay here last fall."

"My own Frank was well cared for here, to the end."

Jo looked up. "Your husband's name was Frank?" she asked, realizing she hadn't known that.

"Yes. Francis G. Kepner. The 'G' was for 'Gilbert,' his grandfather's name, which he never cared for much." Ina Mae opened a packet of crackers. "He wasn't overly fond of 'Francis,' either. Too much junk mail would come addressed to 'Miss Francis Kepner.' " Ina Mae snorted in disgust. "As

108

if a woman would spell it with an 'I.' "

Jo smiled, aware that she never managed to remember which version was masculine and which feminine. She broke off a piece of her muffin and nibbled at it.

"What did he, ah, what was his ailment?" she asked.

"No illness. Frank was healthy as a horse."

"But — ?"

"He was skydiving. He'd done it before, loved it from the first, and decided he was going to treat himself to a jump every birthday. That last time, though — it was his sixty-eighth birthday — things unfortunately went wrong. Parachute problem."

Jo winced.

"He spent five days in a coma, then peacefully slipped away." Ina Mae took a spoonful of her soup. "People, of course, said things like, 'If he hadn't taken such risks, you'd still have him with you.' But the way I saw it was if he hadn't taken risks, he wouldn't have been Frank, so who would I have with me? Some man who wouldn't have enjoyed life nearly as much!"

Ina Mae took another spoonful of soup and dabbed her mouth with her paper napkin. "When it was clear he wasn't going to survive I told him as much, even though I wasn't sure he could hear me. I said,

'Frank, I will miss you terribly, but I'm glad you got to do what you wanted to do.' "

She cleared her voice. "Well, my original point was that this is a very good hospital. Frank's situation was extreme, nothing like Lieutenant Morgan's, but I watched him get outstanding care. The lieutenant, rest assured, is in excellent hands."

"Thank you."

Jo sat for a moment, quietly picturing Russ surrounded by skilled doctors and nurses, all damage swiftly and competently repaired, pain managed, and brow soothed. It was a much calmer image than what had been bouncing about her head until then.

The aroma from Ina Mae's soup drifted toward her as the older woman stirred through the broth. Jo sniffed, thinking it smelled pretty good. She put her hands at the table's edge and pushed back her chair.

"I think I'll get a bowl after all," she said. "Can I pick you up a muffin?"

Jo was dozing in a quiet waiting area Ina Mae had located on the third floor when her cell phone rang. Jerking upright and blinking, she scrambled through her pocket to find and answer it.

"Jo? You still at the hospital? It's Mark. Russ is awake. They said you can see him for a couple of minutes. The ICU's on the fifth floor."

"I'll be right there."

Jo found Ina Mae down the hall, stretching her legs with a short walk. "He's awake," Jo said, hurrying up to her.

"Good. Go ahead. I'll be here if you need me."

Jo ran off, eager to see Russ, but anxious too, knowing nothing beyond the fact that Russ was conscious. Mark was waiting near the elevator when Jo burst from the nearby stairwell, having decided climbing the two flights would be quicker.

"Did they find the bullet?" she asked, puffing. "Was there much damage?"

Mark talked as he led her down the hall to the double doors of the ICU. "They found it. It didn't hit anything vital. Everything looks good."

"Thank God."

The nurse at the ICU cautioned her to be brief. Jo promised, then followed her to the bed where Russ lay among numerous connected tubes and wires. The first thought that came to Jo's mind was that his face looked as pale as Linda's had when they'd wheeled her toward the ambulance, an awful association that she immediately banished.

"Russ?" she asked, softly.

Russ's eyes opened and he seemed to struggle to focus. Then he smiled weakly. "Hi."

Jo took the hand that lay atop his covers. It felt warm and dry. "How do you feel?"

He seemed to have to consider that, finally answering, " 'Kay."

Mark had stayed back, but nurses hovered nearby, busily checking instruments. It wasn't a good time for conversation, all things considered, so Jo simply squeezed Russ's hand and felt him squeeze back. That made her smile, and she lifted his hand to her face, rubbing it gently against her cheek.

Terrible as it was to see someone normally so strong rendered helpless, Jo reminded herself how wonderful it was to see him alive. She remembered her earlier intention to ask Russ for help with her problem. That was obviously out of the question. The only thing Jo wanted to ask of him was that he heal quickly and completely.

After a few moments of simply smiling and holding on to each other, Russ's need for sleep overcame his struggle to stay awake. The ICU nurse let her know she should leave, and Mark walked her back to the elevator, murmuring a few words of encouragement, as much for himself, Jo suspected, as for her. As she rode the elevator back down to the third floor, Sheriff Franklin and his suspicions popped back into her thoughts, but she quickly brushed it away.

She'd worry about it tomorrow.

CHAPTER 9

Jo called Carrie the next morning as soon as she was sure the entire family would be awake, to update her on Russ's condition, something she'd promised to do after convincing her good friend not to come to the hospital the previous night.

"Did you manage to get any sleep?" Carrie asked, and, when Jo admitted to only one or two hours in fits and starts, she urged her to go immediately back to bed.

But Jo knew sleep would be impossible with the adrenaline of the last several hours still coursing through her and instead showered and dressed before heading for the craft shop. It felt good to be back, once she pulled off Main and into the small parking lot beside the shop. Fitting her key into the lock on her front door, she took a look at the wreath hanging there and saw it was time for a change. The red flowers trimming the wreath, while perfect around Valentine's

Day, didn't match the newly warm weather, which was calling out for pastels.

Jo walked through her store, her spirits lifted as they always were by the bright colors of her many craft items — silk flowers, bright ribbons, scrapbooking papers, and stamping supplies — and found it hard to believe she'd only been gone three and a half days. She set up the coffeepot in the back with fresh water and grounds and plugged it in. She was heading toward the front to open up the cash register when Carrie bustled through the door. Carrie stopped dead and looked at her with scolding eyes, her head shaking with exasperation.

"I told you I'd handle the shop," Carrie said, her hands on her hips. She wore a loosely crocheted sweater over a dark T-shirt and drapey pants, an outfit which Jo knew she favored for its ability to camouflage her extra pounds.

"I wouldn't have been able to rest, Carrie, really. Besides, you have a knitting class this morning, don't you? You can't handle that and wait on customers at the same time."

"Our customers will know enough to be patient at a time like this. My class too. My gosh, Jo, I'd be surprised if you could see straight enough to write up a sales slip after the night you've had. How in the world did you even manage to drive over here?"

"Very carefully," Jo said, smiling guiltily. "I'll be fine, though, as soon as the caffeine kicks in."

Carrie tsked and shook her head some more as she walked to the back of the shop to drop off her things. Jo checked the cash register, making sure they had plenty of change, and looked through a few order slips.

"I thought I'd put together a new wreath for the front door," she called out to Carrie. "Something more springlike."

"Good idea. Why don't you work on that in the back, and I'll watch things out front."

Jo smiled, knowing Carrie hoped she'd end up sound asleep at the worktable with her head nestled among the trimmings. But she intended to actually finish the wreath and to this end picked up a basket and wandered into her flower area to look over her choices. The front door opened, and Jo heard the voice of one of the knitting class students, Kathy Vincent, greeting Carrie.

"Am I the first?" Kathy asked.

"Yes, you are. How's the sweater coming?"

Kathy chatted about her knitting progress as she headed toward the chairs Carrie kept in the yarn section for the classes. As she passed the shelves where Jo stood with her basket, Jo turned to say good morning and was surprised to see Kathy freeze.

"Oh! You're here! I didn't, I mean, I thought —"

Carrie broke in, saying, "Yes, I tried to convince Jo to stay home and get some rest, but she wouldn't listen."

Kathy smiled weakly and nodded as Carrie went on to talk about how Jo had spent several hours at the hospital. But Jo had the feeling that wasn't what Kathy had been thinking of when she was so surprised to see her. It was almost as if she *hoped* she wouldn't see Jo that morning. Which didn't make sense, so Jo made a mental shrug and turned back to her wreath trimmings, refocusing on the question of whether the pale yellow rosebuds would work with the light blue daisies.

Carrie and Kathy had just settled down on the chairs when the phone rang.

"I'll get it," Jo said, stepping over to the front counter to pick it up. "Jo's Craft Corner. Jo here."

"Oh!" the voice on the other end said. After a pause, it said, "Um, this is Penny Collins. Can you just tell Carrie I won't make it for the knitting class today?"

"Sure, Penny. Everything okay?"

"Um, yes, I, ah, just remembered I had

another appointment, that's all."

Jo hung up, thinking that Penny had sounded a bit strange, but gave Carrie the message.

Kathy looked up on hearing that and said, "I don't think Lisa will make it either."

"Oh?" Carrie said, loosening a length of yarn from her skein of navy worsted.

"Uh-huh. She thinks the baby might be coming down with something. You know Lisa." Kathy grinned, a bit nervously it seemed to Jo. "Always the worrywart. And actually," she said, "I can't stay too long myself. I have a million things to do. So if you would just show me how to do this sleeve part, Carrie, that'll hold me for a while."

"Sure, Kathy." Carrie reached for the young woman's needles and went into the explanation, but the look on her face told Jo Carrie was thinking much the same thing as she was. That something odd was going on.

It wasn't until Javonne Barnett showed up around lunchtime, long after Kathy Vincent had scurried off and after a very quiet morning, businesswise, that an explanation was offered.

Javonne had been one of Jo's first workshop students back in the fall, and had helped and supported her in many ways over the last several months, as much as her part-time job and full-time family duties allowed. From her white uniform, which contrasted starkly with her mocha skin, Jo knew Javonne had come from her husband's dental office where she helped out.

"Jo, you've got a problem," Javonne said.

Jo smiled. "That I know, but exactly which one are you referring to."

"The one you probably don't know you have yet, girl. People are talking about what happened at Michicomi. I've been hearing them in Harry's waiting room, and some of it's even come up when they're sitting in Harry's chair."

"What? About Linda Weeks?"

"Not just about Linda Weeks but about *you* and Linda Weeks. Somehow everyone seems to have heard that you had some kind of bust-up with her. And now the woman's dead and there's a lot of whispered speculation going on."

"Speculation about what?" Carrie demanded.

"Speculation about Jo. People aren't spelling it out, at least not within *my* hearing, that they actually think you did it, Jo, but they seem very nervous about your connection. Rumors, I'd say, are flying."

"Oh, Lord." Jo looked over to Carrie. "I'll

bet that's why Penny Collins and Lisa cancelled this morning. And Kathy, now that I think about it, wasn't just surprised to see me here, she looked frightened to see me. She probably expected me to be safely locked up."

"That's ridiculous!" Carrie cried.

"Of course it is!" Javonne agreed. "But that never stopped people from thinking such things. Look, I didn't get to the craft festival what with my James down with the flu all weekend, but I got the whole story eventually from Loralee. Not that I needed any explanation to tell me you're innocent, of course, just to get straight on what happened. But people who don't know you like I do just need to get the same facts. Once they understand, the rumors will stop spreading."

"How can I do that?" Jo asked. "Take out a full page ad in the *Abbotsville Gazette*?" Jo framed a headline with her hands. " 'The Truth about Linda Weeks and the Lies She Told about Me?' It would still be only me claiming to be innocent."

"Oh, Jo," Carrie said, looking wretched and wringing her hands.

Jo knew what she was thinking, because the same thoughts were going through her own head. Jo's reputation was going south.

And along with that would go her shop. People wouldn't come to the Craft Corner to buy things or sign up for her workshops as long as they held even an unsupportable suspicion she was a murderer. The business Jo had struggled so hard to build and that had just started to allow her a bit of financial breathing space was in major jeopardy, not to mention what it was going to be like living among townspeople who thought the worst of her. Something had to be done.

"What you'll have to do," Javonne said, "is find out who sent those candies to Linda."

"I'd love to," Jo said. "But I'm sure the sheriff has already tried to do that, and would have stopped looking at *me* if he'd had any success. The person who bought the candy could have gotten it at any of several Kitty's Kandy stores around here. If they paid cash and didn't attract any particular attention at the time there would be no way of identifying them."

"But it would have to be someone who was familiar with this area, don't you think?" Carrie put in. "I mean, most of the vendors at Michicomi come from somewhere else and wouldn't know about our local candy stores."

"Not necessarily," Jo said. "Bill Ewing,

the guy who was so steamed at Linda, for one, is staying with a friend somewhere around here, to take photos. If he's stayed here before he probably knows the area. Gabe Stubbins is going to let me know where this friend is." Jo's thoughts went gratefully to the good-natured toymaker who had been so supportive during the stressful few days at Michicomi, and who also, Jo remembered a bit uneasily, had shown he was familiar with Abbotsville and its environs. That small coincidence, though, she was sure, had no bearing on things.

"Linda had been married," Jo said, moving on to another tack. "I wonder, knowing her, how bitter the divorce might have been and where the ex might be?"

"Didn't you say Meg Boyer mentioned knowing her in high school? Maybe she would know," Carrie said.

"She didn't seem aware of Linda having been married, since she didn't recognize Linda's married name. But it might still be worth talking to Meg. She might have connections to old classmates who do know about Linda's marriage."

"You still holding the paper flowers workshop tonight, Jo?" Javonne asked. "I'd understand if you're not, but maybe if our old gang gets together again we can help you brainstorm."

Jo had forgotten about the workshop, and though she was prepared for it, having planned ahead several days ago, she wondered how she would get through this long day. But with the rapid way things had spiraled downward, taking time out for rest was the last thing on her mind.

"Yes, I'll hold the workshop," she said, "though I suspect the number of people showing up has probably shrunk since I last looked at it."

Javonne flapped a hand. "No matter. Your true friends will be there, and we'll help you straighten this whole mess out." She moved toward the door. "I'm sorry this all comes on top of Russ Morgan's being shot. I've been hearing, though, along with everything else, that he's doing really well."

"Have you?" Jo brightened. "Mark Rosatti promised to keep me updated, but it's only been a few hours since I last saw him and I suspect he's had a few other things to do as well." Jo's thoughts had never been far from Russ. But convinced, thanks to Ina Mae, that Russ was in excellent hands, she allowed herself to worry much less.

"I'd better get back to the office," Javonne said. "See you tonight."

Jo and Carrie each waved Javonne off,

then turned to each other with concern-filled faces. Jo spoke first.

"Well, Meg Boyer works at the Abbot's Kitchen now. What would you like me to pick up for your lunch?"

"How about," Carrie said with a rueful look, "a nice solution to Linda Weeks's murder, all wrapped up tightly and tied with a bow."

Jo smiled and asked, "Did you want fries with that?"

CHAPTER 10

Jo pulled on a thick navy cardigan before heading out, glad she'd brought the sweater with her that morning. The earlier promise of a warm, sunny day had faded as clouds moved in to dim the brightness and chill the air. As she walked, the sight of a clump of daffodils, their sturdy stalks topped with buttery, half-opened buds, gave her hope for pleasanter days ahead — weatherwise, though at the moment Jo held little expectation for that in her life. For the immediate future, it seemed "pleasant" would be defined as "not under arrest" or "not seeing mothers pull their small children inside as she walked by," which hadn't happened yet. But the day was still young.

After Javonne's warning about the rumors flying around Abbotsville, Jo had two customers stop in. Their arrival had at first given her hope that the situation might not be as bad as it had sounded. It turned out, however, that these "customers," two women she'd never seen before, were simply curiosity seekers. While pretending interest in her craft wares they had mainly tossed stares her way in between whispered titters. They had finally left without making a purchase, leaving Jo with a sinking feeling about what lay ahead for her.

She passed the empty shop that had once been Fantastic Florals by Frannie. Jo remembered hearing that the place had been recently leased to an antiques dealer, and she saw signs of rejuvenation inside — painters' drop cloths and ladders. She was glad the shop would be active again, but would miss the feisty little florist who had once manned it. Frannie, for one, wouldn't have put any stock in the murder rumors, Jo was sure. But she had come to know Jo well enough, whereas the majority of townspeople still didn't. That, apparently, was Jo's vulnerability.

She came to the Abbot's Kitchen and reached for the door's handle uneasily, hoping to find the place on the empty side. She had held off coming until after the lunch rush and was relieved, as she pulled the door open, to see she had guessed right. The only face that turned her way was Ruthie's, which crinkled into a road map of creases as she smiled warmly.

"Hi, Ruthie," Jo said, gratefully returning the smile. "How've you been?"

"Working too hard. Good to see you again, Jo, though I'm sorry to hear about all your recent problems."

"Thank you. I appreciate that more than you can know, and I'm trying to resolve at least some of them. Carrie and I would like our usual order to go, and if she has a moment would you mind if I talked with Meg Boyer?"

"Meg? No, I don't mind at all. Something to do with this craft show business?"

Jo nodded. "Meg told me she went to high school with the woman who was murdered at Michicomi. I need to find out a few things about her."

"Meg knew that woman? She never said a word about it! I knew she'd been to the craft festival, of course. She's not much of a talker, is she? Hard worker, though, so I have no complaints."

"You and Bert have done all the work yourselves up to now, haven't you? This must give you a bit of a break."

Ruthie smiled. "All these years, just the two of us. We're starting to think it might be time to let go a little, take some time off, as long as we have the right people to handle things for us. Not easy finding reliable people, though, with what we can afford to pay." Ruthie turned her head toward the kitchen. "Meg! Can you come out here a minute?"

Ruthie lowered her voice and leaned toward Jo. "I wasn't all that impressed with Meg when she first applied. Seemed kinda listless and uninterested, you know? But then I heard she'd been stuck at home a lot with a husband who was kinda controlling. I thought this might be her first try to get out and get hold of her life a bit, you know what I mean? So I decided to give her a chance. It's been working out."

Jo nodded. "I'm glad."

Ruthie straightened up as Meg stepped through the door from the kitchen, a white apron covering the front of her paisley-printed smock and wide jeans. "You wanted to see me?" the younger woman asked.

"Jo, here, wants to talk to you. Why don't you grab a Coke or something and sit down a bit. I'll get Bert started on the order."

Ruthie disappeared into the kitchen, and Jo pulled a bottle of chilled iced tea from the self-serve case and turned to ask Meg, "Coke for you?"

"Uh-huh. Diet."

Jo handed her the can and went over to

128

one of the small tables near the window, Meg following behind. She twisted off her iced tea cap and waited until Meg popped her Coke open, then said, "I wanted to ask you more about Linda Weeks."

Meg shrugged. "Okay." She took a healthy gulp from her can. "What about her?"

"Her former husband. Did you happen to know him?"

"No. I never heard any news about her after high school, so I didn't even know she was married."

"What about other classmates? Did you keep in touch with anyone who might be able to give me a name and information on how to find him?"

Meg stared above Jo's right shoulder, thinking, and Jo saw a spark of interest appear in her eyes. She looked back at Jo. "You know, I might. Hold on." She pushed her chair back and stood up. "My pocketbook's in the back."

Jo sipped her iced tea and watched Meg go into the kitchen, her step a bit livelier than when she'd come out. Jo crossed her fingers that she'd return with a good lead. While she waited, a customer walked through the door, and Jo glanced over, relieved to see it was nobody she recognized — or who recognized her — but sad, at the same time, over that feeling. She had chosen to settle in a small town partly for the pleasure of becoming part of a community. She was discovering, though, that there could be a downside to that. With the way her business had slowed, she needed to clear her name quickly, before "down" turned into "down and out."

Ruthie came out to wait on the customer, and Meg soon followed, holding a large, well-worn handbag. She plopped down in her seat and began searching through it, pulling out things that looked to Jo like they might have been in there for years: old envelopes, rumpled tissues, at least two pairs of sunglasses, a mashed, wrapped Twinkie.

"Ah," Meg finally cried. "Here it is." She pulled out a battered-looking address book and flipped through it, small pieces of paper dropping out in the process. "Yes. Emmy Schmidt. I have her number. If it hasn't changed and I get her, I'll bet she can tell us something."

"Want to try now?" Jo dug into her own purse. "You can use my cell phone."

"Sure." Meg took the phone, then grinned. "I hope Emmy's sitting down when she answers. This'll be quite a shock, hearing from me."

Jo watched as Meg carefully punched in Emmy Schmidt's number, then waited for the connection. Meg drew a breath as someone apparently answered.

"Hi, Emmy? This is Meg Padgett. Remember me? From the Marching Wolverines?" She grinned, and Jo was able to faintly catch the sounds of Emmy screaming in surprise. "Yeah, a long time. Uh-huh. Right!"

Jo waited as Meg went through a brief catching-up conversation, noticing that she offered little of herself other than that she was now Meg Boyer and living in Abbotsville, Maryland. Emmy apparently had much more she wanted to share. Meg traded reminiscences about the high school band, in which she had played the clarinet and Emmy was a majorette, which at least sounded promising to Jo as someone likely to have been friends with Linda. But Jo shifted in her chair, wanting the conversation to get to the point.

Finally she heard Meg bring up Linda, not mentioning what had happened to her recently but only asking, casually, if Emmy knew if she was married or not.

"Oh?" Meg said, making writing motions to Jo, who quickly pulled out a pen and a scrap of paper from her pocketbook. "So she married him after all, huh? But it didn't last? What a shame. I heard she had gone to New York. Is he there too? Oh, really?" Meg scribbled something down. "Wow, that's a surprise. What made him move there, I wonder? Oh. Uh-huh. I see. Well . . ." Meg's side of the conversation lapsed into "mmms" and "uh-huhs" as Emmy apparently took over once again, but Meg pushed the paper she'd written on over to Jo as she continued to listen.

Jo read what was written there and felt her eyes widen. She looked up at Meg, who nodded agreement with Jo's reaction.

Linda Weeks's former husband was Patrick Weeks — a name that meant nothing to Jo — but he presently lived in Marlsburg, Maryland. Marlsburg was the surprising part, since it was probably within twenty miles of Abbotsville.

Jo thought this over, as Meg hung on the line with Emmy. Had Linda applied to come to Michicomi in Hammond County for more reasons than to sell jewelry? She must have known Patrick was living nearby. Did she contact him? And if so, how had that gone?

"Okay, Emmy. Great talking to you." Meg wound up her conversation — with some difficulty, apparently, as she added several more "uh-huhs" before the final good-bye.

She handed the warm phone back to Jo, looking pleased.

"Great work, Meg," Jo said.

"Will you go see him?"

"Yes, I think that'd work better than just calling. It sounded like you knew the guy she married from school. Would you like to come along?"

Meg frowned. "No, I don't think so. I mean, I didn't really know him. I just remembered his name and that he and Linda were a hot couple toward the end of senior year." She cleared her frown. "If I went we might just get stuck talking about high school stuff. Look how Emmy went on and on."

Jo thought Emmy's easiness about sharing information had come from talking to an old classmate and would have liked Meg's help in that way with the ex-husband. But she didn't want to urge Meg into a situation she wasn't comfortable with. Besides, Jo needed to remember that Patrick Weeks wasn't just a source of information, but a possible suspect. How possible remained to be discovered.

"Oh," Meg said, "Emmy mentioned that Pat has his own business, building custom-made furniture. That should make it easier to find him, don't you think?"

"Definitely. He'll at least be in the yellow pages. That's good to know." Jo stood up. "Thanks, Meg. You've been a terrific help."

Meg smiled, and flicked a strand of hair off her face with a toss of her head, a gesture that struck Jo as perkier than her usual half-hearted hand swipe.

As she walked back to the craft shop, lunch order in hand, Jo wondered about the high school version of Meg. What had she been like then? Certainly energetic enough to be in a marching band. Slimmer? Less mousy? Apparently memorable enough to be instantly recalled by the band's majorette. What had changed Meg over the years? An unwise marriage that had gradually beaten her down? Perhaps her husband had been the reason she held back from seeing Patrick Weeks, fearing what his reaction would be?

Jo remembered what Ruthie had said, that she thought Meg might be working on regaining control of her life. If so, Jo wished her the best of luck. Pulling your life back together, as Jo understood from her own experience, wasn't easy, but was well worth all the effort.

On that note, her thoughts flew to Russ, the man whose recent entrance into her life had brightened it so, but whose very presence she found herself feeling so conflicted about. The shooting had certainly demonstrated how important he'd become to her. But it had also frightened her. What if she let Russ mean as much to her as Mike had, only to lose him as she had lost Mike?

At that thought, Jo halted, nearly dropping her lunch bag.

"I don't know if I could bear that again," she said, remembering the pain of that time.

A second question instantly came to mind: *Would you not have married Mike if you'd known what would happen?*

Jo didn't have to think about that. "No, I wouldn't have missed those years for anything. They were precious to me. I wouldn't be who I am today without them."

Well then?

A car horn beeped and Jo suddenly realized she was blocking an alleyway exit. She waved apologetically and hustled out of the way.

"I don't know. I just don't know," she muttered, aware, as she continued on down the sidewalk, that she'd better figure it out.

CHAPTER 11

Jo was munching on her turkey and bacon roll-up at the back of the craft shop when the phone rang.

Since Carrie was in midbite of her veggie burger and struggling to keep control of the straggly bean sprouts that topped it, Jo mumbled, "I'll get it," and swallowed as quickly as she could manage without choking.

"Jo's Craft Corner," she said, having dropped her usual, "Jo, here," after Penny Collins's stuttering reaction that morning.

The caller obviously still picked up that it was she, saying, "Hello, Jo," but didn't hang up. "This is Gabe Stubbins."

"Gabe! Great to hear from you."

"And good to talk to you too. I hope you're doing well?"

"Things could be worse, I guess," Jo said, thinking they didn't have a long ways to go.

"Well, maybe this will help a little. I have

the information I promised to get for you."

"About Bill Ewing?"

"Yes. Got a pencil?"

Jo scribbled down the name and address Gabe gave her.

"Do you know anything about this friend?" she asked. "Is he a photographer too?"

"*She* owns a restaurant. Guess I should have mentioned that. More of a small diner, it sounds like, possibly the kind of place people find by following those knife-and-fork signs near a freeway exit. I gather there's a modest motel connected to it. I suppose Bill's staying in one of the rooms."

"Thanks, Gabe. This should be very helpful. Are you back home now?"

"Yes, I'm here in Pennsylvania for a few days, but I'll be off again to Richmond, Virginia, Thursday." Gabe chuckled. "The wife claims instead of 'His' and 'Her' towels, she should have 'Hers' and 'Welcome Stranger.' "

"I didn't know you were doing another show so soon. A Michicomi?"

"Right. I hadn't been scheduled for this one, but with the show losing Linda they had an opening. I decided to take it. I had plenty of toys stocked up, and Richmond's a good stop."

"I'm sure it is. Well, try to get some rest before hitting the road again. Thanks for getting this information for me."

Gabe wished her luck with it and said good-bye. Jo turned to Carrie, who'd finished her veggie burger by this time and was gathering up the wrappings.

"What are you doing for dinner tonight?" Jo asked.

"I have no idea. I haven't been to the market lately and our pickings are slim. Plus both Charlie and Amanda have after-school things going on, which means having to pick them up instead of food shopping and cooking."

"Perfect!" Jo smiled and Carrie threw her a puzzled look. "I think you deserve dinner out at" — Jo checked her note — "Ginger's House of Home Cookin'."

"I do?" Carrie asked, uncertainly. "Where's that?"

"Just off Route 30, at exit 14. A pleasant drive on a spring evening and a delightful spot for a family dinner. I hope."

Jo explained what Gabe had told her. "I'd go scout it out myself, but I've got the workshop tonight and I was hoping to get to the hospital sometime."

"Oh, of course!" The uncertainty on Carrie's face was replaced by an eagerness to help. "I'll just check in with Dan, but I'm sure he'll be fine with it. What do you want us to find out?"

"Anything you can, I guess." Jo described Bill Ewing to Carrie. "If we're lucky, you'll spot him hanging around there. If not, maybe you can strike up a conversation with the owner, Ginger, and see what you can pick up about him. Anything at all will be helpful."

"We'll do our best." Carrie opened her cell phone to call her husband about the idea, and Jo walked back to the stockroom to gather together the materials she needed for the workshop. She had checked the sign-up sheet to see who was coming and mentally crossed off the names of two people she felt sure would not show up. That left Ina Mae, Javonne, Loralee, and Loralee's daughter, Dulcie.

Considering the topic sure to be discussed beyond their project, Jo thought it should be an interesting evening.

A few hours later, Jo spread out materials for four on the workshop table, thinking, with little satisfaction, that she had been right. Around five o'clock both Ellie Blandsfield and Sally Holloway had called to cancel, each claiming unexpected emergencies. At least they'd been considerate enough to call, Jo thought, and she had responded as courteously, leaving an opening for them to return should they have a change of heart. That was a slim possibility, Jo knew, but she brushed away the thought, not wanting to dwell on the negative.

On the positive side, she had talked to Russ, briefly, and he'd sounded much better than he had the night before. She'd hoped to run over to the hospital before the workshop, but Russ suggested she come by later, explaining there'd been a steady stream of fellow police officers stopping in.

"You won't be too tired?" she'd asked.

"Not for you," he'd answered, which made her smile. "I'll have the nurse put a hold on visitors pretty soon and catch a few z's. You'll be on my approved list."

"Nice to be approved of."

"*Highly* approved of," he'd said, which had broadened her smile even more.

Jo pushed the large box of tissue papers to the middle of the table. She was deciding how much wire and glue to set out when Loralee and Dulcie walked in.

"There she is!" Loralee called out cheerfully with what was becoming her regular greeting. Jo rather liked it, coming, as it did from a good friend. If, on the other hand,

Jo started hearing it from strangers as she walked down the street, as in, "There she is — that murder suspect," *that* would be an altogether different matter.

Dulcie followed behind, and Jo noted the similarities and differences between mother and daughter. Dulcie mirrored her mother's petite frame but hadn't inherited Loralee's blond curls, sporting instead straight brown hair worn in a becoming bob. From the few interactions Jo had had with Dulcie, she seemed to have been blessed with much of Loralee's blithe nature, but tempered with a touch of steeliness. This surfaced particularly when her young family was concerned, much like a protective mother bear. But Jo decided that since she had no intention of ever getting between Dulcie and her brood, it shouldn't be a problem.

Jo welcomed them both, listening politely as Dulcie launched into a detailed explanation of the effort it had taken to arrive on time what with her having to feed and bathe both children plus tidy up and get a couple of loads of laundry going. Since her husband, Ken, was apparently home and not incapacitated, Jo suspected he had long ago realized she was happier doing such things herself — and then being able to exclaim about it — and that his best bet was to keep

141

out of her way.

"How is our lieutenant doing?" Loralee asked, her face pinched with concern.

"Much better," Jo assured her.

Loralee gave Jo's arm a squeeze. "I know this is a difficult time for you, dear. I wouldn't have dreamed of expecting you to carry on with this workshop, except Javonne thought we might be able to come up with ways to help with that craft show problem if we all gathered together."

"I wouldn't be surprised at all if that happened, Loralee. There's something about everyone's ideas being thrown into the mix that always seems to work."

"Like putting together a good potting soil," Dulcie said, looking sage. "A little humus, some fertilizer, maybe a bit of lime, and pretty soon good things get growing."

Loralee laughed lightly, explaining, "Dulcie's been working in the garden lately." Ina Mae and Javonne pushed through the Craft Corner door at that time, and Loralee waved them over, calling out cheerily, "C'mon, ladies. Time to get planting!"

"We can start on our paper flowers before getting into anything else," Jo said, as the women seated themselves around her table. "Loralee, do you remember these?"

"Yes," Loralee said. "I certainly do. Those paper flowers were one of the first things I noticed when we first visited Sylvia and Xavier. They had brightened up that little apartment so beautifully."

"How is the baby?" Javonne asked.

"Even prettier than the flowers," Loralee said, "and growing like a weed," she added with a grin.

"I would have loved to have Sylvia help teach this class," Jo said, "but her hands are pretty full for now. She did give me a few tips, though, and I've practiced by making several myself." And hung them about my booth at Michicomi, she remembered but didn't mention, not wanting to bring up the craft fair problem just yet. Jo reached for the tissue paper. "There are several types of flowers we can make, but we'll start with the easiest one."

Jo picked out a sheet each of white, blue, red, and yellow and laid them evenly on top of one another. "You can use one color or several colors, whichever you prefer. But you'll need four sheets, and we'll cut a square out of all four lined up together." Jo did that, then straightened them up neatly. "Next, keeping the papers together, you'll make small accordion pleats like this all across the square." Jo folded her papers back and forth until she ended up with a skinny rectangle.

"Now," she said, "take a piece of wire and twist it tightly around the center of this rectangle, and voila!" Jo fluffed out her paper layers to form a beautiful, and extremely colorful, flower.

"Wow, neat!" Dulcie cried.

"And remarkably simple," Ina Mae said.

"It is," Jo agreed. "And once you have your flower you can cover the wire stem with floral tape or use crepe paper if you prefer. Make a bunch of these and you've got a vase full of long-lasting decoration."

"Hah," Javonne said. "I don't expect them to last long in my place, between my rough-housing kids and the dog. Maybe if I hang them from the ceiling."

The ladies got down to work, picking out their tissue papers as Jo passed around scissors and rulers. "After you guys finish this one," she said, "I'll show you a few, more intricate flower shapes until we run out of time."

"This would be a piece of cake for Vernon, wouldn't it?" Javonne said, referring to Vernon Dobson, the only male in Jo's past beading workshops. Vernon, a retired butcher, had shown surprising ability at learning that particular craft, and had helped Javonne with it, as she had struggled.

"Oh, Vernon," Loralee said. "Where did they go, again?"

"A cruise in the western Caribbean," Javonne said. "His wife wanted to go, he told me. I think he wasn't too sure about it. He's never been on a cruise."

"He'll enjoy it," Loralee said. "But it's unfortunate for us that he's gone right now. We could probably use his input on Jo's problem."

"Speaking of which," Ina Mae said, "what's the latest, Jo, on the Linda Weeks murder?" She lined up tissue papers she had chosen in varying shades of purple.

Jo had stepped back to pour herself a mug of coffee, wondering as she did how many cups that came to for the day. Her adrenaline from the previous night had begun to run out somewhere near midafternoon.

"I found out a couple of things," she said. "The first from Meg Boyer, when I went over to the Abbot's Kitchen."

"Oh, Meg!" Loralee cried. "Is she happy with her new job?"

"It seems to be working out. Meg was able to find out for me that Linda's ex-husband lives over in Marlsburg. He does custom-made furniture."

"Marlsburg!" Dulcie said. "That's right

down the road!"

"Right, half an hour's drive at most," Jo agreed.

"Hmm," Ina Mae said. "Do you suppose this ex-husband knew Linda was in the area?"

"That's something I plan to find out. I'll drive over to see him tomorrow."

"Would you like me to come with you?" Dulcie asked. She had chosen to make her first flower in a single shade of hot pink and was folding her square carefully. "I'm looking for a corner cabinet for our dining room — they're *so* hard to find — so maybe I could start off the conversation with this ex-husband about making one, and then work things around to Linda."

"A wonderful idea," Loralee chimed in. "I can watch the children for you, so no problem there."

The others nodded, and Jo, who had planned to make the trip alone, thought that it might just work to take Dulcie along. Dulcie had an easy, disarming way about her that could help draw out Patrick Weeks. "Okay," Jo said. "Does one o'clock work for you?"

"Perfect." Dulcie fanned out her tissue paper flower, which had turned out quite well. Dulcie grinned, admiring her first craft creation, and Loralee beamed like the ever-proud mother she was.

Seeing that the group had mastered the basic paper flower, Jo proceeded to demonstrate a petal flower shape, showing them how to cut the tissue paper, into circles this time, then fold the circles into quarters and shape the petals with scissors.

"Once we have the flower part done," she said, "we'll thread the petal shapes onto a wire and add a small center with a cotton ball." She wired and glued, then held her finished flower up to four delighted "ahs."

As she reached for her scissors to begin her second flower, Ina Mae asked, "You said you'd found out a *couple* of things, Jo. What's the second?"

Jo shared what she'd learned about Bill Ewing, explaining to those who hadn't heard yet exactly what her interest in him was. "Carrie and Dan are dining tonight at the restaurant of the friend he's staying with. I'm hoping they can pick up a little more information about him while they're there."

Ina Mae nodded approvingly as she folded her newly cut circles into quarters.

"He's a photographer, you said?" asked Javonne, still picking out the papers for her second flower. "My Harry loves cameras.

He's always playing around with them and picking up new lenses and things — when he's not fixing teeth, that is. Maybe he can be of some help in talking with this Ewing guy."

"Wednesday's his day off, isn't it?" Ina Mae asked. "Perhaps if Jo finds out where he'll be photographing a barn that day, Harry and Jo could accidentally run into him."

Wow, Jo thought, looking over her group of friends who were so rapidly coming up with ways to help her. Tonight's idea mix, she thought, grinning as Dulcie's metaphor came to mind, was beginning to turn her bare-dirt plans into fertile ground.

"That'd be terrific, Javonne," she said. "See what Harry thinks of it."

Jo smiled as she watched four sets of hands work diligently at their budding bouquets. Who knew what an evening of making paper flowers might help her dig up? And hopefully, she added, taking a sip from her coffee mug, quash the seeds of suspicion toward her that had been germinating in Sheriff Franklin's mind.

CHAPTER 12

At nine o'clock, Jo waved off her workshop group and locked the front door behind them, feeling a wave of fatigue wash over her. One more quick cup of coffee, she decided, and then she'd take off for the hospital. She drained the last of the pot into her mug, then tidied up the workshop area quickly between sips, eager to be on her way.

The drive to the hospital was quiet, as Abbotsville streets usually were at that time of night, and the hospital lobby turned out to be even quieter and much emptier than it had been the previous night. Jo thought how she much preferred this calm atmosphere. Last night's had been filled with stress and worry, while the current one gave out a feeling of restfulness and healing, exactly what she wanted for one particular patient.

Russ had been moved from the ICU to a private room. As she stepped off the elevator, Jo spotted a uniformed police officer

149

standing guard. Why, she wasn't quite sure, since Russ's shooter was definitely in custody. She decided it was simply a way Russ's comrades showed extra concern for one of their own. She started to give the officer her name, but he smiled and waved her in before she got more than "Jo" out, saying, "He's been waiting for you."

Jo peeked in and found Russ awake, the head of his bed raised as he watched the news. "Hi," she said.

Russ flashed his old smile, not the exhausted one of last night, which cheered her immensely as well as making her heart skip. He looked much less pale than he had too, though still far from robust.

"You made it," he said, clicking off his TV with the remote.

"Looked forward to it all day." Jo went over to the right side of his bed, his uninjured side. He held out his hand and when she took it, he drew her close. They kissed, but gently, Jo acutely aware that although Russ looked and sounded much better, his strength still had a long way to go. She stroked his cheek, then said, "You shaved!"

"With help. Couldn't greet my date looking like a caveman."

"Your date," Jo said, running a hand through her hair, "probably looks like

150

something the saber-toothed tiger dragged in."

Russ shook his head and started to say something, but was overcome by a fit of coughing. Jo poured fresh water into the glass on his end table and held it out to him. He took a swallow, cleared his throat, then handed it back. "Thanks." He grinned. "You'd make a good nurse."

Jo laughed. "Maybe if serving water were all I had to do. Do you need anything from a real nurse?"

He shook his head, and Jo pulled up a chair and sat down, taking his hand once more.

"How're you feeling?" she asked, leaning closely.

"Hard to tell with all the pain meds they're pumping into me. Ask me in a couple days when the pills start tapering off."

"You scared me half to death, you know."

Russ squeezed her hand. "Sorry about that. My own damn fault for getting in the way of the bullet."

"Mark Rosatti said you were trying to help the girlfriend who panicked."

Russ winced and shook his head. "If she'd only hung on a few more minutes. The situation seemed to be calming down, and we might have walked them both out of there with no problem. I don't know, maybe he said something that really scared her, made her decide to run for it."

Russ's voice cracked dryly and he reached for his water. Jo got it for him, then pulled the tray table over the bed for him to use.

"Turns out," Russ said, after a swallow of water, "the guy had been showing signs of instability for a good while, which they're telling me might have been handled if he'd gotten treatment."

"Why didn't he get it?"

Russ shook his head. "Who knows? Denial? Ignorance? The system? Whatever it was, people ended up getting hurt because he didn't go for help early on."

Jo rubbed Russ's hand, thinking about that. "What is the girlfriend's condition?"

"Bullet grazed her. She'll be okay. And the shooter? Not a scratch. He ended up throwing down his gun and walking out with his hands up." Russ's mouth twisted. "Full of remorse, I hear." He pulled his hand away to rub at his face, which looked fatigued.

"Did you get any rest from your steady stream of visitors?" Jo asked.

"Tried to. Pretty hard to rest in a hospital, I'm finding out. Can't wait to get on home."

"Don't rush it. What about your family, Russ? Have they been called?" Jo knew Russ had a younger brother, Scott, somewhere out west.

"Yeah, Scott called and wanted to come. I told him not to. He can't afford to fly all the way from Seattle at the drop of a hat. Besides, Pam's due pretty soon. He should be with her."

Jo nodded. She also knew Russ had been married before, but didn't ask if there had been any contact with his former wife. He hadn't talked to Jo much about the marriage, other than it had ended five years ago and had lasted barely four. Jo took her cue from his reticence on the subject, aware it was not an area she was eager to get into either.

There was a brisk knock on the door, then a scrub-suited nurse walked in, pushing a cart filled with medical paraphernalia. "Time to do a few things for our lieutenant, here," she said, taking a quick look at his bandaged shoulder. She turned to Jo. "If you'll just wait outside?"

Jo stood up. "Actually, I'd better get going. It's pretty late."

"What's happening with that Michicomi case?" Russ asked, glancing suspiciously at the instruments lined up on the cart.

"Oh, not too much," Jo said, pushing her chair out of the way.

"Franklin arrest anyone yet?"

Jo shook her head, then leaned down to give Russ a good-night kiss, which, while exceedingly pleasant had the additional effect of blocking more questions. She hurried to the door, saying, "Get a good rest tonight. I'll be back tomorrow."

"Promise?" Russ asked, leaning around the nurse to see her.

"Wild horses wouldn't keep me away."

Jo pulled the door closed behind her thinking that wild horses weren't exactly what she needed to worry about. Franklin's deputies showing up with an arrest warrant, however, was a whole different thing. But she wasn't going to think about that yet. What she wanted most right now was to head on home and fall into that wonderfully soft, beckoning bed of hers. Russ might be the one pumped full of sleep-inducing pain meds, but the way Jo felt as she made her way back to the parking lot, she could definitely give him a run for the money on pillow-to-REM speed.

CHAPTER 13

The next morning, shortly after arriving at her shop, Jo spotted the answering machine blinking and pressed Play. The voices of Carrie's two knitting students came on, one after another, and with much hemming and hawing gave convoluted reasons for not being able to come to the class that morning. Jo sighed and called Carrie.

"You might as well take the morning off," she said, explaining why.

"Shoot!" Carrie said. "Why don't I call those two and try to straighten them out?"

"I doubt it would do any good. At this point no one is going to admit they truly believe I'm guilty of murder. But the rumors are probably making them uneasy enough to want to keep their distance. Nothing you say is going to erase that feeling. Only finding the real murderer will do that. Which reminds me, how did it go last night at the diner I sent you to?"

"Well, Ginger's version of home cooking was more like home freezer to home microwave. We didn't leave hungry, that's the best I can say for it. But we did spot that photographer Bill Ewing sitting at the counter. You described him perfectly."

"Did you get to talk to him?"

"It took a while, but yes, around the time we were ordering desserts — I don't recommend the apple pie, by the way — Dan managed to catch his attention by bringing up the subject of tobacco barns with the waitress, and how they were disappearing with all the new development. I saw Ewing's ears perk up when Dan mentioned an old one he knew about that was still standing after many years. Ewing wandered over to ask about its location. He wrote down Dan's directions. I think he plans to go there tomorrow, if the weather holds out."

"Great! Good work, Carrie. When this is over I'll treat you all to a really good dinner, at the place of your choice."

"When this is straightened out, I'd be happier to see you put your money into a big open-house party at the shop to welcome back all your wayward customers."

"Not a bad idea," Jo said, thinking, however, that it depended not only on this terrible situation ultimately being straightened out, but also on how quickly it was. Her budding business had precious little cushion to fall back on. This slowdown of income would hurt her badly if she didn't clear her name soon.

When Carrie arrived, shortly before one, Jo was eager to be on her way to talk to Patrick Weeks.

"Thanks for holding down the fort again," she said, grabbing her pocketbook and keys. "Wish me luck in Marlsburg."

"I do. I hope between you and Dulcie that you can pry everything you need from that ex-husband."

Jo hoped so too, and as she climbed into her aging but still road-worthy Toyota she wondered if she had made the right decision about bringing Dulcie along. She didn't know Loralee's daughter all that well, having spoken to her fewer than a handful of times since she'd moved her family into Loralee's house with its newly attached mother-in-law suite. At last night's workshop it had sounded like a good idea — that Dulcie get the conversation going with questions for Weeks about corner cabinets. Would the discussion get stuck on furniture, though? Jo needed to turn the talk to Linda. Would it have been easier on her own, to simply approach Weeks directly?

By the time she'd reached Loralee's and Dulcie's home Jo had run out of questions as well as time. Right or wrong, Dulcie was coming with her. As Jo pulled up in front of the pretty Cape Cod, she spotted the woman waiting out front beside a blooming forsythia, a red and white cooler sitting at her feet. Jo's first thought was that Marlsburg wasn't a long enough trip to need food. And Dulcie certainly couldn't plan to soften up Patrick Weeks with gifts of home-made soups or baked goods, though Jo wouldn't put that past Dulcie's mother. What did she need to keep cold?

"Hi, Jo," Dulcie called, picking up the cooler and hurrying toward the Toyota. "Let me pop this in real quick, and then I'll get the baby seat."

"Baby seat?" Jo squeaked.

"For Andrew." Dulcie closed the passenger door on her cooler, then returned to the house where a car seat perched on the front stoop.

Jo eased out from behind the wheel. The last she remembered of last night's discussion was that Loralee had volunteered to watch Dulcie's children. *Both* of them.

"Caitlin felt a little warm to me," Dulcie explained, as she lugged the bulky seat to

Jo's car. "I can't take a chance the baby will catch something."

Jo didn't claim to know that much about babies, but it seemed to her that babies were *always* catching something, that it was part of what defined their babyness.

"Is Andrew specially vulnerable?" she asked, suddenly picturing Dulcie's son as living one step away from life in a bubble.

"Andrew's extremely robust!" Dulcie answered, almost dropping the car seat in her shock at Jo's implication. "I make all his baby food from scratch, and he gets absolutely no refined sugar. He's healthier than any other thirteen-month-old I know!"

"But you're so concerned about him getting sick." Jo reluctantly opened her Toyota's back door as Dulcie hefted the baby seat, ready to strap it in.

"He'll be much better off staying with me," Dulcie said in a tone of finality. As she got to work installing the seat, Loralee appeared on the porch, carrying baby Andrew. Jo walked over to meet her.

"I'm sorry, Jo," Loralee said, adjusting Andrew's little knit cap. "I know you didn't plan on having the baby with you. And Ken needed the car today, or Dulcie would have left the baby seat where it was and driven you both."

Or maybe she could have just cancelled altogether, Jo thought but didn't voice to Loralee, who would have been pained. Instead she asked, "How is Caitlin? Does she need to see a doctor?"

"She seems fine, so far. I promised Dulcie I'd check her temperature regularly and call the doctor if it got any higher, but I really think she was simply a little overheated from running around earlier." Loralee leaned closer to Jo and whispered, "Dulcie's a wonderful mother, but a bit over cautious."

Jo smiled weakly, thinking, *now* you tell me.

"Would you mind terribly holding him for a minute?" Loralee asked. "I need to bring out the diaper bag, which is quite bulky."

Jo took Andrew, who, she had to admit, was a cutie with his no-refined-sugar chubby cheeks and big blue eyes. She quickly carried him toward his mother, before it could sink in that he had just been handed over to a complete stranger and therefore needed to work up the required howl.

"There you are," Dulcie singsonged as she reached out for her son, gave him a loving nuzzle, then strapped him securely into his seat. "I've packed plenty of drinks and nibbles in the cooler," she said to Jo, "so he shouldn't be a it of trouble."

Promise? Jo wanted to ask, but didn't. One part of wisdom, she remembered once hearing, was recognizing the inevitable and accepting it, and she decided she might as well strive for a little wisdom. She wished, though, she had striven long before this excursion was first proposed.

Loralee trotted over with the diaper bag, and Jo stowed it in the back, then climbed behind the wheel. They all waved good-bye, with Loralee continuing until Jo turned the corner and probably long after. As Jo caught the final sight of her friend in her rearview mirror, she wondered what Russ would say about a murder investigation starting off in such a manner. Several wry comments came to mind before she realized she was highly unlikely to ever tell him, or at least not for a long time. Certainly not while he was still recovering from his gunshot wound.

The drive to Marlsburg progressed fairly pleasantly. The sun peeked out for a bit, highlighting the white-flowering trees along the road, which Dulcie identified as flowering pears. "There might be a few wild cherries here and there too," Dulcie said, which, if correct, indicated her interest in gardening went beyond plopping a potted mum in a hole or sprinkling a few marigold seeds in a row.

161

Andrew was thankfully quiet, aside from the few squeaks and munching noises Jo heard behind her as he worked at his nibbles. Dulcie kept so busy supplying him with chunks of fruit or sugar-free crunchies that nothing was discussed about the upcoming encounter with Patrick Weeks. Jo hoped this trip wouldn't end up being one long "mother's afternoon out." Dulcie and Andrew might benefit from the excursion, but Jo's situation had little room for such luxuries.

She pulled off of Route 30 at the exit that announced Marlsburg, then drove a mile or two until the sparseness of houses occasionally dotting the landscape changed into the compact density of town streets. Jo checked the directions Dan had printed off his computer for her, and with Dulcie's help reading the street signs, made a few turns until they both spotted the sign: "Weeks Custom-Made Furniture."

"There it is," they said in unison, and Jo pulled into the small parking lot beside the one-story brown building. While Dulcie got busy extracting Andrew from his seat, Jo stepped out to look the place over. Though clearly many years old, the outside had been painted and trimmed attractively, with diamond-paned windows at the front that gave a cozy, Williamsburg feel. Large masonry flowerpots flanked the entrance, which Jo imagined would sport red geraniums or something equally as welcoming once the weather warmed. The overall effect, she felt, was a thriving business, though from the size of the place, probably a modest one. Too modest, she was sure, for Linda to have wanted to be a part of it.

They passed through the door into a small showroom filled with wooden furniture: dining room sets, rockers, dressers, end tables, all glowing with a rich, soft patina. "Oooh, I like these," Dulcie said.

A man stepped out from a back room, wiping his hands on a rag. Of medium height and build, he had thinning, sandy-colored hair and pleasantly even features, though his serious expression told Jo he was probably more comfortable in the back room than dealing with customers. He was dressed in a plaid flannel shirt tucked into jeans.

"Afternoon, ladies," he said, greeting them. "What can I do for you?"

"Mr. Weeks?" Jo asked, and he nodded.

"I love your furniture," Dulcie said, shifting Andrew in her arms.

"Thank you." A smile transformed his face, but only briefly. "We specialize in eighteenth-century styles, but we can make others. Were you looking for anything in particular?"

Dulcie launched into an explanation of the corner cabinet she was thinking of, and as she did Jo glanced around and noticed a girl of about eight peeking out of the back area. "I'm not sure what we can afford just yet," Dulcie said, "but I'd love to get some ideas."

Weeks led Dulcie to a couple of pieces in the showroom, mentioning the alterations that could easily be made as well as the various stains and finishes available. Jo followed, but stopped to examine a lovely, bentwood rocker. The young girl stepped out a little farther. Jo smiled, and she smiled back shyly, then came all the way over.

"I helped my daddy make that," she told Jo.

"Did you? You both did a very good job. It's beautiful."

The girl smiled wider, and Jo looked at her more closely. She had her father's sandy hair, but a shade or two brighter. Her eyes, though, were definitely her mother's. Jo realized with a shock that this must be Linda's daughter. A daughter whose existence Linda had neglected to mention to any of her friends in New York.

164

As the girl ran her hand over the rocker's curved arm, Jo asked, "What's your name?"

"Abigail."

"Abigail? That's a very pretty name."

"Abby," Patrick Weeks called, "would you bring my catalogue from the back?"

As the girl turned and ran to the back room, Weeks explained, "She's out of school today because her asthma was acting up earlier. She's okay now."

"What a shame!" Dulcie cried. "Asthma and allergies can be so frightening in children. But usually they outgrow them, don't they?"

Weeks shifted his weight. "Usually."

Abigail ran back with a catalogue in her hand. Weeks took it and rapidly flipped through to find a particular page. He rolled back the other pages and held it out to Dulcie.

"This is the one I was talking about. Very eighteenth century in style and also in construction. All the joints are dovetail, or mortise and tenon, which gives a much stronger, longer-lasting joint. Plus we sand only enough for smoothness, but still allow the character of the wood to show through."

Weeks went on about stains and lacquers, clearly enthused with his subject, and Dulcie listened closely, obviously enthralled. Jo wondered how serious she was about wanting a cabinet, and since no costs had yet been mentioned, what her budget might allow. The workmanship Weeks was describing was not going to come cheap.

Finally, a price was named, and Dulcie gave a little gasp. "Oh, my!"

"That, of course, would be our top of the line." Weeks flipped a few more pages and began discussing another piece. Andrew, who until then had been quite cooperative, apparently decided he'd had enough and started fussing.

"Andrew," Dulcie said, struggling with the suddenly squirmy child. "What has gotten into you?"

Jo felt a tug on her jacket.

"I have some toys he could play with," Abigail said, shyly but loud enough for Dulcie to hear.

"Do you?" Dulcie said, smiling at the girl. "What kind of toys?"

"A top my daddy made out of wood. And some blocks. We keep them in the corner back there."

"I'm afraid Andrew needs a quick diaper change before he plays with anything. Do you mind?" Dulcie asked Weeks.

"No, it's fine. We get lots of families. Abby, show the lady where the restroom is, okay?"

Abby skipped off, leading the way, and Jo, suddenly pleased to have brought Andrew along, was left alone with Weeks. He looked over to her. "Can I show you anything in particular?"

"My friend is the one who's looking for furniture."

Weeks nodded and started to turn away, but before he got too far, Jo asked, "Does Abby know what's happened to her mother?"

CHAPTER 14

Patrick Weeks looked at Jo, a scowl rapidly darkening his face. "Who are you?"

"My name's Jo McAllister. I knew Linda in New York where we both crafted jewelry."

"You were a friend of hers?"

"I knew her. I found Linda difficult to be friends with."

Weeks gave a low snort. "Then you knew her pretty well. To answer your question, no, I haven't told Abby yet, so I'd appreciate your not saying anything in front of her."

Jo nodded. "Of course. She seems like a sweet girl. Linda never mentioned her to me."

Weeks walked toward the front windows, farther away from the restroom and play area where Abby lingered. "That doesn't surprise me in the least. Abby was two when Linda decided we were holding her back and took off. I could count the times she's seen her daughter since then on the fingers of one hand."

"How sad."

"Actually, I think Abby's better off for it. Linda would have been a rotten mother if she'd hung around."

"What will you tell Abby about her?"

"That's going to be a tough one, isn't it?"

"Daddy, can the baby play with the new toy truck?" Abby asked, running halfway across the showroom.

"No, sweetheart." Weeks cleared the grimness from his face to answer his daughter. "I haven't finished sanding it yet."

"Oh, okay." Abby ran back to where Dulcie and Andrew were, and Weeks turned back to Jo.

"The sheriff was here to inform me of what happened to Linda," he said. "Abby wasn't around, then, thank God."

Jo noticed that all his concern centered on his daughter and the effect such news would have on her, with nothing spared for what had happened to his ex-wife. She wished she could have been there when the sheriff first told Weeks, to see his reaction. Had he been shocked, or merely pretending shock? Would she have been able to tell?

Jo was about to ask if Linda had contacted Weeks when the door to the showroom suddenly opened and a tall, matronly woman breezed in.

"Patrick," she called, spotting him with Jo, "I've decided I want that table made after all."

Jo saw relief fly across the man's face — from having his conversation with Jo interrupted? — and he excused himself to attend to his paying customer. Dulcie, looking over, picked up Andrew and rejoined Jo, with Abby trailing behind.

"Any luck?" she asked.

Jo shrugged, glancing at Abby. "A little." She saw that Weeks and the tall woman had become engrossed in a conversation that looked unlikely to end soon, judging from the papers he began pulling out from behind a counter. Then a young couple entered the store, running further, unwitting interference between Patrick Weeks and Jo. She asked Dulcie, "What would you think of getting a cup of coffee, somewhere around here?"

"Abby tells me that she and her daddy go to Shirley's Café a lot, and that it's right down the street. Is that right, Abby?"

"Uh-huh." Abby ran to the window and pointed. "It's right down there, past the gift shop and the tree that was hit by lightning last summer and now it has a big dark stripe going down it."

"Wow, so we'll get to see that," Jo said. "Thanks, Abby."

"Will you bring the baby back?" Abby asked Dulcie. She reached up to touch one of the little hands Andrew held down to her.

"Maybe not today, Abby," Dulcie said. "But we might come back another time. Your daddy makes beautiful furniture."

Abby nodded but looked disappointed as she waved good-bye to Andrew. Dulcie called out her thanks to Patrick Weeks with a promise that she would think over all he had told her. He looked up from his consultation to acknowledge their leaving. His gaze, Jo noticed, left Dulcie and settled on her as they made their way to the door.

"Thanks for getting me those few minutes to talk with Weeks," Jo said as soon as they were out of the store.

"Thank Andrew," Dulcie said. "He's the one who put an end to the furniture discussion with his squirminess."

If this were Carrie, Jo might have jokingly asked if a well-timed pinch hadn't possibly occurred, but she doubted Dulcie would consider that funny. She also wondered why Dulcie so readily agreed to let her child play with strange toys, but that was soon answered by Dulcie herself.

"It's a good thing I had my disinfectant

wipes with me. I gave those blocks a good rub down before I let Andrew near them."

They stopped at Jo's car to pick up Andrew's sippy cup from the cooler, then continued on down the street toward the café Abby had pointed out.

Shirley's Café turned out to be a small, family-style place with blue-checked curtains trimming its windows and cozy wooden booths and tables welcoming its patrons. The menu displayed near the door featured home-style foods such as meatloaf and chicken with dumplings, and Jo could understand why Patrick Weeks took his daughter there often.

The sole waitress, full figured and friendly, quickly produced a high chair for Andrew, exclaiming over his big blue eyes and generally clucking in a grandmotherly way. When she brought their order of coffee, she asked chattily where Jo and Dulcie were from and what had brought them to Marlsburg — the perfect lead-in, Jo thought, for bringing up Patrick Weeks.

Dulcie explained about their visit to the furniture shop, adding that she wasn't sure she could afford the prices. She righted Andrew's sippy cup, which was filled with apple juice and had rolled over on his high-chair tray, a tray she'd, of course, quickly wiped down before settling Andrew behind it.

"Yes, Pat's prices can be high," agreed the woman, who Jo had decided from her general air of ownership must be Shirley. "It's all high-quality stuff, though. You buy something from him, it'll last long enough to pass on to this little guy here someday."

Jo smiled, trying to imagine Andrew grown-up enough to have a place to furnish. "Mr. Weeks's little girl was there," she said. "She was awfully sweet, eager to help with the baby."

"Oh, Abby's a doll! I just love her to death." Shirley winked and said, "I'm her honorary grandmother, you know. Have the certificate she drew for me, with my name on it and all." Her smile faded. "Poor thing. Abby really *needs* a grandmother. Pat is great with her, but a little girl needs the feminine touch sometimes."

"What about her mother?" Dulcie asked, and Jo waited to hear just what Shirley knew.

"Took off," Shirley said, her eyebrows arching and mouth thinning in disapproval. "Cared more about chasing her own concerns and left that dear little thing behind. Can you believe it? Barely sees her daughter at all, from what I understand."

Dulcie automatically reached out to Andrew, patting his hand as though needing to reassure him of her loving dependability.

"So she hasn't been back here for a long time?" Jo asked.

"Well, no, she was here, actually, just last week."

"Oh," Jo said, muffling her interest. Her eyes flicked toward Dulcie's then back to Shirley. "I guess Abby was happy to see her, huh?"

Shirley sighed, then pulled a chair from an adjoining table and sat down. "I can't imagine what that poor little thing was feeling. This out-of-the-blue visit from her mother must have confused her to pieces. She has asthma, you know, and it's been acting up pretty bad lately, and I blame it all on that mother, what with her suddenly claiming she wanted to have custody again."

"Custody!"

Shirley nodded. "Can you believe it? The girl barely knows her, and now the woman thinks she can swoop down and be a mother again, just like that." She shook her head disgustedly.

"Can she?" Jo asked. "Legally, I mean? Did she ever give up custody?"

"Patrick says they had agreed to joint custody from the first, but she never claimed it before. Said her life was too unsettled, or something. So what's changed? I don't know. All I know is it's going to break my heart if Abby ends up going off with her. And Patrick's too. Not to mention what it'll probably do to Abby." Shirley shook her head sadly. "I just hope he can do something to stop her."

A customer came into the café, and Shirley pulled herself together, calling out as she stood up, "Afternoon, Harvey! How're you doing today?"

Jo looked at Dulcie, sure they were thinking the same thing. *Had* Patrick done something to stop Linda?

Dulcie leaned closer to whisper, "She doesn't know Linda Weeks is dead."

Jo nodded.

"How's your sister doin', Shirl?" Jo heard Harvey ask as he settled into a booth nearby.

"Doing wonderful! Her and Joe's big anniversary party up in Philly went great! We all had a fine time."

"Missed you around here. Nobody makes chili like you do."

Shirley laughed. "That's why I take off once in a while. So people don't take me so much for granted."

So, Shirley had been out of town and hadn't yet caught up with the latest happenings. Jo expected Harvey would fix that, and she was right. Before long Jo heard Harvey lower his voice confidentially. Shirley's hand flew to her mouth as she listened.

"Oh! Oh, that poor little girl!" Shirley looked toward Patrick Weeks's custom furniture shop. "I don't know how she's going to handle this," she said adding grimly, "Pat, though, won't be feeling too bad."

Jo exchanged another glance with Dulcie. That, they both seemed to agree, was probably an understatement.

CHAPTER 15

"So Patrick Weeks looks like a good possibility, huh?" Javonne asked. She carefully made the first fold in her square of paper, following Jo's directions. Javonne, Ina Mae, Loralee, and Dulcie had gathered for the "Beginning Origami" workshop, though Jo suspected their interests leaned more toward murder than origami. Jo had earlier gathered beautiful origami papers for a project that tied in with their previous class on paper flower creations — making an origami tulip — and had demonstrated the various steps involved.

Answering Javonne, Jo said, "He certainly had a good reason for wanting Linda dead."

"From what the woman at the café told us," Dulcie said, looking up from studying the folding diagram Jo had passed out, "Linda was ready to claim her joint custody rights to their little girl."

"And Patrick felt quite strongly that Linda

was not someone he wanted in his daughter's life anymore," Jo added.

"Strongly enough to murder his ex-wife?" Ina Mae asked. She frowned at her still uncreased, rose-colored paper. She seemed unwilling to make that first crucial fold until she had each of the multistepped folds memorized and understood.

"I don't know." Jo picked up the tulip she had folded for the group and turned it about thoughtfully. "He didn't strike me as a violent man, but then Linda wasn't bludgeoned to death. Whoever sent her that doctored-up candy didn't have to be there and watch her die."

"Which isn't to say they weren't," Loralee put in. She was going great guns, Jo noticed, with her folds. A few more steps and she would have her tulip completed.

"No, that's true," Jo agreed. "For all I know the murderer could have been standing right there in the crowd."

"And you didn't know Patrick Weeks at the time," Loralee said, "so you wouldn't have recognized him."

"But was he there?" Dulcie asked. "Or did he send the candy at all? That's still the big question."

"Indeed," Ina Mae agreed, still frowning, whether over the puzzle of the murder or the puzzle of the origami diagram was unclear. "The death of Linda Weeks," she said, "has a twofold effect. It removes her custody threat, but it also leaves the daughter motherless, which could be devastating to a little girl, even for a mother she seldom saw. I think we all understand how children can idealize an absent parent. Would this man be willing to put his daughter through that kind of pain?"

"I'd say so," said Javonne. "He'd probably justify the pain as being short term, whereas her mother taking custody would be life altering, and in a very negative way. Don't you think, Jo?"

Jo shook her head, unsure. "He hadn't told Abby yet about Linda. He was clearly very concerned about the effect it would have on her."

"He'll have to tell her soon," Dulcie said. "Word is spreading. We saw that at the café."

"Yes," Jo said. "Maybe he was waiting for Shirley, the 'honorary grandmother,' to be around to help. If so, it would suggest he's a loving, caring father."

"People have killed in the name of love," Loralee pointed out sadly, and the rest of the women nodded.

But did Patrick Weeks? Jo wondered. She took a stroll around the workshop table, looking over the progress of each woman's tulip. Loralee's was nearly finished. It would soon be ready for the leaf and stem. Javonne and Dulcie were about halfway through, but Ina Mae had just made her first fold. She glanced up at Jo.

"I think I finally appreciate the work that went into those paper airplanes Jimmy Kraus was so fond of sending around my classroom."

Jo grinned. "It'll click," she said. "Everyone approaches origami in their own way. You seem to want to analyze it, like geometry."

"I do. And I see it's bogging me down. The idea that one can make something like that" — she nodded toward Loralee's tulip — "from a single square of paper, without any scissor cuts or glue just boggles my mind."

"Forget the analyzing," Javonne said. She closed her eyes and assumed a Zen-like expression. "Just let the energy flow."

Ina Mae raised an eyebrow, but Jo saw a sliver of a smile as she turned back to her paper.

"What about that photographer, Jo?" Javonne asked. "Was Carrie able to find out where he'll be taking pictures?"

"Yes, she was." Jo told the group about

Carrie's family excursion to the diner that was run by Bill Ewing's friend. "Ewing wrote down Dan's directions and said if the rain held off he'd run over Wednesday morning."

"That's tomorrow," Loralee said.

"And the weather predicted is partly cloudy but dry," Dulcie added helpfully.

"So do you want Harry to meet up with you?" Javonne asked. "I asked him about it and you should have seen his eyes light up! He went and dug out his cameras and fiddled with them the rest of the night."

"He wouldn't mind spending his day off tramping through fields?" Jo asked.

"Mind? He hasn't had the chance to do something like that for ages. He'll think he died and went to heaven!"

The others tittered, but Jo knew Harry's major free-time passion was golf. However, having a man along who was loaded up with cameras could make all the difference in getting the taciturn Ewing to talk, not to mention the safety factor should she find herself in a remote area with a killer. So if Harry was willing to forego the golf greens for the day, Jo decided she was happy to let him.

"Tell Harry nine o'clock, and I'll pay for the film."

"What I'll tell him is not to keep you waiting. That man has no concept of time. I can't tell you how many times . . ." Javonne launched into tales of her only exasperation with the man she dearly loved as the ladies nodded and smiled and turned back to finishing up their origami project.

As they proudly wrapped their flower creation in protective paper for the trip home, one by one the women wished Jo the best of luck for her encounter with Bill Ewing. "Though," Loralee said, "I have a strong feeling you've already met your murderer in Patrick Weeks."

"She'll need to cover all the bases," Ina Mae said.

The group ambled out the door, and Jo, expecting no further business that evening, began preparations for closing up. She was surprised, then, when the door opened and Meg Boyer walked in, carrying a small plastic grocery bag.

"Hi, Meg," Jo said. "Need something last minute for a craft project?"

"No, I was just out picking up a few things and started thinking about your trip to see Linda's ex. I wondered how it went."

"Pretty well, if inconclusive." Jo straightened the small pile of leftover origami papers the group had gathered together for her. "I did learn that Linda had been to see him a few days ago."

"Oh, really? What for? Looking for some sort of reconciliation?"

"No, at least not with Patrick." Jo hesitated briefly but decided she had already brought Meg into the middle of things by asking for her help. "She wanted to reclaim her joint custody of their little girl."

Meg eyes widened. "They have a daughter?"

"Yes. Your friend Emmy didn't mention that?"

"No. I guess I should have asked, but I never thought of it. How old is she?"

"About eight. She seemed very sweet."

"Then I suppose she hadn't been with Linda much." Meg said it without rancor but as a simple statement of fact, which said a lot about what people who knew Linda thought of her.

"Patrick Weeks," Jo said, "seemed convinced that any influence from Linda in their daughter's life would have been very negative."

"Did he seem upset over what happened to Linda?"

"He seemed mostly concerned about how he was going to tell his little girl."

Meg nodded. "I barely knew him, but I

183

have the impression he was a pretty decent guy back then. You don't think he had anything to do with Linda's death, do you?"

"I have a lot more to find out, Meg. But I agree that in that first meeting he didn't come across as someone likely to consider murder."

Meg gave a quick nod, apparently satisfied. "I guess I'd better get on home," she said, shifting the handles of her plastic bag in her hand. "I'll be working tomorrow."

Jo walked her to the door to lock it after her. "How's the job going?" she asked.

Meg smiled. "Ruthie and Bert have been great. They get some weird customers once in a while, though."

"I can believe that, being in retail myself. But craft customers in general are probably much calmer than a hungry person rushing in for a quick meal."

"I had this guy the other day," Meg said. "Ruthie had me running the front counter for her — something I've only done once or twice so far — when he comes in, orders his usual without giving me a clue what it was, then acts real rude when I have to ask. It seems he didn't have time to waste. But I did?" Meg rolled her eyes. "When I turned away for a moment I actually heard him mutter 'fat retard.' "

"Oh, no!"

"I was tempted — really tempted — to slip a few hot peppers in that sandwich of his, but I didn't."

"Can't say I'd blame you. The peppers might have cleaned up his mouth."

"Yeah, but I don't want Ruthie losing customers."

Meg took off, and Jo thought about Ruthie's early impression of Meg as being meek and listless. Her tale about dealing with the nasty customer suggested she was growing in confidence. She hadn't broken into tears or walked off the job altogether, which was a good sign. Jo wondered about Meg's husband. She'd heard hints about his being overbearing. Maybe Meg was also learning to assert herself at home. Jo hoped that things would work out between them.

She straightened up the rest of the evening's workshop supplies, then went around flicking off lights before grabbing her cell phone and calling up its most recently added number. When Russ answered from his hospital room in an encouragingly strong voice, she asked, "Interested in a little company?"

"*Very* interested."

"I'm on my way."

CHAPTER 16

As Jo stepped off the elevator and looked down the hall toward Russ's room, the first thing she noticed was that there was no officer standing guard. That, she thought, was a good sign — the department apparently felt secure enough in Russ's progress that they didn't need to hover anymore. She tapped lightly on his door and poked her head in.

"You awake?" she asked, joking, since she'd just heard a loud protest burst from Russ over a missed shot in the basketball game he was watching.

"Hey! Yeah!" he said, the pained expression from the game immediately changing to pleasure. "Come on in." Russ reached for the TV remote and over Jo's cursory protests clicked it off, which pleased her enough to hurry her over for a good, long kiss.

"Mmm," Russ said when it ended, "nice

to see you too!" He reached out to pull her back but she ducked, laughing.

"You're still recuperating, remember?" She pulled the visitor's chair closer to the bed and sat down.

"I think I just got a lot better."

He did look much better than he had the day before, which cheered Jo immeasurably. "Appetite better too?" she asked. "I picked up a box of cookies from Schwartz's." Jo held up the white box by its string.

"Double chocolate chip?"

"Uh-huh. And raspberry butter and oatmeal raisin, with a few *rugelach* thrown in."

"How did you know?" Russ asked, grinning. Jo laughed, aware they were both thinking of their first date, which had wound up at Schwartz's Bakery. They'd bought a similar assortment and ended up sparring over their favorites, an event that rapidly grew into a tradition.

"I figured I could take you on this time," she said, "with your one arm out of commission and all."

"Don't count on it." Russ reached into the box with his good hand as soon as the string was off and grabbed a large chocolate chip, groaning with pleasure as he took the first bite. "You're an angel."

"I almost didn't bring them. I was afraid a

multitude of other visitors would have overloaded your room with things like this."

Russ waved around the room with what was left of his cookie. "Flowers," he said. "Enough to send more than half off to other parts of the hospital. It was starting to feel like a funeral home."

"No edibles?"

"Nope. Nobody, obviously, is as insightful as you."

"Or as hungry, maybe. I've been grabbing meals on the run the last couple days." Realizing she didn't want to explain exactly what she'd been doing to keep so busy, Jo switched to another subject. "You seem much better than yesterday," she said. "What are the doctors saying?"

"That they might release me pretty soon."

"Really? Are they sure? That seems so sudden!"

"No use taking up a hospital bed when I can sleep in my own bed just as well. Better, actually. They'll probably send a visiting nurse for a few days to check on this," he said, indicating his bandaged shoulder.

"Well, I should hope so!" Jo sputtered. "After all that's happened to you! I don't know about this. It sounds to me like they're rushing things. I really think they should keep you here, just to be sure." Russ gave her a grinning, raised-eyebrow look, and Jo realized how fussbudgety she sounded. "I'm sorry," she said, backtracking. "The doctors must know what they're doing. And you know how you feel. It's none of my business."

"Not at all. I like you worrying about me. I just don't want you to upset yourself. I'll be okay." He reached out to grasp her hand, rubbing it gently. "Especially if I get to see a whole lot of you during my convalescence."

Jo smiled but found herself automatically resisting the feelings that welled up inside her. Thoughts of spending much time with this man whom she'd so recently feared losing were wonderful. She wanted to hover closely and do all she could for him. But at the same time something kept telling her to hold back. That mental roadblock kept popping up inside her whenever she felt inclined to move forward.

Russ seemed to sense her hesitancy and released her hand. "I got a call from Scott," he said, reaching for his water glass.

"Your brother? That's nice."

"Yeah. Pam had false labor, so they spent some time at the hospital out in Seattle. But she's back home now, still waiting."

"That must be frustrating." Jo felt the

distance grow between them and knew it was her fault. She didn't know what she could do to change it. She chatted with him about his brother's situation, then listened as Russ told her about the people from his department who had come to see him and what they had told him about his shooter. All neutral, safe topics, and the longer it continued the worse Jo felt. But she still couldn't bring herself to step around that wall. When it came time to leave she was almost relieved. Did Russ feel the same way? If so, he hid it well. His one-armed embrace was as warm as before, and he seemed genuinely reluctant to see her go.

It wasn't until she pressed the elevator button that she realized he hadn't asked about the Michicomi situation. Apparently no one in his department had thought to bring it up, talk focusing instead on how the case against his shooter was proceeding. As it should. Russ had enough to handle, including his own recovery and rehabilitation, without the stress and distraction of Jo's problems.

She hadn't been contacted by Sheriff Franklin or anyone in his department since Sunday. What did that mean? she wondered as she stepped into the opening elevator. Best-case scenario would be that he had moved beyond thinking of her as a suspect and was, instead, looking at someone else. That seemed highly unlikely, though. Linda's dying words claiming Jo had poisoned her, plus her claim of having had an affair with Mike would certainly keep Franklin focused on Jo. It was up to her to shift that focus, not simply away from herself but toward the true killer.

Jo's reputation was at stake here, as much as anything else. If Franklin's investigation stalled, with not enough evidence to charge anyone at all, she would still be under the gun, so to speak. Gossip, fueled by the lingering mystery, could dog her for the rest of her life. Not a desirable prospect, by any means. Which meant she needed to get moving.

Patrick Weeks had raised several interesting but contradictory questions. Would Bill Ewing, with his simmering anger toward Linda, provide more answers? That remained to be seen.

Jo peeked through her bedroom window the next morning and saw Harry Barnett pulling up in his black Jeep SUV, only five minutes past the appointed time. Javonne, she thought, must have been pushing her lateness-prone husband hard. With Wednesday being the day she closed the craft shop, Jo normally allowed herself the luxury of a longer sleep, followed by a leisurely breakfast. But sleep was a more elusive thing lately, much like the solution to Linda Weeks's murder; she was aware of the link between the two. As for breakfast, she'd downed a piece of toast and sipped coffee distractedly, her thoughts on other things.

Eyeing the SUV, Jo realized what a bonus it might be, something she hadn't considered until that moment. Who knew what the roads would be like in the area they were heading to? Dan Brenner, according to Carrie, had picked the location on the spur of the moment, coming up fast with the only old tobacco barn he could think of. He hadn't had time to figure out how accessible it might still be. Or how upright. Jo crossed her fingers that they — and Bill Ewing — would actually find a structure worth photographing, which hopefully would lead to more interesting developments.

Jo hurried to open her front door and wave to Harry.

"I'll be right out," she called, and saw him wave back. She ran to the kitchen to pull a couple of water bottles from her refrigerator, then grabbed her pocketbook.

"Looks like a nice day," she said as she

climbed into the idling SUV.

"An *excellent* day," Harry agreed. He shifted gears and checked behind him before pulling away from the curb. With an Orioles baseball cap perched on his bald head and a gray sweatshirt topping jeans, he looked very undentistlike. Jo spotted multi-pocketed black bags stowed in the back, which likely held his camera equipment.

"This is so great of you to go with me, Harry," Jo said. "I hope Javonne didn't twist your arm terribly."

"Twist my arm!" Harry said, looking genuinely shocked. "I've been looking for a good excuse to go off like this and try out my new camera. And," he added, grinning slyly, "maybe I'll pick up a few tips from this Ewing fellow while we're at it. He's a real pro, I hear."

"Yes, he's good. I saw some of his work at Michicomi. He's not much of a talker, though, so this might not be easy."

Harry shot her a look. "He's not much of a salesman is what you're saying. But I guarantee you, when two guys loaded with cameras meet, there's going to be talk."

Jo grinned. "Great. By the way, do you know where you're going?" She didn't see any maps at hand.

"Jo, I grew up around here. That barn that

Dan told Ewing about? I used to play there when I was a kid!"

"You did?"

"Yeah! With my cousin Delroy. His folks, my Aunt Eulie and Uncle Ralph, had a place close to there. Del and I used to go looking for garter snakes in the weeds."

"Sounds like fun," Jo said dryly.

"It was! I've been meaning to take the boys out there. It does a kid good to tromp around in the wild once in a while."

Jo smiled and pictured Javonne's reaction to her boys bringing home snakes or dealing with ticks and other creatures of the wild.

"So, where do you want me to lead the conversation, once we get going on photography?" Harry picked up speed as he headed out of Abbotsville and onto the highway.

"The craft festival. I need to get him talking about Linda Weeks."

"Right. So, let's see, I go from, 'What shutter speed are you using there?' to 'Did you hate that woman enough to murder her?' " Harry burst into loud, explosive laughter that drew Jo along with him. She had spent enough time with Harry not to be startled by the sound, but she sometimes wondered how his patients, mouths stuffed with cotton and aspirator, handled having

194

to face Harry's whining drill coupled with his often manic-sounding laughter.

"What's Javonne doing today?" Jo asked.

"She said something about practicing the origami you taught last night. She said it was surprisingly relaxing, even though it took a lot of concentration."

Jo nodded. "I'm glad she likes it. Ina Mae, though, I'm not so sure about."

"What? There's something Ina Mae Kepner can't handle?"

"Oh, she'll get it, eventually, that I'm sure of. She's just not enjoying it as much as I wish she could. She's attacking origami like something she needs to understand fully before she can begin. But some things begin on trust. The understanding comes later."

"Like pulling a sore tooth, huh? Just reach in and yank. You'll most likely get the right one. If not, there's plenty more to try."

At Jo's dismayed look Harry burst into laughter again. "A little dentist humor, Jo," he said, punching her shoulder lightly.

Jo shook her head. "You guys must be a riot at your conventions."

"Almost as much fun as morticians."

"That I can believe."

They had left the highway, and Jo watched as Harry made several turns, each time distancing them farther from strip malls and stoplights and taking them closer to forest and farmland.

"Delroy lived down that road." Harry pointed as they whizzed by. Jo caught a glimpse of a narrow road lined with canopied trees. "He's a chef, now, in D.C. My aunt Eulie was a great cook. He got the gene."

"So we must be close to the tobacco barn?"

"Uh-huh. Right around the bend here. Let's see." Harry slowed down, scanning the roadside carefully. "Should be right about . . . ah! There it is." He swung onto a barely visible farm road whose ruts caused Jo to brace herself on the SUV's sides. They bounced along for a couple of hundred yards through trees that, when fully leafed in a few weeks, would eventually block out most sunlight and turn this pathway dark. Jo saw open field up ahead, and, as they moved into it, a tobacco barn.

"There she is," Harry said. He continued on the farm road, which curved to the left toward the barn. The SUV handled the rough terrain easily — easier than Jo, who continued to hold on tightly — until they pulled up close to the old barn. Harry cut his motor, and the silence of the empty field and barn descended.

The quiet and emptiness made Jo worry. There was no sign of the photographer. "That turnoff wasn't easy to see unless you knew where to look. Ewing might have trouble finding it."

"He might have to drive up and down a few times," Harry acknowledged, "but he'll spot it eventually." He opened his door. "Want to look around?"

"Sure." Jo unbuckled and stepped out. She gazed up at the gray-sided barn as Harry pulled out his camera case. She had seen several such barns from the road as she drove through this part of Maryland, but had never examined one up close. Two stories high and rectangular shaped, it had what appeared to be a rusted tin roof still fairly intact. Clumps of vines covered much of the partially rotted, slatted sides.

"Looks like it hasn't been in use for quite a while," she said.

"Nope. Tobacco isn't the money-making crop it used to be. Thank goodness. You should see the stained teeth of some of my smoker patients. Not to mention the problems that arise from the chewers."

"I can only imagine," said Jo, who really didn't want to. "Can we go inside?"

"Might be able to peek in. I don't know if I'd recommend actually going into it. Might be a few creatures setting up housekeeping in there now."

Harry dragged a rusty-hinged door open and pointed out features to Jo, who took care not to step very far inside. "They used to hang the bundled tobacco up there," he said, pointing to the ceiling above several open cross beams, "for curing."

Jo sniffed and thought she could detect a lingering tobacco aroma mingled with damp earth and vegetation smells. She heard something and pulled her head back out-side. The sound of a car motor grew louder until Jo glimpsed a red vehicle through the far-off trees.

"Looks like Bill Ewing found the road," Harry said.

CHAPTER 17

Jo and Harry watched as the red Chevy Blazer came toward them. It stopped several feet behind Harry's Jeep. Ewing cut his motor and climbed out.

"Mornin'," he said, hiking up his jeans. He wore a multipocketed, safari-style khaki shirt over the jeans, and sturdy-looking boots. "You the owners?"

"No," Harry said. "Just here to take a few pictures."

Ewing scowled. "Who for?"

Harry grinned. "Myself. Got a new camera here — a new digital SLR. I want to see what it'll do."

Ewing grunted. "Thought you might be competition. I'm doing a photo series on tobacco barns for *Mid-Atlantic History* magazine. I don't need it getting cancelled because some other rag beat us to the punch."

"No worry there," Harry said genially.

Ewing simply nodded. "Mind pulling your car out of the way?" He gestured farther down the rutted road and climbed back into his Blazer, assuming Harry and Jo would comply. They did, of course, both climbing into the Jeep, which Harry then backed up slowly, following Ewing until he stopped at least three hundred feet from the barn.

Ewing climbed out and began unloading equipment from the back, ignoring them. Harry shrugged at Jo, then pulled his camera from its case and fiddled with it until Jo saw him glance over at Ewing. His jaw dropped.

"Whoa!" Harry cried. "Is that a Deardorff V4?"

Bill Ewing looked up from the case from which he had carefully removed a large camera, which, to Jo, looked like something out of a 1940s or 1950s newsreel. A tripod lay on the ground beside it. "You know Deardorff?"

"Only from what I've read." Harry's face, Jo thought, couldn't look more impressed. She wanted to ask, "What's a Deardorff?" but held her tongue. As Harry had predicted, suddenly the tight-lipped Ewing was talking cameras, specifically *his* camera, which Jo assumed was the Rolls-Royce of the photography world.

200

Suddenly she was hearing model numbers and letters tossed around that meant nothing to her, as well as terms like "lens focal length," "shutter speed," and "aperture setting." She waited patiently, glad to have Harry warm up Ewing for her, though whether he would rapidly freeze when she took her turn remained to be seen.

Ewing glanced skyward, then picked up his gear and began heading toward the field. Harry quickly asked, "Mind if I watch?"

"Just stay to the rear."

"Great!" Harry said, looking as joyful, Jo thought, as if Tiger Woods had just invited him to share a round of golf. As the two of them tramped off, she wondered if a comparable superstar celebrity dentist existed who would have made Harry as excited, but suspected not. She scurried to keep from being left behind, and when she managed to pull alongside Ewing, broke into Harry's streaming camera talk to ask, "Are you finding enough tobacco barns to photograph for this magazine?"

Ewing turned toward her, answering with a brief, "Yup."

"Mostly around here, or have you had to travel around a lot?"

"Traveled a bit." Ewing stepped over a dip in the ground. "The barns in any one area," he said, keeping his pace brisk, "tend to all look pretty much the same except for condition. The farther out you go, the more variety you get." He stopped, then slid his tripod off his shoulder and began setting it up.

"Down to North Carolina?"

"Haven't been there yet. Virginia and West Virginia. Found a few Mail Pouch barns." Ewing worked at attaching his camera to the tripod, and Jo saw that Harry watched each little movement intently. He obviously had totally forgotten the reason they'd come here in the first place, so getting to the topic she was really interested in had fallen solely onto Jo.

"Oh, Mail Pouch!" she said. "I remember seeing those signs on barns. They were like the first billboards, weren't they?"

"Yup." Ewing looked through his lens, then made adjustments on his camera. "They used only the barns that could be seen from the road. Farmers got a few dollars and a free paint job out of it."

"I don't remember seeing any around here. Where'd you find them? Mostly in West Virginia?"

Ewing nodded and bent down to his camera case to get something. "Found a couple south of Morgantown."

Jo remembered Gabe Stubbins's story of Ewing being ejected from the craft show's Morgantown venue because of his blowup with Linda. She ventured a turn toward that subject.

"Morgantown? Was that after Michicomi?"

Ewing shot her a sharp look. "What do you know about Michicomi?"

"I had a booth in it when it stopped here, at Hammond County."

"You a photographer too?"

"No, jewelry."

"Yeah?" Ewing turned back to his work, acting less than interested. But Jo saw a tightening of his jaw.

"I thought I recognized you," she said. "I stopped at your booth when I had some break time. I was very impressed with your work."

"Yeah?" Ewing glanced back at her, not exactly smiling but a bit less grim. "Buy any?"

"No. I wish I could have, but such things just don't fit in my budget right now."

Ewing snorted softly. "That seemed to be the feeling of most of the Hammond County shoppers. Some of the Michicomi towns are better than others. Unfortunately, they don't let us pick and choose which ones we

203

want to be in, do they?"

"No, they don't. I heard," Jo said, picking her way carefully, "that the woman who died — Linda something-or-other? — had managed to get invited to plenty of good festival towns."

Ewing's jaw clenched once more, and red patches appeared on his cheeks as well as the scalp beneath his light crew cut. This was obviously still a sore subject with him. She pushed harder. "I guess her product was pretty outstanding."

"Her booth was no better than any others! Worse, in my opinion."

"Then how —"

"Sleeping with one of the top guys can get you plenty of favors."

"Oh, gosh! You think she was getting special treatment?"

"I know she was. And let me tell you, lady, it's a pretty sorry state of affairs when an organization handles things that way. Believe me, I would have been done with them altogether if I hadn't spent years building up a reputation with the people who regularly show up at their shows. I can't just start over with another group! But there they were, giving this two-bit newcomer preferential bookings and putting me off with idiotic excuses!"

Ewing had begun gesticulating broadly as his temper rose, one of his flailing arms nearly knocking over his tripod-mounted camera, which Harry leaped forward to steady. Ewing putting his precious camera at such risk told Jo the extent of his anger toward Linda and how much she had affected him.

"Well, I guess your problem with Michicomi is ended," she said.

Ewing stared, suddenly seeming to realize that the object of his anger was dead. Or had he realized what he might have been giving away about himself?

He turned back to his camera. "Tough thing to happen."

"It was. Especially since now they're saying it was murder."

Harry, clearly still enthralled with Ewing's Deardorff, began to interrupt with a question about the film Ewing was using until Jo aimed a not-too-gentle kick at his ankle. Ewing, concentrating on his view of the tobacco barn, didn't seem to notice. Jo plowed on.

"That Sheriff Franklin was talking to a lot of people who knew her, trying to track down the person who sent her those candies. Did he give you a hard time?"

"Why? Because I had a beef with her getting favoritism? If I wanted to take someone out, I'd have punched out the lights of the guy that kept bumping me off the schedule and putting her on it instead."

"But that wouldn't have solved your problem, would it? Picking a fight with one of the organizers would only get you crossed off their list altogether. Removing Linda from the competition would have made more sense."

Ewing's head snapped around. He straightened up from his camera and glared at her. "Are you accusing me of something?"

"Not at all! I'm just saying that might be how the sheriff might look at it."

"The sheriff nothing! He never blinked an eye when I told him I never knew Linda had allergies like that. Sounds to me like you're trying to stir up trouble, lady."

"Hold on," Harry said, stepping in. "Nobody's trying to stir up anything. Jo, here, was just speculating about the investigation."

Ewing wasn't buying it. "How about you two get the hell out of here!"

"Now, just —" Harry began, but Ewing suddenly reached into his equipment case and pulled out a menacing-looking metal rod. He stepped forward threateningly.

"I mean it. Get out of here. You think I

don't know how to use this? Think again. I've run into too many people think they can grab a good camera from me to not be ready to chase them off."

"You think we'd . . ." Harry began to sputter, but Jo pulled him back.

"Let's just go, Harry."

They backed away several steps, Ewing glaring at them, broad stanced, until they turned and walked briskly to Harry's SUV.

"I can't believe that guy," Harry muttered as they climbed into the Jeep.

"Just drive off, Harry. Who knows what else he might have in that case of his."

Once they put a good distance between them and Ewing and were back on the farm road, Jo breathed a sigh of relief. "I'm sorry I got you into that."

Harry shook his head. "It's a good thing I was along. The guy's got a temper, doesn't he?"

"Indeed. I was deliberately aggravating him to see what he might blurt out. But I didn't expect him to go that far."

Jo glanced back, thinking about how Linda Weeks had goaded Ewing. Had she pushed him even further?

CHAPTER 18

After Harry dropped her off, Jo felt too keyed up to stay put. She grabbed her just-delivered mail, shoved it into the side pocket of her purse, and took off for Carrie's place, certain she'd find a receptive ear — and a calming cup of coffee — there.

Carrie, eager to hear all, set down her basket of folded laundry and pulled Jo into her kitchen, which happened to have a pot of freshly perked hazelnut coffee, a blend she favored lately and which Jo sniffed at appreciatively. As Carrie filled two mugs, Jo began her account of her morning's adventure. By the time Carrie had stirred cream and sugar into her mug her eyes were popping.

"He threatened you?" she cried.

"That he did. I was sure glad to have Harry with me." Jo took a long, soothing drink of Carrie's tasty brew.

"You're going to report this to that sheriff,

aren't you?"

"Sheriff Franklin?" Jo set down her mug. "I don't know."

"Jo! Ewing had major problems with Linda Weeks, then was furious when you brought it up. He obviously has a guilty conscience. The sheriff should know about it."

Jo shook her head. "Franklin probably knows about the blowup Ewing had with Linda by now. I think he would have arrested Ewing already if that were enough. Just as he would have already arrested me if bad blood between people were enough to warrant a murder charge."

"But you haven't threatened people with bodily harm."

"Ewing could say he was protecting his expensive camera equipment, which actually is what he *did* say as he chased us off."

Carrie raised a skeptical eyebrow. "Protecting it from a dentist and craft shop owner?"

Jo laughed. "We didn't exactly hold up ID badges for him, you know. We could have been anyone as far as he knew."

"So now you're defending him?" Carrie slumped back in her chair, looking exasperated.

Jo sighed. "I don't know. I'm just trying to

look at it from all angles, I guess. This is tough, Carrie. A murder like this, where the murderer didn't need to be present, means that no alibi is necessary. The candy could have been bought and doctored up at almost any time. So neither I nor Sheriff Franklin can point to any one person and say, Aha, you were spotted at the scene of the crime when you claimed to have been at such-and-such place. Therefore, *you* must have done it. The best we can probably do is look for motive."

"And with someone like Linda Weeks," Carrie said, "a lot of people might have wanted her dead."

"Exactly. I have to admit the thought even crossed my mind, although never seriously."

"So Linda's murderer will be the one person who did take it seriously, who wanted her dead enough to actually kill her. So far, you've looked at her ex-husband and a very angry fellow craft show vendor. Which one looks most likely?"

Jo shrugged. "Patrick Weeks obviously knew about Linda's allergy, and he definitely didn't want his daughter to live with her. But would he cause that daughter the pain of losing her mother completely by killing Linda?"

Jo took another sip of coffee. "Bill Ewing

was furious with Linda about what she was doing and how badly it impacted him. But with a temperament like his, would he be more likely to do something quick and violent like a shooting or stabbing, rather than an underhanded kind of murder like this?"

"Maybe you could ask that friend of yours from the craft festival," Carrie said. "The one who called you about Ewing. Get his input."

"Gabe Stubbins? Good idea." She pulled her cell phone from her purse and found his number. She greeted him when he answered, then asked, "Mind if I run something by you?"

"Sure, Jo. What's up?"

Jo told Gabe about her encounter with Bill Ewing, hearing grumbles and grunts coming from his end as she did. She pictured Gabe shaking his head disapprovingly.

When she finished, he said, "I'm appalled, Jo! If I'd known something like that was likely, I'd never have sent you off to find him."

"What I need to know is, if Ewing had been furious enough with Linda to kill her, would he have been more likely to do so by attacking her quickly, while in the heat of the moment? Would he have been at all capable of the calm, controlled planning that needed to go into sending her the peanut-filled candy?"

There was a long silence on Gabe's end of the phone, and Jo waited. "That's a difficult question, Jo," he finally said. "Sort of a 'lady or the tiger' kind of choice, isn't it? Either one makes Bill a murderer, and that's something I don't like to contemplate. But I understand why you need to know, so I'll do my best."

Gabe cleared his throat. "The Bill Ewing I know had his temper flare-ups, but they were always brief, blowing over in minutes. But he was a professional photographer, remember. Think about the patience his work must call for, having to search for the ideal light and angle, waiting for everything to come together for the perfect shot. So yes, Bill is definitely capable of controlling himself enough to do long-range planning. And his anger toward Linda has apparently remained. So, everything put together, I'd have to say he could have handled the murder in the way it happened. I hope to God, though, that he didn't."

"Thank you, Gabe, for your thoughtful input. I'm sorry if it distressed you, and I won't keep you. You must be getting ready for Richmond." Jo remembered that Gabe

212

was taking Linda's vacant spot at the Michi-comi show there the coming weekend.

"I'm nearly packed up. Had to plan enough for two weeks. They offered me the spot that was open at Rocky Mount the weekend after, and I won't be able to head back home in between."

"Rocky Mount?"

"Nice little town in North Carolina. Call me if you need me. I'll always have my cell phone at hand."

Jo thanked him for that and disconnected, thinking Gabe was certainly keeping busy, and thank heaven for cell phones. She filled Carrie in on what he'd said about Ewing.

"So does that put Bill Ewing ahead of Patrick Weeks in your mind?"

Jo ran her fingers through her hair and rubbed. "Maybe," she said. "It's still hard to say." She looked at Carrie. "The problem is there just isn't enough on anyone. Maybe it's someone we don't even know about. Maybe we'll never know who did it."

"Don't say that! That would be terrible."

Jo nodded, fully aware of what the consequences of that would be. Besides having a murderer at large, the cloud of suspicion hanging over her head would never be fully dissipated. She leaned back and sighed, the movement of her feet knocking over the pocketbook she'd set on the floor, which spilled the mail she'd stuck in the side pocket. Jo bent down to gather it up.

She flipped rapidly through the envelopes, wincing at the high number of bills, fully aware that another set would be waiting for her at the shop. Would her shrinking checking account be able to cover them all? she wondered. The electric company and her craft suppliers wouldn't be terribly sympathetic to the fact that her business had dropped considerably in the last few days.

One envelope, hand addressed in block letters, stood out, and she separated it from the others. She studied it curiously for a moment, then slipped a finger under its flap to open it. A single sheet of paper lay folded within. Jo pulled it out, and as she opened and scanned it, a low groan escaped her throat.

"What?" Carrie asked. "What's the matter?"

Jo held the sheet of paper out to Carrie, whose jaw dropped in shock as she read.

JO MCALLISTER: WE DON'T NEED YOUR KIND IN ABBOTTSVILLE.
GET OUT!

Carrie stared at Jo, her mouth working

214

soundlessly. Finally she asked, "Who could have sent such a thing?"

Jo reexamined the envelope. "There's no return address, and the postmark says 'Abbotsville.' " Her mouth twisted wryly. "Spelled correctly, I might add. Oh, Carrie," she said, dropping her face into her hands. "It's coming to this."

"That's ridiculous!" Carrie cried. "Don't take it seriously, Jo. It's just some stupid person's idea of a joke."

Jo looked back at the to-the-point message, written in ballpoint with all the letters neatly spaced and even. She looked back up at Carrie.

"Maybe, but I'm not exactly laughing."

Back home, Jo dragged herself out of her car and through the connecting door from her garage to her kitchen. She dropped her pocketbook and mail — including the hurtful anonymous letter — on the kitchen counter and continued on to her living room, plopping herself down on her shabby, broken-springed sofa. She laughed grimly, remembering how recently she had entertained hopes of replacing the dilapidated piece with something that had never been owned before, whose upholstery she herself had chosen, and which — wild and crazy dream — might even be comfortable. That desire had been replaced with hopes of retaining a roof over her head.

The blink of the answering machine beside her caught her attention, and she pressed the message button.

"Jo, it's Javonne," the voice firmly stated. "Harry told me what happened! I can't *believe* that man . . ." Javonne went on to rant and call Bill Ewing several interesting names, which brought a wan smile to Jo's lips. Javonne wound up her message by saying she was extremely thankful that Harry had been along, and that Jo should call her as soon as she got home.

The answering machine beeped off, and Jo sat for a moment, contemplating whether she was up to calling Javonne. As she thought, the phone rang, seeming to make her decision for her, and Jo picked it up, expecting to hear her friend's voice. Instead, she heard a strange, raspy-sounding growl. "Jo McAllister. We don't want you here. Go back where you came from."

The phone went dead, and Jo held it out and away from her ear as though it would bite her, barely able to believe what she had heard. She might not have, if she hadn't just read a letter that said much the same thing.

She dropped the phone back into its

216

cradle and was staring at it numbly when the phone rang again. Jo jumped off the couch at the sound and backed away, unwilling to hear the same, terrible message again. It rang four times until her answering machine clicked on, and Jo's hands flew up to her ears. She didn't want to listen. But the voice from the machine penetrated and she quickly dropped her hands.

"Jo," the voice said, "it's Mark Rosatti. Russ has taken a turn for the worse."

CHAPTER 19

The drive to the hospital through lunch-hour traffic took frustratingly longer than Jo's previous late-night drives. Plus the hospital parking lot was more full, the lobby more crowded, and the elevators busier — all elements that combined to keep her from reaching Russ as quickly as she wanted.

Mark had said he'd be waiting outside the ICU, where Russ had been taken, and she spotted him as soon as she burst from the elevator. He was pacing, hands in pockets and staring at the floor.

Jo hurried up to him. "How is he?"

Mark's grim look softened as he turned to her. "Fighting hard."

"You said he developed an infection in his wound?"

"They're going to have to do more surgery to clean it out. He's back in the ICU because of a high fever and blood pressure problems. They're pumping him full of antibiotics, trying to get him stabilized before the surgery. Right now he's in and out of consciousness, so I don't know if you'll be able to talk to him. But I thought you'd want to be here."

"Thanks, Mark. Can I at least see him?"

"I think so, but let me check." Mark went off to talk with one of the nurses and came back nodding. "They said you can go in."

Jo entered through the double doors into the room where Russ had been that first night, a room filled with quiet busyness as efficient nurses bustled about their seriously ill patients whose monitors beeped and IVs dripped. Jo approached Russ's bed quietly, thinking how pale his face had been on the night of his surgery, but how flushed it looked now. She touched his forearm; it felt burning hot.

His head turned at her touch and his eyes opened. His dry lips stretched into a weak smile. "Hi."

"Hi, yourself." She squeezed his arm, happy to find him awake and to hear at least that one word from him.

She brushed a few dark hairs away from his eyes, and he reached for her hand, holding it against his face. "Nice. Feels cool."

"You can put this compress on his forehead," a nearby nurse told Jo, handing it to her.

"Like the hand better," Russ said, his voice getting weaker, but he allowed Jo to replace it with the cold compress. His own hand dropped back to his side.

"What is it with you, fella?" Jo asked, struggling to keep her voice light. "It seems I can't let you out of my sight without you getting yourself into problems."

Russ smiled. "Can't leave me for . . . a . . . minute." His eyes closed. Jo waited, but they didn't reopen.

The nurse looked over. "You can stay for a bit, but then I'll have to ask you to wait outside."

Jo nodded, and sank onto the edge of a molded plastic chair. She held on to Russ's hand and watched his face, the rise and fall of his chest. At one point he began to cough and his eyelids fluttered. She swallowed and blinked the tears out of her eyes in case he reopened his own, but he didn't.

After a while the nurse signaled that her time was up. Jo reluctantly left, glancing back at the motionless form of the man she knew as strong and vigorous. It was painful to see him so weakened, and frustrating to be unable to do anything about it. Jo dug in her purse for a tissue and was swiping at her face when Mark came up to her.

"Will you be hanging around?" he asked gently.

She nodded.

"I hope you don't mind, but I left your cell number as a contact for Russ's brother Scott. I could only get his voice mail, and I have to be in court in half an hour."

"That's fine. Go ahead. I'll be glad to talk to him if he calls."

"Thanks. And don't worry." Mark tilted his head in the direction of Russ's room. "He's pretty tough."

Jo knew he intended to look worry free himself, but he wasn't exactly pulling it off. She smiled. "I know. All you cops are. Goes with the job, right?"

"Right." Mark hesitated a moment, then took off. Jo glanced around for a waiting area and, seeing one a few yards down the hall, headed for it. She took out her cell phone and stared at it. Her first impulse was to call Carrie, but she remembered that Carrie had plans to see Amanda in her middle-school choral group's performance. Knowing Carrie, she would readily give up that pleasure to run over and be with Jo, and Jo didn't want to ask that of her. She would call Carrie later, when hopefully the news would be better.

Jo scrolled through her address book until she found what she wanted. She pressed the Call button, waited for an answer, then said, "Ina Mae? Got a minute?"

"I'm glad you called me, Jo," Ina Mae said when she arrived and gave Jo a brisk hug. "There's nothing worse than waiting through something like this on your own."

Jo nodded, trying hard to smile. "Sitting here by myself, my imagination has been going crazy. These old *People* magazines aren't much distraction."

"What have you heard lately?"

"His fever's slowly coming down, and his blood pressure is stabilizing."

"Wonderful."

"They want to do more surgery as soon as they can — to clean the wound out." Jo tried to keep her tone even but heard herself failing miserably.

Ina Mae looked at her for a moment. "Then we'll just wait here," she said, "until they tell us they're taking him to surgery, at which time we'll celebrate by treating ourselves to a late lunch in the cafeteria."

"Celebrate?"

"Of course, since that will mean our lieutenant's infection is under control and that all they need to do at that point is go in and tidy things up."

Jo had to smile at the idea of the surgeon being compared to a broom-wielding house-maid, but as usual Ina Mae had looked at things with her common sense.

"You're right, Ina Mae. I hated the thought of Russ going through another surgery, but it actually will be a good sign, won't it?"

"Once it's done, he'll really be on the road to recovery. Now, can I get you some coffee or a soda?"

Jo agreed to a soda, hating to send Ina Mae off for it, but hating more to leave the area in case someone came by to update her. She sat, watching staff nurses, doctors, and lab personnel bustle through the hall, feeling more and more like part of the furniture as one and all ignored her in their particular pursuits.

Ina Mae brought cheese-cracker packets along with their drinks, then chatted just enough to distract Jo from her worries. Time dragged by until finally, a nurse came directly toward them.

"We're taking the lieutenant to surgery now," she said, and Jo sighed with relief.

"So his fever is down?"

The nurse smiled and gave a thumbs-up. "All systems are go."

"Wonderful," Ina Mae said and, as the nurse went off, turned to Jo. "Time to celebrate with something like a nice, big taco salad. Sound good?"

Jo smiled. "Sounds great."

As they rode the elevator down to the cafeteria, Jo said, "I'm sorry I interrupted your tai chi class." When Jo had called her earlier, Ina Mae had answered in an uncharacteristically soft voice, and Jo could hear Asian-style music in the background, which required an explanation.

"It's no problem," Ina Mae said as the elevator settled to a stop and the doors opened. "I'm not sure I'll keep on with it after all. It's a lovely program, but I think I prefer more vigorous exercise. Plus there's all those moves to learn, which are giving me a bit of trouble. Much like the origami did." She smiled. "Could be my Scottish genes just don't mesh well with Asian traditions."

"It might be a stretch for you. No pun intended," Jo added as she pictured the class, "but I'd hang in there. I've heard so many good things about tai chi that I've thought of getting a DVD to practice it myself at home. Trouble is, by the time I get home, exercise is the last thing I feel like doing."

"Well," Ina Mae said, guiding Jo toward the food line, "it's supposed to be a very good stress release. And Lord knows you could use that. There's the taco salad, by the way," she said, pointing to a colorful dish, "and it looks very good, doesn't it?"

"Actually, I think I'll go for the tuna salad sandwich. But why don't you get the salad? My treat."

Ina Mae hesitated, then chose a smaller version of the salad and an iced tea, passing by the dessert section. She urged dessert on Jo, though, who finally picked up a cup of rice pudding, mostly to pacify her friend who seemed eager to pack calories into her, having commented more than once in the past on Jo's need to, as she put it, bulk up a bit more. They carried their trays to a quiet table and unloaded them, then settled down.

As Jo took her first sip of water, her thoughts immediately flew back to Russ and his fever. "I'm still shocked over that infection popping up so quickly. Russ looked so completely wiped out from it."

Ina Mae opened up a sugar packet. "Post-surgical infections are not all that rare, from what I hear." She shook a small amount of sugar into her iced tea. "Especially after a wound of the lieutenant's type. Hospitals are quite capable of taking care of it."

Jo shook her head. "Just last night he seemed to be recovering so well. He was talking of going home soon."

"There's going to be ups and downs. Count on it and you'll be better able to handle it."

"Good advice, Ina Mae, but not always easy to follow. I'm afraid some of my downs have made me hypersensitive." She looked at her sandwich, fiddling with it, then said quietly, "I'm not sure I can handle roller coaster rides anymore."

Ina Mae looked at her. "You can," she declared. "The downs are just going to hurt a bit more because of that tenderness. Completely understandable, of course, after what happened to your husband. Emotional wounds may take longer to heal than physical ones, but they do heal, Jo. Believe that."

Jo lifted her sandwich and took a bite from it. After a moment she said, "I'm sure you're right, but just the memory of the pain can make a person pretty skittish. Ina Mae, I care about Russ very much. Obviously, or I wouldn't be here, wringing my hands over his latest crisis. But I can't help feeling he deserves someone without all the baggage I'm dragging around."

"Why don't you let him make that decision?" Ina Mae said with a slight smile.

"Because, because . . ." Jo shook her head. "I don't know. Because I want to make it for him, I suppose. And that's not fair, is it?"

"No, it isn't." Ina Mae scooped up a forkful of her salad. "And you'd be hard put, you know, to find anyone without some kind of baggage," she said. "Most people tend to keep it tucked in their back rooms, but it's still there." She pointed at Jo's plate. "Keep eating. You need the energy."

Jo grinned. "Yes, ma'am." She took a bite from her sandwich, gazing over it at Ina Mae and thinking that she couldn't imagine this sensible and upfront woman having any hidden baggage to her life. But who knew? As this wise friend had just implied, people's lives were complicated, and it generally took a long time to get to know everything about a person. It just happened that Jo's major problems were the kind that were impossible to keep private. She was reminded of her anonymous letter and phone call. She told Ina Mae about them.

Her friend's eyes flashed as she listened. "Such rubbish! The last thing you need is harassment of that type. It's clearly the ignorant action of one cowardly person, and I wouldn't give it a moment's attention."

"The trouble is, it probably reflects what many people in town are thinking."

"It's ridiculous! Why should anyone assume you're guilty? You haven't been charged with a thing!"

"I imagine my having known Linda in New York, and the real problems between us along with the ones she simply claimed, make me look suspicious. Then there's those murders that happened not so long ago around here. It all adds up to a pretty negative picture."

"Those past incidents were completely cleared up, thanks to you. They should have nothing whatsoever to do with whatever rumors are presently going around. I haven't heard a thing said against you, by the way, but then I tend to associate with sensible people." Ina Mae huffed and reached for her iced tea. "The best way, of course, to put an end to this kind of thinking is to uncover the actual murderer. What did you learn from that photographer this morning?"

Jo told Ina Mae about her encounter, finishing her tuna fish sandwich in the process and moving on to her rice pudding. Ina Mae's reaction was much like Carrie's, other than not urging her to immediately share this with Sheriff Franklin. She did suggest, however, investigating Bill Ewing more intensely.

"Harry and I were discussing that on the drive back," Jo said. "He reminded me that you can find a lot of things on the Internet if you know where to look. I don't have a computer yet — I was hoping to be able to afford one for the store before long, but now . . . Well, anyway, he offered his own for me to use, or there's Dan's too. I was just over at Carrie's and could probably have used Dan's computer then, but getting that anonymous letter pushed everything else from my mind."

"Of course. And now there's Russ to think about. I wish I could help, but I'm afraid I'm just starting to learn my way around computers. Another class at the senior center," she said with a smile.

"You're helping enough just by being here, Ina Mae," Jo assured her. She took a last drink from her water glass and reached for her pocketbook. "If you're done, I'd really like to get back to the fifth floor."

"Certainly." Ina Mae helped Jo tidy up their table, then followed her back to the elevator. They rode it silently up to the ICU, the elevator stopping along the way to pick up or discharge various hospital workers or visitors. Once there, Jo inquired after Russ at the nurses' station.

"He's still in surgery for the debridement," a woman in green scrubs told her. "It shouldn't be too much longer."

Ina Mae told Jo, "Go ahead to the waiting area. I want to make a quick phone call."

Jo headed down the hall and as she settled onto the tan vinyl settee, heard her own cell phone ring. She pulled it out of her purse and looked at the display. The number was unfamiliar, and she answered it questioningly.

"Jo McAllister?" a male voice asked.

"Yes. Who is this?"

"This is Scott Morgan. Russ's brother."

CHAPTER 20

"Scott! Hello." The vinyl cushion beneath her crackled as she sat forward. "Mark Rosatti said he'd given you my number. I'm glad you called."

"How is Russ?" His voice sounded eerily like his brother's, and Jo pictured a younger version of Russ with the same dark hair and even features. How much younger Scott was, she couldn't remember.

She explained about the fever and required surgery to clean out the infection. "Apparently, this kind of thing is not too unusual, especially with gunshot wounds. I spoke to Russ very briefly before they took him up, and I'm hoping to see him again once it's over and he wakes up."

"Thank you for being there for him. I feel rotten that I can't be."

"Russ told me about your situation. You couldn't possibly leave your wife at a time like this."

"Yeah, it's been touch and go with her having false labor and all. If we weren't so far away . . ."

"Russ understands that, Scott. And he's in excellent hands, so there's really nothing to worry about." Jo found herself reassuring this man of what she'd had trouble reassuring herself.

"I appreciate that. It's just that Russ was so great when we went through a rough time with our first one — Ryan. This was when we were all still living in Cincinnati, of course, so the logistics were easier. But Russ was still getting over his son's death, so his being there for me meant all that much more."

"Russ had a son?" Jo's mouth had suddenly gone dry, and she had trouble getting the words out.

"You didn't know? Well, I'm afraid it's something he doesn't like to talk about. The baby lived only a few hours after his birth. It was really tough. Tough on both Russ and Laura. It probably was what led to their split, even though they hung in there for another year. That kind of thing can put a lot of stress on a couple. You did know about Laura, didn't you? I mean, I'm sorry if I'm dropping too much on you."

"No, I knew Russ had been married."

Though I never heard her name before. Jo thought back to the woman she had seen meeting Russ for lunch at the Abbotsville Country Club the day Jo had set up a craft show there. Had that been Laura? Or someone else?

"So, when will he be out of surgery?" Scott asked.

"The nurse said not too much longer. I can call as soon as I hear anything."

"Would you? That'd be great." Scott gave his number, then added details about where he might be, which went over Jo's head for the most part as her thoughts went back to that one, stunning fact: *Russ had a son.*

She was closing up her phone as Ina Mae rejoined her. Knowing she must have a dazed look on her face, Jo explained about Russ's brother having called, though not what he had shared with her. That she needed to absorb for a while.

Ina Mae nodded, then said, "I just spoke to Dulcie."

"Oh?" Jo said, not having any idea why Ina Mae would call Loralee's daughter.

"Dulcie," Ina Mae said, "is, as they say, computer literate."

It took a moment for Jo to pull her focus completely away from Scott's call and understand Ina Mae's point. "Oh!"

Ina Mae nodded. "She's going to see what she can find about Bill Ewing on the Internet. Her husband, of course, uses their computer for his work. But since he works from home, she'll be able to hop on as soon as it's free."

"Good idea! Ina Mae, I'm glad at least one of us has her head screwed on straight."

Ina Mae flapped a hand. "I'm not the one getting hit from all sides at the moment."

That's the truth, Jo thought, Scott's information immediately flying back into her head. When was Russ going to tell her about that? she wondered. How painful must it continue to be for him if he still avoided talking about it?

Ina Mae sat down, bringing up lighter topics meant to be distracting for Jo, and Jo did her best to pay attention. She couldn't, however, keep her thoughts from wandering back to Russ, and though Ina Mae probably assumed she was dwelling on his surgery, *that* had suddenly taken second place. Russ's hidden emotional pain — his baggage — had taken center stage.

Sometime later, as Jo sat groggily flipping through magazines whose stories and pictures she barely saw, a smiling nurse stepped into the waiting area. "The lieutenant is awake," she said.

"How did it go?" Jo asked, instantly alert.

"Very well. The area was cleaned out and he has a new drainage tube inserted. He's not fully out of the anesthesia, but you can see him for a few minutes."

"Excellent," Ina Mae said. Jo hopped up to follow the woman back through the double doors into the ICU.

Struggling to ignore the bandages, tubing, and beeping monitors, Jo concentrated on the fact that Russ's eyes were blinking but open, and were looking at her. She stood at his bedside once more and murmured soft nothings, and he mumbled mostly indecipherable responses. Their main connection came through the touch of his hand in hers, warm, but not feverishly hot, and firm, which told her he was glad she was there. They held on until the nurse said their time was up, then reluctantly released, sliding palm to fingertip, then a final good-bye with promises of return.

"He's doing fine," the nurse assured her back in the hallway. "He'll sleep for several hours now."

Jo nodded and thanked her. She pulled her emotions together and called Scott. "Russ is back from surgery," she reported. "Everything went perfectly."

"Fantastic!" Jo heard the relief and joy in the younger brother's voice, which echoed her own. They chatted for a minute on minor details, then ended with the probability that Scott would talk to Russ himself the next morning.

Jo returned to Ina Mae. "All is well," she said.

"Of course," Ina Mae said briskly, but her eyes were bright. She turned away to start tidying up magazines and gathering her things. "Feel up to a stop at the Tylers' before you head on home?"

Jo had to think a moment before the name clicked. "Oh! Dulcie's place?"

"Yes. I heard from her while you were otherwise occupied. She's been surfing, as they say, on the Internet. She found something she'd like to show you."

Jo pulled up behind Ina Mae's blue Chevy Malibu in front of Loralee's — or rather, as she supposed she should now call it, the Tylers' — house. As she turned off her motor, she pulled out her cell phone to call Carrie to quickly tell her about Russ's surgery.

As expected, Carrie's first words were: "Why didn't you call me right away!" which meant, of course, "Why didn't you tell me to come over?"

"It was nothing to worry anyone about," Jo said, playing down the potential seriousness of Russ's infection as well as her own worries. When Carrie protested that she could have quite easily come to the hospital to wait with her, Jo decided not to remind her of Amanda's choral performance but simply emphasized that Russ's surgery had been routine and simple. *Easy for me to say* popped into her thoughts.

Carrie groused a bit more but eventually came around to being glad to hear that Russ had come through it well. She began to speculate on what she could bring Russ when she eventually came to visit. "Something edible," was Jo's advice, and they ended on a good note, Carrie apparently having forgiven Jo for not having seriously disrupted her own plans for a pleasurable afternoon in order to sit beside her for hours doing nothing much.

Ina Mae tapped at Jo's passenger window, and Jo climbed out to head up the short walkway with her to the house.

Dulcie opened the door before they reached it and welcomed them in. Five-year-old Caitlin hovered behind her mother's khaki pants, clutching the edge of her blouse with her fingertips. Blonde Loralee-like curls framed her face as she peeked out curiously.

"Caitlin, you go upstairs with Daddy now," Dulcie directed her daughter. "Help him get Andrew ready for bed, okay?"

Caitlin dragged herself off reluctantly, throwing many backward glances at her mother's guests, and Jo smiled as she watched. Remembering Dulcie's strong impulse to control all things child or house related, the fact of her having actually delegated away a bedtime task to her husband indicated to Jo the high measure of importance she must put on her Internet find.

Dulcie led Jo and Ina Mae through her tidy living room and shiningly clean kitchen to the basement steps. "The computer's down in Ken's office," she said. "Would either of you like something to drink before we go down? Coffee? Soda?"

Both Jo and Ina Mae shook their heads, thanking her. "We're very interested to see what you found," Ina Mae said.

"I ran it past Mom earlier," Dulcie said, leading the way down her basement steps. "She thought it was well worth calling you about. She's off, by the way, picking up some curtains for her kitchen, or she'd be over to say hello."

238

"Things are working out with that new addition to the house?" Ina Mae asked as she trotted downstairs between Dulcie and Jo. The question was rhetorical since all Loralee's friends knew she was absolutely delighted to have Dulcie and Ken move into the main part of her house while she shifted to the smaller, more manageable addition.

"It's been perfect," Dulcie declared. "Mom loves being close to the children. And we both enjoy working on the garden together. We can hardly wait to start picking out annuals as soon as the last frost is over."

Jo nodded, thinking of her own scraggly yard. Then she thought of her own far-from-scraggly mother who lived in her retirement community in Florida. Would the two of them have teamed up as well in a living situation like this? Knowing her mother's strong preference for avoiding unpleasant or upsetting situations, Jo doubted it. Having one's daughter under suspicion of murder definitely qualified as both unpleasant and upsetting and was the reason Jo hadn't called her lately. Needing to sound cheery and upbeat for forty-five minutes straight seemed like more than she could manage lately.

"Okay," Dulcie said, plopping into the desk chair and reaching for the computer mouse. "Let me pull this site up."

As Dulcie clicked and double clicked, Jo glanced around. The basement area had been roughly divided in two using bookcases and a desk. The office part, which Ken used for his accounting business, showed attempts at organization with file cabinets and shelving. But the shelves overflowed with books and papers, cabinet drawers bulged partially open, and the desk was piled high with folders and paper scraps. Since the play area beyond was amazingly tidy with all games and small toys neatly stored off the floor in see-through containers, Jo could only assume that Ken had declared his office off-limits to Dulcie's cleaning needs. What sort of strains Dulcie might therefore be feeling or urges she was controlling at the moment, Jo could only imagine.

"Here we are," Dulcie said, looking up at them to explain. "I started off by doing a search on his name, using 'Bill Ewing' first, since that's the name you said he goes by for his photography work. But that only got me his photo credits on several magazines' sites, and his own website that talks about his work.

"So then I went with William Ewing. It's not an uncommon name, so I had to sift through a lot. Did you know there was a

William Ewing who was governor of Illinois back in the 1830s? I didn't even know Illinois was a *state* then. The things you learn. Anyway, I finally found this." Dulcie gestured to her monitor.

Jo leaned forward and saw that Dulcie had pulled up an archived newspaper story. It was short, and she read it quickly. "Oh, wow!" she said, straightening up.

Ina Mae asked to see, and Dulcie gave up her chair to give Ina Mae better access. "I'm sure it's *our* William Ewing," Dulcie said, "because it happened near the site of a Michicomi craft show that was going on at the time in Albany. I checked that."

"All the details certainly fit him," Jo agreed.

"Well!" Ina Mae said, looking up. "So our Mr. Ewing has had a criminal charge against him. That's interesting."

"A charge but not a conviction," Jo pointed out. "It was the owner of the camera shop who claimed he saw Ewing leaving the area after the rock smashed through his store window."

"Shortly," Ina Mae said, "after they had had an altercation over the expensive, secondhand camera Ewing bought from the shop's owner."

"Which Ewing claimed was defective, but

the shop owner refused to take back," Jo added.

"So apparently Ewing stomped off in a rage but returned later to hurl the rock through the man's window, damaging merchandize that was displayed behind it as well."

"Again," Jo said, "all according to the shop owner."

"Whose name," Dulcie said, jumping in eagerly at that point, "was Clayton Pellet. I wasn't able to find anything about how the criminal charge played out, so I did a search on Pellet's name. Let me show you what I found." Dulcie reclaimed her chair and clicked away until the monitor displayed what she wanted.

Jo looked over her shoulder to read it. It was an obituary for Clayton Pellet, camera shop owner. She checked the date. "He died before it went to trial!"

"He did?" Ina Mae cried. "From what?"

Jo straightened up. "All it says is 'died suddenly.' "

"Hmm. And his sudden death, therefore, ended all charges against our Mr. Ewing, since Pellet was the only witness. Charges that might have been highly damaging to Ewing's future."

"Absolutely," Dulcie said, looking triumphant. "What if Clayton Pellet's sudden death came from an allergic reaction?"

"That would certainly be very highly suspicious," Jo agreed. "But we don't know that."

"Maybe we can find out," Ina Mae said, "though it might mean tracking down relatives of the man to ask." She looked doubtful.

"Let's think on that a bit," Jo said. "Maybe we can come up with another, less intrusive way. Dulcie, that was terrific work! Things are looking very incriminating for Bill Ewing. I don't, however, want to forget about Patrick Weeks yet. Could we do a search on him next?"

"Sure," Dulcie said, her eyes shining. "But let me check on how things are going upstairs. Why don't you get started?" She gave up her chair to Jo. "Can I bring anything down for you two when I come back?"

"You mentioned coffee, I believe?" Ina Mae said.

"Absolutely. Jo?"

Jo agreed that she could use a cup as well. It was stretching into a long day. She got down to work at the computer while Dulcie ran up to check on her husband's progress with the children.

"I have to admit," Ina Mae said as Jo

clicked away, "that I hope you don't find anything too bad on Patrick Weeks. From what you told me, he sounds like a devoted father. I'd hate to see that little girl of his lose a second parent."

"I know what you mean. But if anything's there, we have to find it. Nobody would want that child to be raised by a murderer."

"No, of course not." Ina Mae sank down.

Jo glanced over at her and saw the frown on Ina Mae's face. Finding out negative things about people was never pleasant, as Jo had certainly learned in the past. She turned her focus back to the computer and gradually began to appreciate the extent of Dulcie's accomplishment. The Internet was a wondrous ocean of information, but narrowing the sea down to a trickle, she found, was a major effort, especially when you couldn't say for sure what you were looking for.

She heard faint lively childish squeals overhead and assumed Caitlin was being guided toward her own bed. Before long, clinks and clatters sounded from the kitchen, then footsteps padded down the carpeted steps toward the basement. Jo glanced up to see Dulcie carrying a small tray with coffee mugs and cookies — probably homemade, Jo figured.

"How's it coming?" Dulcie asked as she came into the cluttered office. She glanced around for a place to set her tray, and Ina Mae moved a pile of folders from a low filing cabinet to the floor to clear space.

"Little by little," Jo said. "I found several mentions of his furniture making — very positive ones. And there was something from his and Linda's high school alumni group. A twenty-year reunion being planned."

Dulcie poured out coffee for them both, and Jo reached for hers gratefully, along with an oatmeal cookie. She sipped and nibbled quietly as she sifted through mentions of other Patrick Weeks, P. Weeks, Pat Weeks, and just plain Weeks. "Oh!" she suddenly cried and almost spilled coffee all over Ken Tyler's keyboard.

"What? You found something?" Ina Mae asked. She set down her own mug and stepped over to peer at the monitor. "What is it?"

Jo pointed to the section that caused her reaction. It was a list of recent arrests in the Ohio town where Patrick and Linda's high school was located. Ina Mae read, then sighed deeply, ending with a head-shaking tsk. "Drugs," she said. "Unfortunate."

"Drugs?" Dulcie asked. "Patrick Weeks

245

was arrested for drug use? When?"

Jo checked the date of the story. "Nine years ago."

"Then it was before his daughter was born," Dulcie said. "Thank goodness for that."

"And it was for possession of drugs, not for selling, which would have carried a far worse penalty," Ina Mae said.

"Nine years is a long time," Dulcie said. "He certainly looked fine the other day. And he's built a thriving furniture business, which indicates to me that he's living a steady, drug-free life now."

"I would hope so," Jo said. "I imagine we'll be able to find that out if we keep looking. However, he still has this on his record." She looked at Ina Mae. "If he hoped to fight Linda's intention to reclaim her parental custody, it would certainly be a strike against him."

"Indeed," Ina Mae said. "What you found, Jo, gives Patrick Weeks a very strong motive for murder."

CHAPTER 21

With Carrie's knitting students continuing to cancel, Jo had told Carrie to take the day off, suggesting she might like to finally get to the doctor's for her itchy eyes and runny nose. But instead, Carrie stopped in around two with a box of freshly baked brownies, having apparently decided, once again, that looking after herself was a low priority.

"I thought I could run these over to Russ," she said. "But I don't mind watching the shop, Jo" she said, "if you'd like to take them instead."

"No, Carrie. I'd rather wait until later tonight. It's quieter then. There's a couple of things I might like to talk to Russ about, assuming he's up to it."

Carrie looked at Jo curiously but didn't pry, something Jo greatly appreciated. She hadn't told Carrie — or anyone — about what Russ's brother Scott had shared with her. She wasn't sure whether she would bring it up with Russ, but it had been weighing on her mind, along with the half dozen or so other things that had popped up in the last twenty-four hours. She had, of course, told Carrie what they found on the Internet concerning Bill Ewing and Patrick Weeks. But about Russ — that would have to wait until Jo sorted it out for herself.

"Well, then," Carrie said, "I think I'd like to run to the hospital now, so I can be back before school lets out. Amanda might need a ride home after her science club meeting, if Lindsey's mom can't pick them up." Carrie set down her box to pull out a tissue and surreptitiously wiped at her itchy nose.

"Go ahead. Things have been so slow lately, it really doesn't take two of us to mind the shop anymore."

Carrie's face puckered. "It's just temporary, I'm sure." She picked up her box of brownies. "Russ may not be up to eating any of these yet, but I'll put them somewhere handy for when he is. Any message you'd like me to give him?"

"Just that I'll be by tonight. Give him a hug for me."

"I will."

Carrie took off, and the jingling of the bell as the door closed behind her reminded Jo how little she was hearing that sound anymore. After a minute or so, two women strolled into view outside her window and slowed. Jo hoped they might come in to shop. But they only peered in curiously. Jo saw their heads bend toward each other as though exchanging comments — about her? — after which they moved on.

Jo sighed and turned toward the back of her shop, deciding it was best to keep busy — and out of sight. She had another workshop coming up for her regulars that evening — a collage workshop — and she needed to get ready for it. Jo was pulling out poster board and gesso in her stockroom when she was surprised to hear the jingle. She leaned out to see Meg Boyer.

"Hi, Meg," Jo called, walking out to meet her. "Finished work?"

"Uh-huh. Ruthie mostly needs me during the lunchtime rush. I thought I'd pick up a scrapbook on my way home. Talking to Emmy the other day reminded me that I've got a bunch of stuff from my old high school days that I never did anything with. It'd be nice to organize it all." Meg's cheeks were a touch rosier than they had appeared before, and Jo thought the added color was nice. She had also perked up her hairdo a bit so that it wasn't falling over her eyes. A definite improvement.

"Good idea. The albums are right over there." Jo pointed to the scrapbooking section. "See if there's something you like."

Meg went over and began to browse. Jo was ready to head back to the stockroom, thinking Meg would need time to decide, but within moments Meg was carrying a floral-covered album up to Jo's checkout counter.

"Nice one," Jo commented. Meg also set down some photo adhesive, and Jo began ringing it all up.

"I was at Dr. Barnett's office yesterday for a small tooth emergency," Meg said as she dug through her purse for her credit card. Since it was the same large, overfilled bag as the day before, it was taking a while.

"Oh? I'm sorry to hear that."

"Nothing too bad, just an old filling that fell out. Dr. Barnett was nice enough to come in on his day off to fix it for me. His wife came in too. She told me about what happened when you and Dr. Barnett went to talk to that photographer from the craft festival."

"She did?"

"Yeah, she was pretty keyed up about it. I guess she knew about me helping you find Pat Weeks, so she figured I'd be interested."

"That's right, I did tell her about you calling your friend." Jo took Meg's card and swiped it, handing it back along with the slip for her to sign. "Which was very helpful," Jo added as she watched Meg sign her name.

Meg shrugged but looked pleased. "So this guy, Bill Ewing, came across as pretty suspicious, huh?"

"His reaction to my questioning yesterday sure put him in a negative light," Jo said, "and we're digging up other things from his past that show he doesn't much like being crossed."

"Are you going to the police with it?"

"No, I want to hold off until I have something more concrete. Right now it's simply indications, like what we found on Patrick Weeks too."

"Patrick? You found something on him?" Meg's eyes widened with curiosity.

"Yes. I don't want to say exactly what, but it was something that Linda might have used as leverage to gain full custody of their daughter. I think it gives Patrick a stronger motive for killing Linda."

"Boy, that would be awful, wouldn't it? I mean, it'd be bad enough if he did it, but really sad for his little girl."

"You're not the only one who feels that way."

Meg stood shaking her head for a moment, then picked up her purchase and pulled the strap of her bulky purse up to her shoulder. "Well, I'd better be going. I want to get started on this." She patted her new album inside its bag.

Jo wished her good luck and watched her go. Meg's mention of the dental office reminded Jo that she'd never returned Javonne's call after being summoned to the hospital by Mark. In her message, Javonne had sounded pretty indignant over Bill Ewing's actions, and Jo could imagine her ranting about it as poor Meg sat in the dentist's chair, a captive audience of one with her mouth stuffed with cotton and an aspirator. Jo grinned at the picture. She was glad she'd see her friend tonight. There was plenty to update her about.

Javonne appeared at the shop that evening carrying a small package. As she handed it to Jo, her lips curled to one side. "It's from Harry," she said.

Jo took the flat-shaped item, which was protected by a brown paper bag, wondering what in the world Harry would be sending her. She drew out the contents and laughed with surprise. It was a photo of the tobacco barn, taken with Harry's digital SLR. He had printed it out to an eight-by-ten size and framed it.

"Very nice!"

Javonne grimaced. "I told him I couldn't imagine why you'd want a souvenir of that awful day, but Harry didn't see it that way."

"He's proud of the photo he took, and rightly so. It's beautiful."

The other workshop ladies soon arrived and admired it as well.

"Harry has hidden talents," Loralee exclaimed. Javonne shrugged but seemed pleased and somewhat mollified over what she'd thought an ill-considered gift. As the group settled about the workshop table, Ina Mae and Dulcie filled her in on their Internet discoveries. Loralee, of course, had already learned all from Dulcie, and she quietly sorted through the clipped magazine pictures she had brought in for her collage project, nodding along with the explanation.

"Well, well, well." Javonne's eyes sparkled with interest. "So it looks like you might have the last laugh on Mr. 'Don't touch my fancy camera' Ewing."

"Don't forget about Patrick Weeks," Dulcie said. "He's always been a strong contender, and that drug use charge we found on him bumped him up a few notches on the suspect list."

"But that was so long ago," Loralee said. "Nine years! Surely, from the looks of things, it's been all put behind him, a foolish, youthful mistake. No judge deciding custody would give it any weight, would they?"

"Maybe, maybe not," Ina Mae said. "The important thing is did Patrick Weeks think it would have mattered?" She turned to Jo. "But we should probably get started on our collages. I've got my pictures, and I see you've provided the poster board. What's our first step?"

"You're right," Jo said. "We'd better get started. We can talk more later. The first thing to do, ladies, is to lay out your pictures on the poster board and play with them a little, moving them around until you're happy with the arrangement. You can trim your pictures in interesting ways with your scissors, or even tear the edges for a different effect. Then, when you're satisfied with the overall look, you're ready to start gluing."

Jo could see from the look on Ina Mae's face that this project was much more to her taste than origami. She had brought in several pictures from *National Geographic* magazines as well as sections of old road maps, which Jo thought would make a very interesting travel-themed collage.

Loralee, on the other hand, had cut out pictures of fuzzy baby animals, which she planned to arrange into a collage for her little granddaughter. Dulcie, Jo noticed, hadn't yet cut out any pictures but was leafing through old gardening catalogues, checking the pictures for possibilities.

Jo looked to the table area in front of the fourth member of the group, but Javonne seemed too intent on solving the murder mystery, or rather, too intent on pinning it on Bill Ewing who had so infuriated her, to settle down yet. Loralee, however, changed the subject by asking after Russ, and Javonne's look of righteous anger immediately softened.

"He's doing pretty well," Jo assured them, "all things considered. Carrie popped over to see him this afternoon and called with a good report. I plan to go tonight."

"Give him all our love," Loralee said. "Tell him I've been freezing a few good, nutritious meals to take him when he comes home."

"Which we hope won't be before he's 100 percent ready," Ina Mae said. She was trimming a picture of Blarney Castle to fit between one of the Great Wall of China and the Acropolis. Places she had been, Jo wondered, or places she hoped to see?

As the ladies worked busily, Jo pulled out a project of her own, something she'd had an idea for and wanted to try out. Dulcie looked up at one point and said, "Oh, that's cute! Will we do that next?"

"If you like. But not tonight. I'm still figuring out the steps as I go along, but I think it's turning out pretty well."

"What are you doing?" Loralee asked. "Decorating boxes?"

"Yes, gift boxes. I thought it'd be fun to decoupage gift boxes with scrapbooking paper — inside and out."

"I like the effect of the printed paper on the outside, but solid color on the inside." Dulcie said.

"And" — Jo held up a cellophane-wrapped scrapbooking sticker of a dragonfly — "this is going to be glued to the inside of the lid."

"Ooh! So you see it when you open it up!" Dulcie cried. "What a nice surprise that will be. Maybe you could use it for a gift for Lieutenant Morgan."

Jo smiled. "Well, Russ might prefer something a bit more masculine. I doubt pastel-colored dragonflies are quite his thing."

Ina Mae smiled as well. "Possibly not decorated gift boxes either. That looks like something the giftee might enjoy saving to keep special things in, which I'd say is more a feminine thing. I can see one of my daughters using it to store all her little scented candles."

The others agreed and were coming up with other uses for Jo's decorated boxes when the Craft Corner's bell jingled. Involved in their conversation as well as their own projects, most didn't notice, but Jo, whose ear was alert to the sound, immediately looked over. She was surprised to see Meg Boyer coming in.

Jo called out, "Hi, Meg," which caught the others' attention, and they added their greetings to hers. "Need something more for your scrapbook project?" Jo asked.

But Meg, instead of heading for the scrapbooking area, came straight back to the workshop table. She had the look of a woman on a mission.

"I was talking to Kevin tonight," she said, and Jo assumed she referred to her husband. "He was away for a couple of days on a sales trip, so I didn't get a chance before tonight to tell him about that photographer, Bill Ewing. You're not going to believe this," she said, "but Kevin knows him."

"He does?" It seemed to Jo as if all five of them had cried out at once.

"From the army," Meg explained. "They were both stationed at Fort Leonard Wood in Missouri for a while. Kevin worked as a clerk, but Bill Ewing — Sergeant Ewing, he was then — was doing photographic work for the army."

"Did he know him very well?" Ina Mae asked.

"They weren't good friends or anything, but Kevin is pretty sure Ewing will remember him if he calls and invites him out to lunch."

"Oooh," Javonne said, obviously interested in the possibilities.

"How does Kevin feel about doing that?" Jo asked, thinking that Meg's husband, from what she understood, preferred to make all the decisions in their household.

"Oh, he's up for it!" Meg said. "I've explained all about how you want to find Linda's killer. Kevin says Bill Ewing always seemed like a powder keg ready to blow up. He feels if Ewing murdered someone, he needs to be brought to justice."

"Amen," Ina Mae said. "But how does he think he can do that by meeting with the man?"

"Well," Dulcie said, jumping in, "Kevin's

in sales, right? So he must know how to draw people out. And they have their military years in common to put Ewing at ease. He should be able to get the man relaxed and talking, maybe after a couple of beers?"

"Exactly!" Loralee agreed. "It's a wonderful idea, Meg."

Meg beamed, obviously proud of having come up with it.

"Please warn your husband to be careful," Jo said.

"Yes," Javonne said firmly. "Tell him to make sure they meet in a very public place, so that if Ewing gets upset, there'll be plenty of people around for protection."

"I'll tell him, but Kevin is pretty good at taking care of himself. Anyway, Jo, I wanted to run that by you, to make sure it wouldn't interfere with anything else you planned. Then, if it's okay, I'll need to know how Kevin can get in touch with him."

"If Kevin's willing to give it a try, that's great, Meg. I can use any help I can get." Jo gave Meg the name and location of the combination restaurant and motel where Ewing was staying. "He's probably been eating most of his meals there, so an invitation to go elsewhere should appeal to him."

Meg tucked away the paper on which she'd written all the information. "I'll let you all know how it turns out."

"Come join us for Jo's next workshop," Loralee invited. "You'll love the things she teaches us. And we're a pretty good group."

Meg smiled, clearly pleased at the idea. "Maybe I will!"

She took off to the friendly farewells of them all. As the door jingled behind her, Loralee said, "Such a nice young woman. I can see a real difference in her since she's taken that job at the Abbot's Kitchen."

"Does anyone know her husband?" Jo asked, and got four head shakes.

"With him having to travel so much," Loralee said, "I guess he's always preferred to keep to himself on his days off." She hesitated. "Meg has hinted that he somewhat unreasonably expected her to do the same, that is, stay at home most of the time and keep to herself. But apparently that's changing. Looks like they're both starting to reach out more to their fellow townspeople. I'm so glad."

"If he can get something on Bill Ewing that Jo can take to the sheriff, I'll be even gladder!" Javonne declared. She glanced around the workshop as if seeing the ongoing collage projects for the first time. "What did you say I should do with this poster board, Jo?"

CHAPTER 22

Jo closed up shop after the ladies took off and headed to the hospital to see Russ. She reflected on the fact that this was perhaps her fourth or fifth trip there, taken with as many different emotions — fear and dread, relief, then back to worry. What emotions rolled through her this time she'd be hard put to pin down and label, but they'd been churning ever since her talk on the phone with Russ's brother Scott. What she was going to do about them she hadn't the faintest idea.

She tapped on Russ's door, which led to the old room he'd been returned to, and pushed it partway open.

"Hi," she said tentatively, feeling unexpectedly shy, as though the man she had come to see was someone she barely knew. But once Russ turned his head toward her and smiled his familiar smile, all her hesitancy disappeared.

"Feeling up to company?" she asked, stepping in. His eyes were shadowed and somewhat sunken, and she noticed his television wasn't on.

"Been staying awake just for you," Russ said as he reached out with his good arm to pull her close. She set down the poster board that she'd brought with her before leaning over to give him a kiss. His lips were dry but, thankfully, nonfeverish. His cheek, she noticed as she rubbed her own against it, was pleasantly smooth.

"You got a shave again," Jo said.

He grinned. "Gotta find something to keep them busy."

"Oh, you've kept everyone here plenty busy lately. It's time to let them move on to the other patients."

"And start doing things for myself? What's the point of being in the hospital if you can't be waited on hand and foot?"

"I don't know anyone less likely to enjoy being waited on. You know you're itching to get all this over with."

Russ laughed, and joked, "How little you know me." The words struck a chord with Jo, but she managed to smile.

"What's that?" Russ asked, looking at the poster board she had leaned against the bed.

Jo picked it up. "It's something I made for

tonight's collage demo, but I put it together with you in mind." She held it where he could see and watched the amusement grow on his face as he looked it over. It was a collage of police-related cartoons that she'd clipped from old *New Yorkers* and other magazines that Ina Mae had given her.

Russ's amusement increased to laugh-out-loud.

"I hoped you'd like it."

"Do I get to keep it?"

"Of course. I can tape it to the wall, there, if you like."

"That's good. Then when Mark comes by next time he won't miss it. That one about the burglar in the rabbit suit will ring a few bells for him."

"Oh?"

"I'll let him tell you about it. It's a good story."

"Mark's been a good friend." Jo took out the tape she'd brought with her and began fixing her cartoon collage to the wall beneath the television. Several get-well cards had been taped there as well, and Jo noticed one or two new flower arrangements in the room. Carrie's box of brownies perched on the table beside the bed, its cover ajar.

"Mark's the best."

"I also got to talk to your brother Scott

while you were in surgery."

"Yeah, Scott told me. He called this afternoon."

"He seemed very sorry he couldn't be here."

"I told him not to worry about it. We'll get together after the baby's born."

Something in Russ's voice had changed, and Jo looked over at him. She came back to the bedside and pulled the chair close, sitting down.

Russ looked at Jo silently, then said, "Scott told me what he'd blurted out. He apologized, said he assumed you would have known about Laura's and my son. He was right. I should have told you."

Jo took Russ's hand with both of hers. "There's no *should* about it. You share things when you're ready to. Not before. Scott, unfortunately, pushed things forward."

Russ shook his head. "You told me all about what you went through with Mike's death. I owed you that much in return."

Jo squeezed his hand. After a moment, she asked softly, "Did he have a name?"

Russ nodded. "Jarrod Russell, the Jarrod after Laura's father who died when she was little." He smiled. "I intended to call him Bud. Never was too crazy about 'Jarrod.'

But I hadn't mentioned that to Laura."

Jo smiled back. "Was that Laura who met you for lunch? Last September, when the country club's craft show was going on?" Jo remembered her surprise that afternoon when, basking in the success of the first local craft show she'd been asked to organize, she had spotted Russ — he was still Lieutenant Morgan to her then — affectionately greeting a very attractive woman at the doorway of the club's restaurant. The surprise had been at her own pained reaction, her first clue that she had budding feelings toward this man.

Russ's eyebrows twitched in surprise. "You saw her?"

"Just a glimpse. I was heading for the restroom."

"Yeah, that was her. She was passing through the area and suggested we get together. We've managed to stay on fairly good terms. She's seeing someone now. I hope it works out for her."

"I'm sorry for what you went through," Jo said.

Russ squeezed her hand. "It was tough. But it was tougher seeing Laura deal with it. I tried to help her, but it seemed like the harder I tried the more she pulled away. I have to admit that things weren't perfect between us before that. We probably hoped starting a family would fix things — always a mistake, I've since learned. So when the seas got rough, the water rushed through the cracks."

Jo nodded. "I'm sorry if this is painful to talk about."

"I'm glad that now it's all out. It's a relief. That part of my life was something I wanted you to know about, but I could never figure out how to bring it up. The longer things went, the harder it got, until it became some kind of secret. I didn't want there to be secrets between us."

Jo winced, thinking of all that she'd been keeping from Russ since he'd been shot — for his own good, she had been convinced, so that he could concentrate on getting well. Was that a valid enough reason? She'd certainly thought so when his situation had been so critical. What about now? Was he well enough to handle that added stress and burden? Or might it be good for their relationship to tell him about her trouble, but terrible for his health?

She looked at his eyes, so shadowed and tired. No, she decided, not yet. Bringing back his sad memories had been hard enough on him. She had to allow him more time to rest and gather his strength. If, when

266

he finally learned what she had been doing, Russ was upset that she'd kept it from him, she'd have to take the chance that he'd also be able to understand and forgive. She looked at him and realized with a rush of feeling how important that chance was to her.

Russ, unaware of the thoughts going through her head, simply smiled and reached up to stroke her face.

CHAPTER 23

Jo noticed a subtle change at the craft shop the next day. Customers were coming in, which was a good thing. And many were buying — a very good thing. However, during their browsing periods Jo found she was picking up on a lot of whispering. And from the glances thrown her way she couldn't help but assume the whispers were about her.

There was nothing overt enough to counteract. When merchandise was brought to the front counter — small bunches of dried flowers, a scrapbooking paper or two, or ribbons — the faces of her customers were always blandly smiling, where earlier she was sure she had detected furtive, suspicious looks. Carrie noticed it too, having come in to check her yarn stock.

"I'm getting the feeling of being watched," she said to Jo during a quiet time, "but when I look up, whoever's nearby is busy examining whatever's in their hands."

"I have that feeling too," Jo said. "And have you noticed, most of our customers today are people we've never seen here before? It's as if they suddenly heard about the Craft Corner and drove across town to check us out."

"Yeah, but check us out for what?"

"That's what I'm wondering. I suspect there's less interest in my craft supplies and plenty in whatever gossip they might be hearing about me."

As if to illustrate her point, two young women, strangers to Jo, entered the shop and paused just inside the doorway to stare at her.

"Can I help you?" Jo asked.

"Oh, ah," the taller of the two stammered, "are you the owner? Jo McAllister?"

"Yes, I am."

"Oh! Well," she said, grinning somewhat nervously, "we just wanted to look around. Okay?"

"Go right ahead. If you have any questions, just ask."

The two scurried off to the stamping section and began picking up stamps and papers and embossers, turning them about in their hands but looking back toward Jo more than at the merchandise. Jo sighed and wished she could just hang a sign around her neck that said, "Ask me if I did it!" Instead, she tossed a weary glance to Carrie, who had moved off to tidy up the rack of knitting needles. Carrie responded with a shrug and a look of her own that said, "Hang in there."

The pair eventually left without buying, after having wandered over nearly every inch of the shop. Jo was glad to see them go, though she bade them a good day with a courteous smile.

"This is getting me down, Carrie," she said. "I don't know which is worse — no business at all or business of this sort."

"No business is definitely worse," Carrie said. "These people might be coming for the wrong reasons, but at least some of them are plunking down their dollars to step in here. Once things are cleared up, they'll come back, having remembered what nice things they saw here."

Jo wasn't sure she agreed, though she appreciated the sentiment. The phone rang, and she went to answer it, hoping mightily it wouldn't be a "Get out of town!" call.

"Jo McAllister?" a male voice asked. It sounded familiar but Jo couldn't immediately place it.

"Yes?" she asked, warily.

"Patrick Weeks here."

"Oh! Hello. What can I do for you?"

"I'd appreciate it, *Ms.* McAllister," he said, his tone laced with barely controlled anger, "if you'd stop sending your spies over here."

"My spies! What are you talking about?"

"Don't give me that. You and that woman with her baby came here to check me out because of Linda. That was bad enough, with Abby here and all. But then a third one of your band showed up. That's more than I'll put up with. I want it to stop. Do you hear me?"

"I didn't send anyone there, Mr. Weeks. Who was it?"

"I don't know, but I know very well what she was after. It's harassment, and I won't put up with it. I'm warning you."

"What did she look like?" But Weeks had slammed down the phone.

Jo looked at Carrie, who had caught enough to stare worriedly. "Linda's ex-husband," Jo explained. "He thinks I've sent a spy to watch him."

"What! No way!"

"Of course not. At least," Jo hedged, "I hope not. He knows Dulcie, so it couldn't have been her. And I can't see Loralee running there on her own. You don't suppose Javonne or Ina Mae would have taken that on themselves, do you?"

"Oh, dear. It doesn't seem likely, but do you think you should check?"

Jo did think so, just to be sure. She called Javonne first.

"Me?" Javonne asked. "When would I have the time to do that? No, Jo, it sure wasn't me. Besides, you know I'm convinced the murderer is Ewing. I wouldn't waste the time — if I had any — spying on the ex-hubby."

Ina Mae's response was similar. "It wasn't I. And frankly, I think it's possible it wasn't anyone. Mr. Weeks just might be blowing smoke to throw you off track."

"He sounded pretty steamed up."

"I'm sure he did. But was his anger over a supposed spy, or was it because he fears you're getting too close to the truth?"

"You're right. The woman from the café — Shirley — could have told him what she said to us."

"Quite possible." Ina Mae's voice grew serious. "Jo, you know I'm hoping this man isn't the murderer, for the child's sake, but this latest development is very worrisome. You need to be on guard. A murderer who knows you are suspicious of him can be very dangerous — as you've learned before."

Jo nodded. She *had* learned that and

didn't particularly want to repeat mistakes from the past. She thanked Ina Mae and hung up.

"Neither of them?" Carrie asked.

"No, and Ina Mae suggested that Patrick Weeks may be trying to scare me off."

"Oh, Jo," Carrie said, "I think you should go speak to that sheriff."

Jo didn't have a chance to answer just then because more customers entered the store, one of whom stared curiously at Jo.

"May I help you?" Jo asked.

"Just looking," the woman said, smiling somewhat smirkily. She wandered off to join her companions, who had started whispering to each other.

Jo closed her eyes, shook her head, and sighed.

Later that afternoon, Carrie was just getting ready to leave when the phone rang, and since she was nearest, she picked it up.

Jo paused at the doorway of her stockroom, waiting to hear if she was needed, and saw Carrie's face growing more and more distressed over whatever she was hearing. Jo's heart jumped to her throat with the dreadful thought that it might be about Russ. She hurried closer, fearing the worst when she heard the words "hospital" and

"ICU." But Carrie never looked her way. Finally she hung up and turned toward Jo.

"Meg Boyer's husband is in the hospital. It sounds critical."

"Meg's husband! What happened?"

"I don't know except that he suddenly took very ill. Oh, Jo," Carrie said, her face a picture of woe, "he met with Bill Ewing today, remember?" She sank onto the high stool beside the register and looked up at Jo dolefully. "And," she said, "we sent him there!"

CHAPTER 24

Within minutes of Carrie's phone call from Loralee, Javonne burst through the Craft Corner doorway. "I told you! I told you it was that awful man!" she cried, her face a mix of triumph and distress. Her convictions had been verified, but at the same time a man had been put in the hospital and might be in danger of losing his life, so where was the satisfaction in that?

"What do you know about Kevin Boyer's condition?" Jo asked. "Have you heard more details than we have?"

"I know he's deathly ill, that's what I know." She began pacing the open space in front of Jo's checkout counter, the fabric of her white dental office uniform making little swishing noises.

"What were his symptoms? When did he actually get sick?"

Javonne stopped her pacing to think. "Sara Killian came in to get her teeth cleaned, and she said she had popped into the Abbot's Kitchen on the way to pick up a sandwich for later. That's when Ruthie told her that Meg had been summoned to the hospital and that one of Meg's neighbors had called an ambulance. They found Kevin collapsed on his driveway."

"Could it have been a heart attack or a stroke? Something natural, I mean?"

Javonne shook her head. "Sara said Ruthie had the impression it was stomach related. The poor man was probably poisoned during his lunch with Bill Ewing!"

"Maybe it was appendicitis," Carrie put in hopefully.

Javonne shot her a look of pure skepticism.

Jo took the neutral ground. "We need more information. It's useless to speculate at this point. How long ago did this happen, Javonne?"

"I'd guess an hour or two."

"And Loralee told you," Jo asked Carrie, "that he was in the ICU?"

Carrie nodded.

"Did Loralee say how she knows that? Had Meg called her?"

Carrie shook her head. "Loralee's next-door neighbor's daughter works at the desk of the hospital laboratory. She told her mother they got a whole lot of stat test orders on Meg's husband from the ICU."

"Well, that tells us he's sick, but not much else."

"Loralee also said she was heading over to the hospital to be with Meg."

"Good. That's very nice of her, and hopefully she can soon provide us with more details. I'm very sorry for Meg and for whatever happened to her husband. But until we know more," she said to Javonne, "we can't be running around accusing anyone of poisoning."

"I just hope Ewing doesn't take off for parts unknown in the meantime," Javonne said, sniffing. "Or," she added significantly, "try to poison someone else."

Javonne left to return to the dental office, and Jo urged Carrie to go on home to see to her family's dinner. "I need to work on my bills. I'll call you if I hear anything from Loralee."

"Call me the instant you hear. Don't worry about interrupting our dinner." Carrie grabbed her things, then paused as she was partway out the door. "It just occurs to me," she said, "if it turns out Kevin Boyer was actually poisoned, then, terrible as it is, it might finally end those rumors flying around about you, Jo. You were here all day with me and in plain view of plenty of customers, so you obviously couldn't have slipped Kevin anything."

Jo sighed. "The way things are going, someone will probably come up with a theory of how I could have done it by long distance."

Carrie clucked over that, but left, wishing Jo luck with her bills. Jo sat down at her desk to immerse herself in her store's finances, which bad as they were should have totally absorbed her. But her thoughts kept wandering over to the hospital, wondering what was happening in the ICU, then moving down a floor or two to Russ's room.

When she thought about her last talk with Russ, she wondered about that barrier that had always stood between them and if a significant chunk might have been taken out of it. It felt that way, and Jo found she liked what she was glimpsing on the other side. She chewed on the end of her pen. Was she falling in love? She didn't know, but she thought she might at least have grown more ready to fall in love. Did that make any sense? She shook her head. Probably not.

Her electric bill, which sat on top of the pile, caught her eye, jolting Jo out of her musings. Had she really used that many kilowatts in the last month? And the rates had definitely jumped up without her noticing. The days were getting longer, which might make a difference in the cost of lighting the shop in the future, but then she'd soon need to use the air conditioner, which would gobble up that difference. Ugh!

With thoughts of her shrinking checking account leading to worse ones about whether she would even have a viable business to keep cool and well lit by summer, she switched back to thinking about Kevin Boyer. What was happening with him? What *had* happened to him? As those questions ran through her head, filling it with images of Kevin meeting with Bill Ewing and what might have occurred, the phone suddenly rang, making her jump. She retrieved the pen she had dropped and reached for the receiver.

"Jo, dear, it's Loralee."

"Loralee! Are you at the hospital? How is Meg's husband? And Meg?"

"Kevin, I'm afraid, is in a coma. Meg's terribly distraught."

"A coma! What caused it?"

"The doctors don't know at this point. They've ordered lots of tests, including toxicology ones, which sounds ominous. Meg is convinced that Bill Ewing put something into Kevin's food."

"Was she able to talk with Kevin? Did he tell her what happened between Ewing and him?"

"No, Kevin hasn't been conscious since they found him on his driveway. But Meg said he definitely went off to meet with Ewing, and that he had hinted to her before he left that he knew something from their army days that reflected badly on the man."

"Only hinted?"

"I'm afraid so."

"Does she know where they were meeting?"

"No, Kevin never told her that either."

Why do men like to keep so many things to themselves? Jo wondered, tapping her pen in frustration. Aloud, she said, "It looks like we'll just have to wait for those toxicology results."

"If I learn anything more, I'll let you know, dear."

"Thanks, Loralee. Please give Meg my best." Jo rang off and gave Carrie a quick call to share the latest. Then she mulled over this development.

What could have happened between Kevin Boyer and Bill Ewing that would have caused the photographer to take drastic action? If Ewing had poisoned Kevin, he must

280

have come prepared to do so, Jo thought, which led her to think it might have been based on whatever Kevin knew about Ewing from the past. But how would that have connected to Linda?

Jo thought about Gabe Stubbins. Would he possibly have any knowledge of Bill's past that might help? Something that might have slipped out during a late-night beer or two? There was one way to find out. She pulled out her cell phone and scrolled down to his number. To her disappointment, she got only his voice mail. She left a quick message and hung up, dissatisfied, then remembered the card he had given her with his home number on it as well. Perhaps she could reach him there? A search through her purse failed to turn up the card, and she realized she must have left it at home.

Jo thought for a moment, then picked up her store phone and called Information. She hoped she correctly remembered the town in Pennsylvania that Gabe had mentioned and waited while the operator searched for a number for a Gabe or Gabriel Stubbins. Then, as the wait grew longer, she hoped Gabe hadn't chosen to be unlisted. Finally the woman's voice came back on and to Jo's relief, recited a number. Jo thanked her and quickly punched it in. An older woman's voice answered.

"Mrs. Stubbins?" Jo asked, and when the woman said she was, Jo identified herself.

"Oh, yes, Jo. Gabe has mentioned you."

Jo was glad to hear a smile in the voice. "I tried to call Gabe's cell phone," she explained, "but it wasn't on. I thought maybe he was there?"

"Oh, Gabe's down in Richmond now. The Michicomi show, you know."

"That's right," Jo said, shaking her head. "So much has been going on around here, I've lost track of the days. I remember now about the Richmond weekend. He must have been down there hours ago."

"No, he probably arrived later than he normally would because there was someone he was hoping to see along the way — in Maryland."

"Oh?"

"Yes, an old friend of his from the shows. Maybe you know him too. Bill Ewing, the photographer?"

"Oh!" Jo said, surprised. "You said '*hoping* to see.' Do you know if they actually did meet?"

"No, I'm afraid not. Gabe will probably call me later tonight. And if you left a message for him, perhaps he'll get back to you too." Her tone told Jo that any further questions she had would best be asked of her husband, so Jo thanked her very much and ended the call.

Jo stared at her phone, wondering why Gabe had wanted to meet with Ewing. And if they had met — considering Ewing had met Kevin Boyer for lunch — when had that been?

CHAPTER 25

Jo woke early the next morning with her thoughts going in several directions at once. Had she actually slept? she wondered, or had her brain simply kept on running after her eyes had closed, like a factory chugging on with its night shift? If only her brain had been as productive. What she woke to seemed more of a tangle of raw material than any finished product. Now she had to sort through and try to make some sense out of it.

Making her way to the kitchen and the coffeepot, she thought about how she wished she could have seen Russ the night before. She had called before closing the Craft Corner, hoping to run over, but caught him in the midst of a noisy gathering, all the off-duty people from the station having apparently decided to visit him at the same time.

"This crew doesn't look like they'll be

leaving for a while," he had said, then suggested, "Why don't you hold off until tomorrow?" which sounded like the most reasonable thing to do, though Jo hadn't liked it much. She had tried to comfort herself later at home with a scoop or two of Cherry Garcia from her freezer. But, not surprisingly, it hadn't done the trick.

Jo hadn't heard back from Gabe, but Loralee called her to say that she was heading home and that Kevin's condition had not changed. As Jo scooped out coffee grounds, she wondered once again what Kevin might have known about Bill Ewing that he had only hinted at to Meg. If Kevin hadn't seen fit to confide in his wife, might there have been a friend that he had? Jo realized she wanted to know more about Meg's husband. The best place she could think of to begin would be with his neighbors, most of whom she might be able to catch at home on this Saturday morning.

But where did Meg live? Jo didn't know, but Ruthie, of course, did, and the Abbot's Kitchen opened early for coffee and breakfast buns. If Jo stopped there before heading to the Craft Corner, she could check with Ruthie and maybe even have time to run out to Meg's neighborhood. After plugging in her coffeemaker, Jo went off to

285

shower. It looked as though she'd need a brisk one, as her day was once again going to be full.

"Meg's address?" Ruthie handed a breakfast croissant and coffee over to one of her early-bird customers, a middle-aged man dressed for golf, who, to Jo's relief, hadn't given Jo a second glance when she joined him at the counter. Apparently not everyone in town gave a hoot about whatever gossip might be flying around about her. "Hold on a sec," Ruthie said. "I'll be right back."

Ruthie disappeared into the back of the Abbot's Kitchen, returning soon with Meg's job application form. "Shame what's happening with her husband. You planning to take a fruit basket or something to the house?"

"No. I believe Meg's been spending most of her time at the hospital while Kevin is in this coma." Jo looked at the address Meg had filled in: "422 Asher Court, Abbottsville, MD." She scribbled it down on a scrap of paper, then asked Ruthie, "Any idea where Asher Court is?"

"It connects to Ridgeway Avenue. Just a short ways past the post office."

"Great, that should be easy to find." Jo tucked the paper away. "I hope things haven't been too busy for you without Meg to help?"

"Oh, we've been managing," Ruthie said, with a slightly odd look on her face. Before Jo could ask about it, another customer came forward to give his order, so she said a quick thank-you and took off. She checked her watch as she left the sandwich shop. Did she have time to get over to Meg's neighborhood and talk to a few people before the Craft Corner needed to be opened? Maybe she should make sure Carrie could cover for her.

"Sure, Jo, no problem," Carrie said after Jo called her from inside her car and explained what she needed time for. "Though from the impression I have of Kevin Boyer, I can't picture him being on close terms with his neighbors."

"Well, if that's the case, at least I will have learned that much about him. I'll try not to be too long." Jo hung up and pulled away from the sandwich shop, heading for Asher Court.

Meg's house was a modest, one-story ranch style that looked at least a couple of decades old. Jo had no idea what Kevin's job paid, but from what she understood, his had been the only income for the household until very recently, and Jo well understood the challenges of stretching a single income to cover all expenses. Meg had only lately stepped out to take her part-time job at the Abbot's Kitchen. If she had been somehow held back from working until then, the downside of that showed in the condition of their house, whose siding looked in need of painting, if not replacement, and whose driveway was cracked and in need of resurfacing.

Jo parked in front of the house and wondered which of the surrounding ones to try. As she pondered, the garage door of the house to the left began to rise. In moments a man stepped out, pushing a wheelbarrow loaded with tools and inadvertently making Jo's decision for her. She climbed out of her car.

"Good morning," Jo called, walking toward the weekend gardener. She saw, as she drew closer, that a bag of mulch also lined the wheelbarrow.

The man, gray-haired but slim and fit, paused in his forward movement and responded to her guardedly, possibly expecting a sales pitch of some kind. Jo quickly introduced herself and explained that she was a friend of Meg's. This brought a relaxation of the furrow between the man's brows, and he introduced himself as Jack

McKendry.

"How's Kevin doing?" he asked.

"Not too well, I'm afraid. He hasn't regained consciousness yet."

McKendry shook his head sympathetically. "That was quite a scare yesterday," McKendry said, his face reflecting the anxiety he must have felt at the time. "I was out here working on my bushes — I'm retired, now," he explained. "Anyway, I happened to look over and there he was, sprawled on his driveway. At first I thought, well, I don't know what I thought, but it sure surprised me. I saw his wife's car was gone, so I went over to ask was he all right, but all he did was groan. I hustled back to the house and called for an ambulance. Best I could do. I don't know anything about first aid."

"That was exactly the right thing to do," Jo assured him, which drew an appreciative smile. "Do you know Kevin well? I mean, are you friends beyond the 'nod and wave' level?"

"Friends? I don't know." McKendry shook his head. "We never saw much of him, with him traveling so much and all. I can't say I knew him very well, no. Why, you planning some kind of 'welcome home' party for when he gets out? We'll be glad to come, of course, but —"

"No, nothing like that. I've never actually met Kevin. But I needed to know something about his time in the army and hated to bother Meg at a time like this. So I guess you never got into conversation with him about his time spent at Fort Leonard Wood?"

"Afraid not. Rick Gurney, across the street there," McKendry said, pointing out a beige two-story, "might be able to help you. I saw them talking together a few times. But I never even knew Kevin was in the army. Wouldn't have guessed it, to tell the truth, a guy like him."

"Oh?"

"Well, you know," McKendry said, then shook his head. "That's right, you said you never met him. And maybe I've just got an old-fashioned, outdated idea of what army material is. They probably need all types nowadays."

"What type would you say Kevin was?"

"Oh, I don't know," McKendry said, beginning to look sorry he'd got himself onto the subject. He obviously wasn't someone who was comfortable analyzing casual acquaintances. "Bookish, maybe? Quiet anyway, and not real athletic. But as I say, they probably have a use for all types."

290

He started fiddling with the tools stacked in his wheelbarrow.

"Well, thanks," Jo said, taking the hint. "I'll run over and give Rick Gurney a try and let you get to work." She noticed that a pickup sat in the driveway of the house McKendry had indicated, which looked hopeful for finding somebody at home.

"Yeah, Rick should be able to help you." McKendry gave her a big smile then, and whether he was wishing her luck or just happy to be rid of her Jo couldn't tell. But she thanked him again and crossed the street to knock on the door of the beige house.

As she waited, a light blue sedan came down Asher Court and pulled into the drive behind the pickup. A slim, red-haired woman of about forty, wearing jeans and a yellow pullover, climbed out holding a plastic grocery bag. She looked at Jo curiously, and Jo stepped off of the house's stoop, ready with her explanation. But Jack McKendry beat her to it, calling out helpfully from his yard, "Susan, that there's Jo. She's a friend of Meg's and wants to talk to Rick."

Susan Gurney immediately smiled, and Jo waved gratefully to Jack McKendry. She was happy not to have had her full name mentioned, which avoided the possibility of Susan Gurney recognizing her as *that woman who's under suspicion of murder.*

"Rick's probably in the basement," Susan said, closing her car door, "which is why he's not answering the door. You're a friend of Meg's? How is Kevin? I heard about what happened yesterday."

Jo told her what she had told Jack McKendry, and Susan reacted much the same, shaking her head in sympathy as she crossed in front of Jo to open her front door. "C'mon in," she invited. "I'll get Rick for you."

As Jo followed Susan into the house she picked up the aroma of cooked bacon. The scent grew stronger as they made their way down the short hall to the kitchen, which sported dirty breakfast dishes on the table and a greasy frying pan on the stove.

"That man," Susan said with good-natured exasperation. "Can't pick up a thing for himself." She set her bag on the counter, then took the few steps over to a door at the other end of the kitchen and pulled it open. "Rick! You down there? Someone here to see you."

Jo heard a muffled response that sounded close to, "Be right up," and said to Susan, "I hope I'm not interrupting him from anything important."

Susan flapped a hand. "Don't worry about it. Saturday mornings he likes to putter down there. He claims he's working on a project, but it's mostly just puttering. I don't mind. It's his way of relaxing. I just wish," she said with an eye roll, "he'd put a few things in the dishwasher first."

She unloaded her grocery bag, chatting in a friendly way as she did. "We're going to a potluck dinner tonight, so I picked up a few things after I dropped the kids off at soccer practice. Want some coffee? There's some here I can heat up."

"No, thanks." Jo handed Rick's breakfast plate and mug over to Susan, who had started tidying up. "Did you know Meg and Kevin well?"

"Well?" Susan paused thoughtfully, Rick's dishes in hand. "Not as well as you'd think I should, living right across the street from them and all." She scraped crumbs from the plate into her sink before loading it into her dishwasher. "Of course, we've only been here about a year or so, and they don't have kids to come play with our kids. They kind of keep to themselves anyway, though. Except when Kevin came over sometimes to ask Rick's advice on his furnace. They seemed to have a lot of trouble with their furnace."

"Yeah." Rick suddenly stepped out of the basement, dressed in a sweatshirt and jeans. He was a tall, husky man with a receding hairline and friendly face. He wiped his hands on a brown-stained rag. "That furnace of his is on its last legs. I told Kev he'll need to get a new one before next winter comes around."

"Jo, this is my dishwashing-challenged husband, Rick. Jo is a friend of Meg's."

"Yeah? How's Kev doing?"

Jo told him, and Rick said to his wife, "We should get over to the hospital. Take him something. Don't you think?"

"Yeah, we should," Susan agreed, looking less than eager.

"So, you're good friends with Kevin?" Jo asked, beginning to seriously doubt that.

"Oh, yeah!" Rick insisted. "He's a great guy."

"They had a few beers together," Susan clarified. "After talking furnace talk."

"Did he ever tell you about his time in the army? When he was stationed at Fort Leonard Wood?"

"The army? Uh, I don't remember him ever mentioning that. Why, do they need some records or something at the hospital?

294

Meg probably can tell them whatever they need."

"Yes, you're probably right." Jo sighed inwardly. Rick obviously wasn't the confidante of Kevin that she'd hoped he be. "I guess I thought I could save her a little trouble. But thanks." She picked up her pocketbook and turned toward the hall, Rick moving forward to escort her to the door.

"I really only met Meg a short time ago," Jo said, "so I don't know much about either of them. I kind of got the impression Kevin was a bit domineering, and that was why she kept to herself a lot, because that was how he wanted it. Was I mistaken?"

"Kevin? Domineering?" Rick gave a quick laugh. He had an incredulous look on his face. "I wouldn't say that. Would you, honey?"

Susan shook her head. "He seems like a pretty nice guy to me. In fact," she said to her husband, "remember how you had to nearly beg him to borrow your chainsaw when he was ready to go out and rent one?"

"Oh, yeah, when that big tree limb came down in their backyard. I even offered to come over and cut it up for him, but he said he'd be okay doing it himself." Rick grinned. "I could hear him having trouble keeping the saw going at first, but eventually he got the hang of it."

Jo smiled. "Guess I was mistaken, then. Hey, thanks again for your time."

"No problem. Tell Meg to let us know if there's anything we can do, okay?"

Jo said she would. As the door was closing behind her she heard, "We should run over to the hospital this afternoon, Sue, don't you think?" Jo smiled to herself and shook her head as she stepped off the low stoop, sure that with kids to pick up from soccer practice and a potluck dinner to prepare for, that no, Sue most likely didn't think.

Jo stopped at the end of the driveway, thinking. Unfortunately, neither Jack McKendry nor Rick Gurney were knowledgeable about what Kevin had hinted to Meg. She decided she might as well keep trying and crossed back over the street to talk to the neighbors on the other side of Meg. She followed that with knocks on more doors up and down the block. The responses she got from all were, surprisingly, nearly identical in substance: nobody knew Meg or Kevin beyond having exchanged a few words here and there, and nobody seemed to have the impression that Kevin was a difficult man to get along with.

Was that simply because they didn't know

him well? Jo wondered. The darker side of people, she knew, could be easily hidden in casual encounters. But Rick and Susan Gurney, who may have interacted with Kevin the most, had actually scoffed at the idea of Kevin being overbearing. Jo thought back to how she had formed the idea and thought it might have been mostly due to Ruthie's comments. Jo had already decided to pick up lunch for Carrie and herself on her way back to the shop, and thought she'd ask Ruthie about it.

Chapter 26

"Ruthie," Jo called out as she entered the shop, glad to see it empty for the moment of other customers, "can I get our regular sandwich and salad to go?"

Ruthie looked up and smiled. "Sure thing. You find Meg's place all right?"

"No problem." Jo waited until the older woman gave the order to Bert, in the back, then asked, "Didn't you tell me once that Meg's husband was a controlling kind of guy?"

Ruthie nodded. "That I did. From things Meg let drop now and then, it was hard to miss."

"What kind of things?"

"Oh, just little things. Hints, kind of." Ruthie slipped her pencil into her gray hair. "Let me think." She scratched a bit, then said, "Meg told me once, when she came in a few minutes late one time, that she was held up because her husband needed his shirt ironed before she left. I remember I asked her why he couldn't have ironed his own shirt and she got a kind of shocked, scared look on her face. She said something like, 'Kevin doesn't do women's work,' or something like that."

Ruthie thought a bit more. "Then there was a time I saw her chopping up onions kind of slowlike and she was rubbing her wrist like it was sore. When I asked her if she'd hurt it, she said, 'It was my fault, I shouldn't have said —' and then she stopped real suddenlike, as though she'd said too much. I got the feeling he maybe got mad at her and twisted it. I asked her was there something she wanted to talk about, but she said no and got that closed-down look on her face, so I let it drop and told Bert he should do the chopping and let Meg do something else."

Ruthie looked at Jo. "Why do you ask?"

"I just wanted to make sure I hadn't misunderstood. Talking to some of Meg's neighbors, I was getting a different impression of Kevin."

"They wouldn't see him like she does."

"I thought of that possibility too."

"Working here with us," Ruthie said, "Meg might be letting things out about him for the very first time. You can't help feeling sorry for the woman, and I am glad to have given her the chance to get out and assert herself some." Ruthie let out a big sigh. "But I have to tell you, she has a ways to go to learn how to do that, especially dealing with the public like we do here. But I'm sure living in a situation like hers takes its toll on you."

"I guess it would, but what do you mean as far as dealing with the public? Does she have a problem with it?"

"Well, you know, if you've been living under someone's thumb for a long time, it must make you afraid to stand up for yourself. And unfortunately we run into situations here, once in a while, with certain customers who never learned that you don't treat service people like they're something to walk all over. If anyone tries to give me a hard time, though, I just give them my icy stare and let them know they have a choice of cleaning up their act or leaving. I shoulda known that Meg wasn't up to that when I let her work the front counter for me."

"What happened?"

"Darryl Feggins — not my favorite customer by any means — came in, and when Meg didn't wait on him to his satisfaction, he let loose with some nasty stuff. I was taking a break in back, and next thing I know

Meg's stomping in, eyes blazing and muttering all sorts of things under her breath. She was mad as Hades, and she paced around the kitchen back there looking like she wanted to pick up something breakable and throw it against the wall. She didn't, of course, just paced all madlike until we calmed her down. But I had to take over out front and have her stay back with Bert, though my legs were killing me that day and I sure could have used a little more sittin-down time.

"Was this the man who called her a fat retard?"

"She told you about that? Yeah, that was Darryl. Never one for sweet-talkin', was Darryl."

"That's too bad. I guess she just wasn't ready to handle that sort of thing." Jo thought back to Meg mentioning the incident to her when she'd stopped in at the Craft Corner. Her version had ended somewhat differently, putting her in a much better light. Jo wondered if that might be attributed to Meg's desire for being better able to handle such situations in the future. Kind of a 'this is how I *wished* it had ended.'

"So I've kept her working in the back since then," Ruthie said. "But with not being able to get help from her up front, and her being less than reliable sometimes in back, I was beginning to think maybe we should let her go. But I can't do that now, of course, with her husband in the hospital and all."

Ruthie's phone rang, and as she took an order for a takeout, Jo noticed that Meg's application was still sitting on the counter, anchored down and partially covered by a metal napkin dispenser. Jo went over to pick it up, glancing over the form once again as she did. Meg had clearly filled it out in a hurry, with some letters scribbled over and at least one misspelling apparent. Jo pictured her nervously trying to write as customers crowded the little shop, possibly distracting her. When Ruthie hung up, Jo handed the sheet to her.

"You might want to file this away," she said, and Ruthie, seeing what it was, laughed deprecatingly.

"A lot of senior moments seem to be happening to me lately," she said. Jo's order slid through the slot on the back counter and Ruthie picked it up. "Did you put an extra dab of sauce on Jo's?" she asked her husband.

"Sure did," Bert's answer floated back, and Jo smiled, feeling her salivary glands kick in. Life could often get bumpy, but

Bert's turkey and bacon smothered in his special sauce always managed to mellow it out for her, at least for a while.

"I brought you something to eat," Jo called out as she walked into the exceedingly quiet Craft Corner. Apparently the curiosity of the noncustomers that they'd dealt with yesterday had been satisfied for the time being.

Carrie looked up from the knitting she worked on as she sat behind the counter. "You didn't have to do that," she said, smiling. "But thank you. That will save me a little time."

"Does Amanda have a soccer game this afternoon?" Jo set her bag on the counter and pulled out Carrie's salad and her own sandwich.

"Yes, and Dan will be there, of course, since he's coaching. But I'd love to run over and watch it for a few minutes. Unless," Carrie quickly amended, "you need to go out again?"

"Not at all," Jo said, which was true. But it was also true that Jo would sooner close up the Craft Corner altogether for the day than keep Carrie from attending one of her child's activities. Carrie did enough for her as it was, for which Jo was exceedingly grateful.

"Did you have any luck this morning? Find any confidantes of Kevin Boyer?" Carrie carefully tossed her salad, which was chock-full of hearty items beyond the usual lettuce and tomatoes, coating all with the spicy, but low-fat, dressing.

"I'm afraid not. And I'd sure like to know what he might have had on Bill Ewing."

"Why would Kevin have agreed to meet with Bill Ewing," Carrie asked, "if he knew something about the man that might put himself in danger?"

"That's a good question. I don't know Kevin Boyer at all, and I've been getting conflicting opinions of him, so it's hard to say. He's either a bully or a decent guy, and if he's a bully, maybe he hoped to blackmail Ewing."

"Could be."

Jo chewed on her sandwich a bit. "Or perhaps he just didn't think what he knew about Ewing was all that harmful. Maybe he simply thought it was a way to get a conversation going that might lead to more interesting things."

"It's frustrating, isn't it? I mean, to only be able to speculate but not really know." Carrie had by then picked out most of her favorite things from her salad — egg slices, artichoke pieces — and was searching under lettuce leaves for more.

"It's also frustrating not to hear back from my craft show friend, Gabe. His wife told me he planned to see Bill Ewing on his drive to the Richmond Michicomi. If he did, he might have helpful information."

Carrie had finished her lunch and was picking up her things. "This Gabe has been getting extra Michicomi shows after Linda died, hasn't he? From what you told me about Bill Ewing's frustration at losing spots, how do you suppose that would sit with him?"

"I had the impression Gabe and Bill always got along pretty well. But that's a another good question."

Carrie glanced at her watch. "I'd better go if I'm going to get over to the park in time. Thanks very much for the salad. Are you sure you'll be okay here on your own?"

Jo glanced around the empty shop and grinned. "Since not a single customer has come in since I've been back, I think I'll be able to handle things."

"Oh, Jo. I don't know what kind of horrible things are going through people's heads lately about you. But it will clear up. It has to. And all your old customers will be back in droves, full of apologies."

"Thanks, Carrie. From your lips to God's ears." Along with a lot more work to nail down Linda Weeks's killer, Jo added silently. She waved off her friend then looked down at her sandwich, which was nearly gone. Jo realized forlornly that she had barely tasted it, so absorbed had she been in the problems of Kevin, Bill, Gabe, and others.

With so few pleasures coming her way lately, it was annoying to have wasted this one. She glanced around, wondering if Carrie had possibly left behind a cookie or two.

CHAPTER 27

Jo was dusting off the plastic wrappings of some of her origami papers when her phone rang. She put down her lamb's wool duster and went over to answer it.

A familiar voice said, "Jo, I understand you've been trying to reach me."

"Gabe!"

"Sorry to take so long to get back to you, but you know how busy it can be setting up at a new show."

"Yes, I do, which is why I so appreciate your taking the time to squeeze in this call. I'll get right down to what I need from you. First of all, when I spoke to your wife, she said you wanted to meet with Bill Ewing on your drive down to Richmond. Did that happen?"

"Afraid not," Gabe said. "Guess I should have planned ahead more, but this Richmond thing popped up at the last minute. Anyway, I tried to reach Bill while I was on the road but couldn't get through to his phone. I did stop at that diner I told you about — Ginger's — but all she could tell me was that Bill was out, probably with his camera, but nothing more helpful for tracking him down."

"That's unfortunate." Jo explained what had happened to Kevin Boyer after he'd returned from a meeting with Bill, possibly around the time Gabe had been trying to find the photographer.

Gabe predictably reacted with horror, then asked, "You said this man Kevin wasn't able to tell anyone what had occurred?"

"No, he was found unconscious and has remained so."

"I just can't believe Bill would do anything of that sort."

Jo told Gabe about Kevin's hints about Ewing. "Gabe, do you know anything about Bill's time in the army? Anything at all?"

"I do remember he mentioned that he learned quite a bit about photography while he was in the military."

"Did he tell you about anything he wouldn't want generally known, perhaps after a couple of late night beers?"

"No, nothing, Jo. Bill could get mad pretty quick, but at the same time he was quite closed mouthed about himself. A drink or two only made him close up tighter, not start blabbing."

Jo sighed.

"Do the doctors know yet what put this man into a coma?" Gabe asked.

"No, not that I've heard."

"Perhaps it will turn out to be something completely unconnected to Bill," Gabe said, sounding faintly hopeful.

"Perhaps, though I'm pretty sure they've ruled out all the natural causes at this point."

It was Gabe's turn to sigh. "Please keep me informed, will you, Jo?"

Jo promised, and ended the call feeling discouraged. Even the arrival of an honest-to-goodness customer — Mary Chatsky, who was in need of scrapbooking papers for her ongoing project — wasn't enough to perk her up, though Jo put on her best "cheerful shopkeeper" face.

Mary was a down-to-earth woman who enjoyed doing a variety of crafts and caring for her family, and didn't seem to worry much about what her neighbors did or said, which, Jo figured, was probably why she still patronized Jo's Craft Corner. She asked Jo's opinion on one or two points of her scrapbook, paid for her purchases, and pleasantly wished Jo a good day. This helped to chase off a bit of Jo's gloom, but it returned as she noticed a few people peering curiously into her shop but not deigning to come in.

Jo halfheartedly picked up her duster and returned to her cleaning and shelf straightening, two activities that left her mind free enough to mull over the many bits and pieces of information she had packed into it in the last few days. She thought back to the candy box that had been left on her counter at Michicomi. Why *her* booth? Was that accidental — her jewelry booth being mistaken for Linda's? Or was it deliberate?

Then she thought about how Linda had alienated so many people during her short lifetime, going as far back — from what Jo knew — to high school and the boyfriend Linda had married and later dumped, on through her years in New York, then her connections at Michicomi. How many others did Jo not know of? Had she scraped off only the tip of the iceberg of Linda's enemies?

Jo realized she had cleaned just about every surface in her shop that could hold dust and headed toward the stockroom to pick up the very few items she had noticed needed replacing. As she did, the phone rang, and Jo veered off her path to pick it up.

"Jo, it's Mary Chatsky. When I was at your shop, I was intrigued with a vase you had there, a really pretty, multicolored one. It was over near the window and I loved the way it caught the light. Anyway, on the way home I talked myself into getting it — an early birthday present to myself," she said, chuckling. "But I can't get back there right away. How late are you open?"

"I close at six on Saturdays. I know which vase you mean. I love it myself. Would you like me to put it aside for you?"

"Please do. I can get there a few minutes before six for sure, but I don't like the idea of somebody maybe snatching it up before I do."

"Not to worry, Mary. I'll hold it for you," Jo said, not mentioning the extreme unlikelihood that another customer would be in before Mary returned. She went over to pull the vase off the shelf as promised and was setting it beside the register when the phone rang again. Had Mary had a change of heart? To Jo's surprise, it was Gabe, and he sounded excited.

"Did you remember something?" Jo asked hopefully.

"No, I just heard from my wife, who got a call from Amy Witherspoon. Do you remember Amy? She ran the leatherworks booth

311

that was next to mine at the Hammond County show."

Jo did remember. How could she forget that hard, accusing look Amy had given her after Linda was carried off on the stretcher?

"Amy wanted to know how to get in touch with you, which my wife, of course, didn't know. Amy's cell phone battery unfortunately was running low, but she managed to ask my wife to pass on the information that she was heading back to the Hammond County Fairgrounds to pick up an item she'd left behind that they were holding for her. She hoped you could meet her at the office there, at six."

"Me? Did she say why?"

"Amy's phone, as I said, was getting weak, but my wife said she understood that Amy wanted to apologize to you. That she'd learned something that convinced her you had nothing to do with Linda's death."

"Wow! But she didn't explain what that was?"

"No. But this sounds terrific, doesn't it, Jo? I mean, if Amy, who I know was highly suspicious of you, has done a complete turnaround, she must have found out something that will put an end to all of this."

"Indeed! She wants me to meet her at the fairgrounds office?"

"Yes, she was passing through on her drive to Delaware but hoped to be there at six. I'm guessing that besides the information, she might have something concrete to pass on to you. However helpful what she has turns out to be, it's at least good news that she no longer thinks so badly of you. Don't you think?"

"Yes, of course."

"Amy has a soft heart and was surely drawn in by Linda's convincing tales of persecution and woe, so don't think too badly of her for how she judged you."

"I won't. Thank you for passing this on, Gabe."

"Good luck. Let me know how it works out."

Jo put down the phone and thought about the drive to the Hammond County Fairgrounds, which would take at least thirty minutes and meant she would have to leave by 5:30. But Jo had promised Mary Chatsky that she'd be open until six. Carrie was presently off enjoying her daughter's soccer game, and Jo didn't want to interrupt that. But would Charlie have given up his Saturday afternoon to watch his sister's middle-school game? Jo guessed not and called their house.

"Charlie, I'm glad I caught you. Can I ask

a big favor?"

"Sure, Aunt Jo. What's up?"

Jo heard NASCAR noises in the background and hoped Charlie wouldn't mind tearing himself away from the television for a while.

"I have to leave the shop early, but I promised Mary Chatsky I'd be open until six so she could come get a vase I'm holding for her. Do you think you could use your mom's key to get in here around a quarter to six and handle the sale?"

"Sure, no problem."

"That's terrific. Thanks, Charlie." Jo told him where the vase would be, what the price was, and that he could just lock up and leave after that one transaction.

Jo glanced at the clock. Four thirty. She had plenty of time, but should she leave early to avoid getting caught in traffic? With Amy passing through as she was, there was a greater chance of missing her. What would Amy have to tell her? What could have made her do such a complete turnaround? Jo thought about the icy look on Amy's face when Jo gave Gabe a farewell hug. This was a woman whose opinion of Jo had been low and firmly entrenched. She had clearly believed, to the depths of her soul, the worst about Jo. Whatever she discovered would have to be astounding and convincing to bring about this change of heart.

Jo sank down onto the stool beside the register and ran through several possibilities. The more she thought, however, the more her frown deepened. Was this too good to be true? Other "not quite right" feelings she had experienced before began to come back to her, bits of information she had originally ignored but which now seemed worthy of a second look.

Another glance at the clock told her ten minutes had gone by. Jo got up and headed for her desk where she pulled her pocketbook out of the bottom drawer. She drew out her cell phone and studied it for several moments. There was someone she wanted to talk to before she left. Someone who might be able to clear up questions that had popped up as Jo reexamined those uneasy feelings. Jo pressed a few buttons, found the number she wanted, and pressed Call, then sat down and waited for her connection to go through.

CHAPTER 28

Jo could hear her Toyota driving noisily. Her muffler was in need of replacement and had been for several weeks now. It was an expense she'd been putting off until her budget was in better shape, though that consideration was the least of her concerns now. The skies had darkened since she'd left the shop, and a few drops began to dot her windshield. When they covered it, she turned on her wipers, glad to see that at least they worked properly.

As the drizzle increased to a deluge, Jo thought about what Carrie had once said about the fairgrounds' unpaved parking lot, how it had turned into a sea of mud last summer after a thunderstorm. Strange how long ago it seemed that comment had been made, though it was actually little more than a week. So much had changed in those few days — from simple things like the spring-blooming trees along the highway leafing out, to major ones, like the alterations to the lives of Jo, Linda Weeks, and the many people linked to both of them.

Jo saw the entrance to the lot she was heading for and turned in. The rain pelted the roof of her car, and she knew she would be soaked as soon as she stepped out. But getting wet was, again, a minor problem. The major concern was what lay ahead. What would be said? How would things unfold?

Jo turned off her motor and reached for the jacket she'd tossed onto the passenger seat, tenting it over her head as she climbed out. She ran toward the door that was barely visible through the downpour, managing to reach it without slipping on the mud-filled torrents running underfoot. She wrenched it open and paused for a moment inside to catch her breath and shake off the rain. Then she headed to the elevator, pressing the button after she stepped into it for the fifth-floor. ICU.

Jo found her sitting in the same waiting room Jo had occupied so recently. She wore the same blue denim jacket with the incongruous Kokopelli figure Jo had first seen her in, and her head tilted down as she flipped through a magazine. Where were her thoughts? Jo wondered. On the glossy pages in front of her? On her husband, fighting for his life just a few steps away? Or at the Hammond County Fairgrounds?

"Hello, Meg."

Meg's head jerked up, and Jo watched the range of emotions fly across her face — shock and confusion, then a flash of fear, which was instantly covered with a stony blankness. All she said was, "Jo."

Two other people who had been talking quietly with each other looked over, full of interest, and Jo walked over to Meg. "Let's go somewhere private."

Meg opened her mouth to protest, but Jo quickly said, "We need to talk."

Meg shrugged but picked up her large purse and stood, following Jo wordlessly as she led the way out and searched for an empty waiting room. She finally found one two floors down. Russ's floor. Jo went to sit on one of the tan vinyl settees, and Meg took the one opposite her. She looked at Jo questioningly, but only mildly so, her face retaining most of its stolid blankness.

Jo plunged right in. "I thought I'd save you the trouble of driving up to the fairgrounds to meet me."

Meg's eyes flickered, but her expression didn't change. "I wasn't going anywhere, Jo.

I've been waiting to see my husband."

"I think you were planning to leave in a few minutes. The fairgrounds would be a good, isolated spot for your purposes, and empty right now. The perfect place to do away with someone who was starting to figure things out."

"I don't know what you're talking about." Meg had held on to the magazine she'd been flipping through earlier, and she reopened it on her lap.

"Did one of your neighbors tell you I had been asking questions? Maybe Rick Gurney or his wife, Susan? Rick seemed anxious to come to the hospital. He thinks Kevin is a really great guy."

Meg flipped a page.

"That was pretty clever of you, Meg, to set things up as though Amy Witherspoon wanted to help me out."

Meg's eyelids quivered.

"I suppose you picked up on everything that was going on between the Michicomi vendors when I let you watch my booth for me. You probably gathered names and business cards with contact information on them, right? It was a simple matter, then, to call Gabe's home and fool his wife into passing on what she believed was a message from Amy."

"You're crazy, Jo."

"Not crazy, but pretty lucky. When I asked you to call your friend Emmy about Patrick Weeks, it was dumb luck that I handed you my cell phone to use. Emmy's phone number was then stored in it. I talked to Emmy myself, just a little while ago. She had a lot to tell me."

Meg's head jerked up, her stony expression suddenly flashing anger. "You had no right to call Emmy."

"No? Didn't I have a right to find out what you had against Linda Weeks?"

"Everyone had something against Linda! She was an awful person who ruined people's lives."

"She hurt yours pretty badly, didn't she?"

Meg closed down again, her mouth clamping shut. But her eyes had turned dark, and Jo had a good idea what memories might be running behind them.

"Emmy tossed off the story lightly," Jo said, "as though it was no big deal, just something that happened all the time in high school but didn't really matter. That's because it didn't happen to her, though. It was a very big deal to you, Meg, wasn't it?"

Meg had dropped her gaze back down to her magazine and she turned another page, but Jo doubted she saw any of it. Meg's chest was heaving.

"You pretended to me that you barely knew Patrick Weeks, but in fact you two were dating — seriously dating. Until Linda came along and stole him from you."

Meg kept her eyes on her lap as she spoke. "She could have had almost anybody else. She was one of the popular ones, part of the 'in' crowd. I never had a boyfriend until Pat. We started dating during our summer jobs at the pool, and Pat told me he liked that I was so down-to-earth. We had a special relationship."

"Until Linda ruined it."

Meg's face lifted, her eyes looking beyond Jo. "During senior year," she said, "I made the mistake of making her look silly. It was in history class, in front of her friends. She had to give a report — something to do with World War Two — and she wasn't ready for it. She tried to wing it. But I asked a question, just something that popped into my head. I didn't mean it to be sarcastic, but it came out that way and it broke everyone up. Her cliquey friends teased her about it for days afterward, plus she got a D on the report. She had to get even with me. The best way was to steal Pat."

"That must have really hurt."

Meg's eyes focused on Jo, filled with the

321

pain she must have felt all those years ago. "He was the only boy I ever cared about."

"Did you go to Patrick's furniture shop the other day?"

"I had to see him. I knew he wouldn't recognize me, and I didn't want him to. I've put on weight, but I'm going to take it off. I wanted to see what he looked like now, and he looked great. I saw his little girl too. I liked her. I didn't know about her until you told me. But Linda would have been a terrible mother. She *was,* of course, since she left her daughter and barely saw her anymore. I would be a much better mother for her. I would trim down and be like I used to be in high school. Patrick would love me again, and we could be a family, a happy family."

"But you had to get rid of your husband first?"

Meg jerked her head as though annoyed to have Kevin brought into her fantasy.

"Meg, what did you give Kevin that made him so sick?"

Meg stared back down at her magazine.

"If you tell the doctors, they can do something to help him before it's too late."

Meg stood up, slipping the strap of her large handbag onto her shoulder, and walked to the window. She stared out at the rain, her back to Jo. The water ran down the outside of the window in jagged rivulets, and Meg put her finger up to the glass to trace the path of one. "I don't want Kevin to get better," she said, her voice taking on a distant tone.

"Meg, you can't let him die."

"I should never have married him. It's his own fault, talking me into it. He should have known I would always love Pat."

"He doesn't deserve to die for that. What did you give him, Meg?"

Meg turned to face Jo, tears running down her face. "Why should he live when my life is over?"

"Your life isn't over."

"It is, Jo. All I wanted was to be with Pat. Was that so much to ask for? I did everyone a favor getting rid of Linda. You know I did. But now they'll want to punish me for it. I deserve to be thanked, but instead they'll keep me from Pat. After I've waited so long."

What could Jo say to that? Of course Meg would go to prison for murdering Linda, and of course her hopes of living happily ever after with her first love had never had a chance. But there was still the man who was fighting for his life in the ICU to think about. How could Jo get Meg to think about him? To care about him before it was too late?

Jo stood up, thinking only of talking reason to Meg, when Meg suddenly reached into her bag. She pulled out a gun and pointed it at Jo.

"Stay back, Jo!"

Jo froze. "Meg, what are you doing?"

"Don't come near me, Jo. I'll shoot you if I have to. But I don't want to. I want to kill myself. And I will, so don't try to stop me. I'll shoot anyone who tries to stop me."

"Meg, this is insane."

"Is it? Would you want to live if you were me?"

Meg had begun waving the gun, gesticulating with it. Jo's first thought was that it could go off at any time. What if someone else came into the room? Jo could try to overpower Meg, but what were the odds she could take the gun from her without it going off in the process? She suddenly thought of Russ, whose room was right down the hall. If he heard a gunshot he'd know right away what it was and his policeman's instincts would kick in, making him act. But he was in no condition to do so, and who knew what might result from that? Jo had to calm Meg down, to keep her from firing that gun. But how?

"Meg," she said, thinking rapidly, "it's not too late."

Meg stared. "What do you mean?"

"I mean, you can still be with Patrick."

Meg continued to stare, but Jo thought she saw a glimmer of hope flit through her eyes.

"He's probably been thinking of you all these years too, you know. But he doesn't even know you're here. Think how devastated he'll be if he finds out how close you were all this time."

Meg's eyes softened for a moment, but then flashed angrily at Jo. "You wouldn't let me go to him. You'd call the police the minute I left here."

"I wouldn't, Meg. But just to be sure you can take me with you. I'll drive you to Patrick."

Meg appeared to think that over, her desire to be with her lost love possibly overwhelming whatever sense of logic and reality remained. "If you tried to do anything on our way out, I would shoot you, Jo."

"I know, and don't worry. I won't. I want you and Patrick to be together. I know what it's like to lose someone you've loved. I want you to get him back, Meg."

Meg hesitated but then nodded. "You

325

walk beside me, Jo. We'll go to my car, but you'll drive. If I see you try to signal anyone, I promise I will shoot — first you, then them, and then myself."

"Understood. But it will be all right. Just let me get my jacket."

Meg nodded, watching sharply as Jo stepped back to grab her jacket and then her purse. Meg moved up beside her and slipped her gun just inside her own pocketbook. "I have my finger on the trigger, Jo," she said, and nudged Jo to begin walking slightly ahead of her, heading out of the room and toward the stairwell. Jo found herself breathing easier the farther they got from Russ, the nursing staff, and all the innocent patients and visitors that wandered the halls.

Though her own legs trembled.

CHAPTER 29

It amazed Jo, at first, how few people took any notice of them — two women whose strained expressions alone should have signaled that something was very wrong. But she reminded herself that hospitals were full of crises, although of a very different sort, and that everyone they passed must have had stresses of their own to deal with. They therefore left Jo and Meg to their own.

Their slow progress, once they'd left the building, should also have struck anyone watching as suspiciously odd — walking, not running, through the pouring rain. But apparently no one watched, and the two of them reached Meg's car unchallenged.

Once in the car's passenger seat, Meg heaved a relieved sigh. She pulled the gun out of her pocketbook and rested it on her lap, in plain view. Risky, perhaps, should anyone happen to look in, but on this rainy day not likely to happen. Jo mopped the rain off her face as best she could with her jacket sleeve, put Meg's keys into the ignition, and started their journey.

In minutes they were on the street and heading out of Abbotsville, Jo thinking rapidly to what lay ahead. She had promised Meg that she would take her to Patrick, which meant driving to his furniture shop. But Jo realized now that Pat's young daughter was likely to be there too. Bringing Patrick into this situation was bad enough, but there was no way Jo would endanger Abby.

"Meg," she said, "I'm wondering if it's the best idea to go to Pat's shop."

"I'm going to meet Pat," Meg said firmly.

"Yes, I didn't mean that that should change. I'm just remembering that his shop is in a busy part of town. There would be too many people around, people who could tell the police later that they saw the two of you take off together. It would be much better to have Pat meet you somewhere else, somewhere more isolated."

Meg didn't say anything for a while, and Jo drove — on the highway by then — and waited, wondering what else she could say to convince her.

But then Meg said, "He could come to the fairgrounds."

Jo shook her head. She had already pictured the empty expanse around the buildings there, which would make any kind of covert approach by a rescue team next to impossible. "I know you thought it would be an isolated spot to bring me to, but actually they started constructing several more buildings there right after the Michicomi show ended." A huge lie, but Jo hoped Meg would believe it. "There'll be plenty of security people around, keeping an eye on the equipment."

Jo had thought of a place to take Meg that she might agree to and that would also offer Jo hope of escaping. "I was thinking of the tobacco barn where I met Bill Ewing. He wouldn't be there, of course, with this rain. It would be very private, and it's in a very pretty spot."

Meg appeared to think it over. "Okay. Go to the barn. I'll tell Pat to meet me there." Jo glanced over and saw Meg smile slightly. Did she find the thought of a reunion at an old tobacco barn romantic? Did she truly believe Patrick would be overjoyed to hear his high school sweetheart was waiting for him and expecting him to run away with her?

Jo turned her focus back to her driving. Her next problem was finding the way to the barn. Harry had driven the only time she'd been there, and Jo's thoughts then had been on Bill Ewing more than roads. She hoped she'd be able to spot the final, barely visible turnoff while under pressure. Jo's cell phone suddenly rang from inside her purse, making both of them jump.

"Let it ring," Meg said.

"I'd better not, Meg. I asked Carrie to call me about an important shipment we're expecting for the shop. If I don't answer, she'll know something's wrong. Carrie's a real worrywart and she'll start calling people."

Meg pulled the phone out of Jo's purse and handed it to her. "Okay, but keep it short."

Jo flipped the phone open. "Carrie?"

"It's me, Aunt Jo," Charlie said, sounding incongruously cheery. "I'm at the shop. Mrs. Chatsky got the vase and all, but now she wants another one. I checked, but you only have the one. I said you'd order another, okay?"

"That's great, Carrie."

"Huh? Aunt Jo, it's me —"

"So the shipment got there all right?"

"Shipment? What ship—"

"Good. Do they need any help getting it in, Carrie?"

"Aunt Jo, what's going on?"

"Hang up, Jo," Meg said.

Jo glanced at Meg. "Okay, but make sure they don't knock off that photo I hung near the stockroom. The one that Harry took."

"Hang up!" Meg had picked up her gun and was pointing it at Jo. Jo closed her phone. Meg took it and slipped it into her pocket.

Jo looked back at the road. Would Charlie understand what she was trying to tell him? Or would he decide she was sliding into early senility, shrug, and go back to his NASCAR races?

"Pat is going to be so surprised," Meg said.

Jo glanced over and saw that Meg had quickly put aside her concern over the phone call and had taken on a dreamy look.

"It must have been so rough for him," Meg said. "Poor Pat, married to that awful Linda. She probably told him terrible lies about me at the start, things that lured him away from me."

"Yes, I suppose she did."

"But I'm sure he eventually saw through those lies as he began to see through Linda. How he must have regretted his mistake. He must have thought about me so much."

So much that he didn't even recognize

Meg when she came to his store, extra weight or not? But the last thing Jo wanted was to burst the bubble Meg was so contentedly floating in. How long, though, would it remain intact?

Jo had left the highway and driven into the farming area she recognized from her trip with Harry. Before long she spotted, with some relief, the narrow road Harry had pointed out as the site of his cousin Delroy's boyhood home. She slowed considerably, scanning the roadside for the farm road that would lead to the barn. Everything looked different because of the rain and lower light, but eventually she found it.

"We turn in here," she said.

"Here?" Meg asked, suddenly distressed. "How will Pat find this? You can hardly see it!"

"He must know this area," Jo assured her. "He's lived nearby for long enough. But I can help direct him if necessary." Jo said this in as firmly soothing a voice as she could manage. Keeping Meg calm and positive, now that they had arrived, was Jo's next priority.

They bumped along the road, Jo relieved to find its tamped-down surface still firm thanks to the overhead canopy of tree branches that deflected much of the rain.

But it also reduced much of the light, which gave Jo the feeling of driving through a dark tunnel — too much like her present situation. Jo brushed that thought aside and managed to keep her speed up, and they soon reached the area where the field opened up.

"There it is," she said as the barn came into view — to their left and not far from the dense tree line.

"Oh!"

Jo glanced over to see a glow of excitement on Meg's face. Instead of the weed-cloaked, rotting-wood barn that stood there, she seemed to be seeing an ivy-covered castle, the site of her long-awaited reunion with her lost love. Meg quickly fumbled through her purse to find her cell phone. "I have to call Pat. You have to tell him how to get here."

That bubble was suddenly in danger of being smashed to smithereens. Jo quickly said, "Let me make the call, Meg. You're so excited, and it will take so much explaining. I'll hand it over to you as soon as Pat understands."

Meg blinked at Jo. "No," she said, frowning. "I can do it." She scrolled through her list of numbers and Jo cringed, wondering what she could do if Meg became upset and erratic over Pat's response.

Jo pulled up close to the barn and turned off the ignition as Meg put her call through. It seemed as though each of them held their breath while the phone at the other end — in Patrick Weeks's furniture shop — rang. Jo thought she heard the faint sound of a voice answering, but Meg didn't respond. Instead she closed her phone.

"He's not there. I got his answering machine."

Jo exhaled.

"I forgot this was Saturday," Meg said. "He probably closes early on Saturday. We'll have to go there after all. We'll find someone who will tell us where he lives."

"No," Jo said. She had to keep Meg here. "I'm sure he's open until seven. I saw his hours posted on his door when I was there. He must be working in the back, that's all. He'll come out and check his messages. You'll have to leave one, so he can call you."

Meg looked uncertain, but she called the shop again, saying, when the answering machine's message came to its end, "Pat, it's me, Meg. Call me back right away. I have to tell you where I am." She gave her cell number and hung up.

"Maybe I should have said more?" she asked, looking doubtfully at Jo.

"You can explain everything when he calls," Jo assured her.

"What if he doesn't?"

"He will, Meg. Just give him a few minutes." Jo glanced back at the dense part of the farm road they had just come through, which was too visible from where they sat in the car. "Why don't we wait in the barn," she said. "It's getting steamy in here." As she said it she wondered if her hopes of any help coming were futile. Was the message Jo tried to give Charlie too obscure to understand? Meg had both cell phones in her possession. Could Jo somehow get one of them away and call for help without Meg noticing?

Meg still looked fretful about not having reached Pat, but she opened her door. She grabbed hold of her gun and signaled to Jo that she should get out first. Jo climbed out and hurried through the rain to the partially open barn door. She heard Meg's door slam shut and Meg's footsteps behind her as Jo dragged the barn door farther open.

They entered into the dim interior of the barn, lit only by slivers of light that came through the slatted walls. The scent of tobacco seemed to have intensified in the dampness, and Jo could hear a few drips making their way down from the leaky tin roof above. The floor of the barn was dirt and weeds, and possibly — Jo thought, uncomfortably — hiding spots for all sorts of creatures. Meg, however, seemed unaware of the seediness of the spot, only caring about bringing Pat to it as soon as possible.

Jo rubbed at her arms in an effort to ward off shivering in her wet clothes. Wanting to get Meg's thoughts off of Pat as much as possible, but also because she wanted to know, she asked, "Why did you poison Kevin, Meg? Why couldn't you have just left him?"

Meg stared at Jo, looking as though she was having difficulty remembering who Kevin was, much less why she had tried to kill him.

"I had to," she said finally, and when Jo waited for more, added, "You were trying to pin Linda's death on Pat. I had to make it look as though that photographer had done it."

"So you were willing to kill Kevin just to keep Pat in the clear?"

Meg nodded, apparently pleased to see that Jo understood.

"But," Jo said, "since you were the one who killed Linda, the best way to protect Pat would be to simply confess, wouldn't it?"

Meg scowled, impatient now with Jo's turn toward denseness. "I killed Linda so Pat and I could be together! We wouldn't be together if I was sent to prison, would we?"

Jo saw that all actions were judged justifiable by Meg by the higher good of she and Pat being reunited. "What did you give Kevin?" she asked.

Meg's face closed down. "It doesn't matter."

"But it does, Meg. Kevin could still pull out of this if the doctors know what to treat him for soon enough. There's no reason to hide it anymore, is there? By the time Kevin recovers, you and Pat will be long gone."

"I'm going to call Pat again."

Obviously it had been a mistake to mention Pat. He was the only one Meg wanted to think about. Don't bother her, she seemed to say, with lesser problems. She called the furniture shop's number but apparently got the answering machine again.

"Pat, are you there? Pat, it's me, Meg. You have to call me right away. We don't have much time." She paused, then added, "You can bring your little girl too. She can come with us — it'll be all right."

Jo could only imagine what Pat would feel once he heard those words and understood all that was behind them. Bring his cherished daughter to meet up with a madwoman? Jo looked at Meg. Not quite mad, perhaps, but on the brink. Clear thinking had obviously left her long ago, though she'd managed to camouflage it for the most part. The few people who'd encountered Meg in Abbotsville might have thought her odd, but had probably blamed it on her abusive husband. Meg had, in effect, used Kevin as an alibi for all her shortcomings.

"You were very clever, Meg, making Kevin look like a terrible person."

Meg looked up from her phone, once again appearing to have to work at understanding who Jo referred to.

"I mean," Jo said, "all those subtle hints you dropped to Ruthie that convinced her Kevin was abusing you."

Meg nodded then, her lips turning up in a small, self-satisfied smile. "It wasn't easy. I had to make it seem like things slipped out accidentally." Meg's expression turned defensive. "Maybe Kevin didn't actually beat me, but he never made me happy either! Not like Pat would have."

Poor Kevin, Jo thought. He was, in fact, the one being abused, just for being who he was — or wasn't. First Meg had chipped away at his reputation, then she'd made an attempt on his life. Which might yet prove successful — a thought that appalled Jo, and about which she could, at the moment, do nothing. Had she done the right thing, luring Meg away from the hospital to this remote spot? In the heat of the moment it had certainly seemed necessary. Meg had been ready to kill herself — which meant never giving up the secret of Kevin's poison — plus she was more than ready to shoot anyone who got in her way. Innocent people.

At least Jo had taken her away from the many hospital workers and patients — including, most important, Russ. But what could she do next, to save Kevin, and possibly herself?

CHAPTER 30

Meg had begun to pace, gun in hand, as the wait for Pat to call her back stretched out. Jo eased close to the wall facing the farm road and peeked through a slit. She couldn't see any sign of life out there, human or otherwise. The rain had slowed to a drizzle, but the light was fading. Jo began to worry that once it grew too dark Meg would insist on leaving and tracking down Pat in person.

Meg stopped and called out to Jo, "What made you call Emmy?"

Jo quickly turned away from the slit. "Emmy?"

"Yes, Emmy, my high school friend. What made you call her? Was it just from what Rick Gurney said — about Kevin?"

Jo shook her head. "No, Rick and the other neighbors weren't confirming my impression of Kevin, but I was willing to believe it was simply because they hadn't seen both sides of him. Abusers, I've heard, can be quite charming to those outside their household. It was when I went to the Abbot's Kitchen the second time and glanced again at your job application that I caught my major clue. I'd missed it the first time."

"Missed what?"

"How you had filled out your address. The first time I read it, I was focused on your street address, and the fact that you misspelled 'Abbottsville' didn't catch my attention. But when I looked at it later on — after talking with your neighbors — that misspelling popped out at me like a spatter of hot grease."

"What are you talking about?"

"How you spelled 'Abbottsville.' With two t's, just like in the anonymous letter I got that told me to get out of town. How did you put it? 'We don't need your kind in Abbottsville.' The words stuck in my head. The misspelling too."

Meg stared at Jo. "I never could get that straight. It always seemed like if Abbotsville had two b's, then it should have two t's."

Jo stared back, taking in the fact that the problem of spelling "Abbotsville" correctly was more interesting to Meg than the hurtful message she had used it in.

"I guess that was you who called me too," Jo said, "telling me much the same thing as was in the letter."

Meg actually smiled. "You didn't recognize my voice, did you, Jo? I practiced that for a while. I wanted you to think it was a man. Did you think I was a man, Jo?"

Was Meg really expecting Jo to say what a good job she had done? It seemed so, and, galling as it was to do so, if it helped keep Meg from rushing off to Patrick's place, Jo could manage it.

"You fooled me, Meg. I couldn't tell if it was a man or a woman, much less that it was you."

Meg nodded, apparently satisfied.

A cracking sound from outside made both their heads swivel toward the door.

"What was that?" Meg asked.

Jo shrugged. "A tree branch must have fallen."

Meg turned suddenly wary. She rushed to the door and peered out carefully around the edge. "Did you let someone know where we were?"

"Of course not. How could I do that?"

Meg stared back at Jo, thinking. "That phone call! Did you tell Carrie?"

"Meg, you heard everything I said. It was all about the shipment. Nothing else."

"I don't believe you. Someone's out there! I'm sure of it."

"It was just a tree branch. Or maybe an animal."

"I saw something moving. Something big."

Meg leaned her head against the inside of the door, looking at Jo but listening to what might be outside.

"Whoever's out there, stay back!" she shouted. "I have a gun and I will use it!"

Jo heard nothing but silence for several moments, broken only by the sound of Meg's and her own breathing. Then a voice called out sharply, causing both of them to jump.

"Meg Boyer, this is the police. Throw out your weapon and come out with your hands up."

"You called them!" Meg accused. Her eyes had grown huge, but worst of all she pointed the gun right at Jo.

"I didn't. Truly, Meg, I didn't call the police."

"I don't believe you! They're out there, and it's because of you. You promised! You promised you'd help me run away with Pat."

"I tried, Meg. But I didn't know you wouldn't be able to reach Pat."

"You lied to me!" Tears had sprung to Meg's eyes, tears of anger and frustration. She still pointed the gun at Jo, but her hand shook with emotion, making Jo fear an accidental trigger pull as much as a deliberate one.

Light suddenly flooded the outdoors, seeping through the slatted walls into the barn. "Meg Boyer! We have you surrounded. Throw out your weapon and come out."

Jo thought she recognized Mark Rosatti's voice, distorted though it was, by a bullhorn. Jo flashed back to Mark's description of what had gone wrong with the situation when Russ was shot. The woman who had been held hostage at that time had panicked and run, causing her frenzied boyfriend to let loose a stream of bullets, one of which caught Russ. Jo didn't want Mark, or anyone else who had come to help her, to get hurt — or worse. Jo certainly wasn't going to panic and run, but she couldn't let Meg fall apart either, causing an exchange of bullets.

What could she do to diffuse the situation? The boyfriend in Russ's situation had been drunk. Meg wasn't drunk, but her mental state wasn't far from drunkenness with its cloudy thinking. She had already swung within minutes from thoughts of suicide to giddy plans for an impossible future, to threats on people's lives. Reasoning wasn't likely to get through to her. But what would?

"You better go away!" Meg screamed. "I'll

shoot her if you try to come in here."

"You don't have to shoot anyone, Meg," Mark's voice said. "You can end this now by coming out. No one needs to get hurt."

"I'll hurt anyone I have to!" Meg cried, then said to Jo, "They probably think I don't know how to use this, but I do. Kevin got it for me, to protect myself when he was gone, and I know how to handle it. So don't think I don't."

"I never thought that, Meg," Jo said. "I could see you were expert with it. You must have practiced a lot, right? At a shooting range?"

Meg nodded.

"That was very smart of you."

Meg didn't answer, but Jo thought a bit of the wildness in her eyes had receded. She still breathed heavily, and her eyes shifted rapidly between Jo and the scene outside, as glimpsed through the slits in the wood. The blazing light made it impossible to see little more than shadows behind it, which gave the entire area a surreal look. Mark and whoever else was with him must have come through the woods and barricaded themselves just beyond the tree line. Jo could only imagine what Meg must be feeling, caught in this trap when only moments ago she had been immersed in her fantasy life.

The ring of a cell phone startled them both. It came from one of Meg's jacket pockets. Meg made no move to answer it. The ringing continued, then stopped as Meg's voice mail likely kicked in. Suddenly Meg's whole body jerked.

"That might have been Pat!"

She scrambled for the phone and flicked it open to hear the message, her expression changing quickly from excited to angry. She snapped the phone shut. Within seconds it rang again. She ignored it. Then the third cycle began. This time she opened the phone by the third ring and angrily demanded, "Stop calling me!"

Assuming it was Mark on the other end, Jo watched Meg listen for a few moments, then say, "No, I'm not going to let her go. I'd be a total fool to do that, wouldn't I?" More listening, then Meg said, "I'll tell you what I want, Lieutenant Morgan, I want everyone out there to go away! That's what I want."

Lieutenant Morgan! Jo clutched her throat and would have rushed to press her eye against one of the wall slits if it weren't for the fact that Meg was still pointing the gun at her.

"I don't want to hear about that," Meg

cried into the phone and angrily ended the call.

"That was Russ?" Jo asked. "He's out there?"

Meg shook her head impatiently. "He's at the hospital. He said Kevin was getting worse." Meg snorted. "Like I should care?"

Jo exhaled. At least Russ hadn't somehow dragged himself to the scene. But he had found another way to participate and seemed to be trying to stir sympathy in Meg for the man she'd been married to for several years. Meg had hung up on Russ, but perhaps Jo could carry on what he had started.

"Kevin wasn't a bad husband, Meg, was he?"

Meg scowled at Jo. "He wasn't Pat."

"No, of course not. But he couldn't help that, could he? I'm sure he loved you, to want to marry you. He must have seen the same things in you that Pat did. How long did you date? Very long?"

Meg frowned but shook her head. "A couple of months. I was working at a shoe store. I hated it, and I was lonely. Kevin came along and he seemed better than nothing, which is what I had at the time." Meg's face contorted. "Because of Linda."

Wanting to keep Meg's thoughts on her

husband, Jo asked, "Was this after Kevin was in the army?"

To Jo's surprise Meg's expression suddenly cleared. "I made that up," she said. "Kevin was never in the army. I just wanted you to think that was how he knew that photographer."

"I did think that. You fooled me, Meg."

"Kevin never went to meet with the guy. He didn't know anything about it. I just sent him out of town to pick up mulch for the yard. I fixed him coffee to take along, and put that stuff in it. I didn't know how fast it would work or when he would actually drink it, but I figured someone would find him, wherever he ended up. And everyone would think the photographer had poisoned him."

"That was very clever, Meg." Jo said it as smilingly as she could manage, though inwardly cringing. Jo badly wanted to ask what Meg had put in Kevin's coffee, but she was sure Meg would immediately shut down. At least now she was talking, and not about shooting Jo or anyone else.

"So Kevin was never in the army?"

Meg shook her head dismissively. "They wouldn't have wanted him."

"But he's a decent man, isn't he, Meg? He treated you well. He worked hard enough for you two to buy a house."

"Pat makes beautiful furniture. He set up his own business from scratch."

Meg's phone rang again. Jo saw the inner struggle. *Should she answer or ignore it?* When it reached the fourth ring, Meg opened the phone. "Now what?" The words were impatient, but the tone was less so. Meg's eyes suddenly grew large.

"Pat's coming? Coming here!"

Jo wondered how Russ had managed that?

"How soon will Pat be here?" Meg asked. "Yes, I'll talk to him. Of course I will!" Her face suddenly contorted. "If you're lying to me —"

Jo didn't know what Russ answered but it must have been reassuring enough since Meg's expression cleared, though it remained wary. "I don't want to talk to you anymore. I'll talk to Pat when he gets here." She closed her phone and gazed at Jo, though Jo doubted she was seeing her at all. What expectations Meg had of the imminent appearance of Pat, Jo had no way of knowing. Nor could she imagine what the police would allow Pat to say or do. Obviously, taking off with Meg would not be included, though Jo couldn't help but suspect Meg had delusions in that direction.

"Pat's on his way," Meg said.

"I heard. That's wonderful."

Meg smiled. She ran her hand through her hair, which the rain had plastered flat to her head. "I left my purse in the car," she murmured, and Jo guessed she was thinking of the brush and makeup that were stowed in it.

"You look fine, Meg," Jo assured her.

Meg looked unconvinced, so Jo added, "Pat won't care if you're not perfect, you know. He liked that you were down-to-earth, remember?"

"Yes," Meg agreed, her eyes shining. "He did." Her expression turned puzzled. "How did Linda ever get anywhere with him? She was not his type at all, with her perfect hair and her painted-on face."

Jo shrugged. "Men can be blinded sometimes."

"Yes, that's it. He was blinded. Linda was good at that. She fooled so many people, at least for a while. Poor Pat. How awful he must have felt once his eyes opened and he really saw who he was married to."

"You didn't poison Linda for Pat's sake, though, did you, Meg? I mean, you knew by the time you killed her that they had divorced."

"I hated her. All those years I hated her.

She took Pat away from me. And then I found out at the craft show that she hadn't even cared enough about him to keep him. It was like she took him just to hurt me. I finally had my chance to hurt her back." Meg smiled smugly. "I was there, you know, when her throat started closing up. I watched her being wheeled off to the hospital. It was so great. I kept my fingers crossed that they wouldn't figure out what was wrong with her until it was too late."

"So you knew she was highly allergic to peanuts."

"I overheard her talking about it to the school nurse. She said her sensitivity to peanuts was getting worse instead of better. I figured if that were true, by now she might be supersensitive and that maybe eating even one candy filled with peanut paste could actually kill her. It was worth a try, anyway."

Jo remembered believing Meg when she'd claimed to be unaware of Linda's allergy. But then Jo, and many others, had believed a lot of things about Meg that turned out to be lies. Meg seemed to have enjoyed the pretenses, as though fooling people proved how much smarter she was, rather than how devious she could be.

A voice suddenly boomed across the clearing. "Meg? Are you there, Meg. This is Pat."

Meg whirled toward the door at the sound of Patrick Weeks's voice.

"Pat! Is it really you? I'm here, Pat. I'm here."

Jo saw that Meg's face had gone through a transformation, as though she were suddenly sixteen again and her date for the big dance had finally arrived.

"Meg, they'd like you to come on out. Will you do that?"

"I can't, Pat! Not yet. Tell them to go away first. Please? Then we can talk."

"They won't go away. Not until you stop threatening to shoot people. Why don't you just throw that gun away and come on out of the barn with Miss McAllister? Okay?"

"Pat," Meg said, ignoring his words, smiling, "I keep remembering that lake we went to on our days off from the pool. Do you remember, Pat? We'd take a picnic lunch and spread out our towels and just lie there and talk for hours. Remember that, Pat?"

"I remember."

"And remember that time we rented a boat and rowed all the way out? And it started raining, but we stayed out anyway because then we were the only ones out there? It was like we were the only two people in the world. Do you remember, Pat?"

"Those were good times, Meg."

"Let's go back to that lake, Pat."

There was a long silence, and Jo could imagine Pat looking to Mark Rosatti for guidance on how to answer. Or was Russ coaching by phone from the hospital? Where was Pat's little daughter, Abby? Back in Marlsburg, Jo hoped, safely watched over by Shirley.

Finally Pat spoke again. "That was a long time ago, Meg."

"No, not so long. Everything that happened since then has been erased. Isn't it wonderful? It's like it never happened! Linda's gone. Kevin's gone. There's nothing standing between us anymore. We can be Pat and Meg again, back at the lake. The two of us, just like it used to be."

Jo thought she heard a long sigh come from Pat. Though he'd probably dropped the bullhorn away from his face, some of his reaction still came through.

"Nothing is like it used to be," he said, his voice cracking slightly. "*We're* not who we used to be, Meg. I've changed, you've changed. It's no good."

"Don't say that, Pat! We *are* the same. We have to be! I want it so badly, Pat."

353

Tears had sprung to Meg's eyes.

"Wanting something doesn't make it so, Meg. It's too late. It's all too late."

"It's *not* too late, Pat! It's not. I don't want it to be."

Silence.

"Pat? Did you hear me? It's not too late! Really, it's not too late." Meg's tears began running down her cheeks. She made no move to wipe them.

More silence, then Pat said tiredly, "Meg, why don't you just come on out like they want you to? I don't want to see you get hurt."

"But I've been waiting so long, Pat! I came here so we could finally be together. Don't ask me to give that up! I haven't changed, Pat. I haven't. Not inside, I haven't. I promise!"

Pat didn't answer.

"Pat," Meg called, "are you there? Answer me! Don't you see? It's not too late!"

The silence drew out, magnifying the few, tiny sounds of raindrops dripping from overhead leaves.

Meg backed against the wooden door. "He doesn't believe me. Why not?" she asked. "Why won't he listen? How can he do this to me?" Her voice turned hollow. "I waited so long. For nothing."

Jo said nothing, unsure what to say or do. Then, with horror she saw Meg numbly raising the gun to her own head.

"For nothing," Meg repeated.

"Meg, wait!" Jo cried. She gestured toward one of the slits as though seeing something through it. "Patrick!"

Meg's head jerked. She turned, and the hand holding her gun moved away from her head as she did so. Jo reacted instantly, leaping forward and slamming Meg's gun hand against the door. A shot burst from the gun, causing Jo's ears to ring, but the bullet flew off into the barn's eaves. Jo struggled for the gun with both hands, leaning her shoulder against Meg, but Meg fought back, punching and kicking at Jo, then grabbing at her hair with her free hand.

"Let go!" Meg cried, yanking at Jo's hair hard enough to snap her head back. Several of her kicks connected, but Jo managed to keep hold of Meg's gun arm. One particularly painful kick nearly buckled her knee. Jo snapped her own foot back with all her strength at Meg's own legs, knocking her feet out from under her.

Meg went down and the gun flew from her grasp. Jo jumped atop of Meg to keep her from scrambling after it and felt the fight suddenly go out of her.

Meg went limp. "Why didn't you let me kill myself?" she cried. She pulled her knees up into the fetal position and buried her face in her sleeves; her words came out in a high-pitched wail between sobs. "I want to die! There's nothing left. All I had to live for is over."

The sobs grew heavier as Meg lay there, curled tightly, heaving.

Jo stood and limped over to where the gun had spun. She bent down to pick it up and let her breath out in a long sigh, then looked out toward the bright lights.

They could turn them off now, she thought.

It was over.

CHAPTER 31

Her ordeal ended, Jo was rapidly surrounded by Mark and the others who insisted she be taken immediately to the hospital. She readily agreed, though not for medical attention. Her bruises could wait. What she really needed and wanted was reassurance that Russ was all right, that he hadn't badly strained himself while working on her behalf.

Once Mark understood that, he saw that she was escorted directly to Russ's room — the same one she'd last visited him in, though it was not nearly as peaceful as it had been then. The room was packed with fellow police, civilians, and medical personnel, all joyously celebrating the successful end to the hostage situation.

"So this is command central, huh?" Jo called out, standing on tiptoe just outside the doorway.

Heads turned in surprise, then cheers and

welcomes broke out. Arms engulfed her, hugging and propelling her slowly toward Russ, who sat propped up in his hospital bed, surrounded by equipment and people. Carrie was one of those people, and at the sight of Jo, she cried out and scrambled her way through to her. Carrie hugged Jo ecstatically, then immediately scolded her soundly for putting herself in such a dangerous position.

Ina Mae, Dulcie, Loralee, and Javonne also appeared from various parts of the room to surround her, confirming Jo's suspicions of who had been called on to help. Jo was happy to see them but began to wonder when she would reach the person she had first and foremost come to see.

Finally, she worked her way to Russ, who had been not-so-patiently waiting. He pulled her to him, and she sank against his good shoulder and pressed her cheek against his wonderfully scratchy one. They remained that way for a long time, not speaking, until Jo realized that the room had grown much too quiet. Peeking up, she saw far too many pairs of eyes focused on them, and she reluctantly pulled herself out of Russ's one-armed but still powerful embrace saying, "Let's resume this a little later."

Russ nodded, grinning.

"So," she said to her hovering craft shop friends, "there was a major team effort going on here, huh?"

"The lieutenant got us here lickety-split," Loralee said. "As soon as Charlie contacted the police."

"Charlie!" Jo cried. "Where's Charlie?"

"Over here, Aunt Jo." Charlie's voice came from near the window, and Jo looked to see a hand waving behind a couple of tall patrolmen. They parted to let Charlie through, and Jo hurried over to give him a big hug.

"You're my hero, Charlie!" she said. "If it weren't for you who knows what might have happened."

Charlie shrugged and grinned modestly. "It was just lucky Mrs. Chatsky wanted another vase, so that I had to call you."

"But you understood what I was trying to tell you, Charlie. I was afraid you might think I had lost my mind."

"You did throw me for a bit, but I could tell from your voice that you were really serious. I mean," he said, grinning, "I know you don't drink much, Aunt Jo. I also knew from the background noise that you were on the road. Mentioning that photo of the tobacco barn was all I needed to figure out where you were headed."

"Many people would have needed a lot more," Ina Mae said, patting Charlie on the shoulder.

"We'll have to sign this boy up for the department," an officer Jo didn't recognize said, slapping Charlie on the back.

"Let's let him get his driver's license first," Dan quipped from nearby, bringing general laughter.

Jo hated to spoil the mood, but there was an important thing she needed to know. "How is Kevin Boyer? Russ, you told Meg he was doing worse."

"That was just part of the pressure I tried to put on her. Actually, he's coming around, last I heard."

"They discovered what she had given him?"

"As soon as we knew it was Meg you were with — a couple of on-the-ball nurses gave us that information — we sent a search team to her house. They found quite a cocktail of ground-up prescription drugs and who knows what else that she'd mixed together, and rushed it to the lab for analysis. Kevin's been getting the treatment he needs ever since."

"Thank God."

"They also found some other interesting items," Carrie said, her eyebrows raised.

360

"What do you mean?"

"Copies of letters she'd printed out and was apparently sending all over town."

"Letters?"

"Anonymous letters that said much more than the one she sent you. They accused you of poisoning Linda Weeks and getting away with it, and asked if anyone wanted a murderer living in their town."

"So of course people were looking at me as though I had two heads."

"We never got one of those," Javonne said. "She must have known better than to send them to the people who really know you."

"Carrie, you said the letters were one of the things that they found at Meg's house. What else was there?"

Russ answered. "Photos of Patrick Weeks, lots of them, taken recently and when he obviously wasn't aware of it."

Jo nodded, not too surprised. "Meg told me she had gone to his shop. She didn't mention having taken her camera. Pat didn't recognize her, I know, and thought I had sent her to spy on him."

"The photos clued us in on his connection to her. That and a scrapbook full of thoughts she had written down about what their life together was going to be like. Weeks was floored to hear about it. I doubt he'd even thought about her for years. Once it sunk in what she'd done and what was happening at the barn, he was more than willing to help us."

"She must have been one sick person to do everything she did," Dulcie said.

"I can confirm that," Jo said. "She had reason to be angry with Linda, certainly, but a healthy person would have been able to deal with it long ago and move on. She nursed her grudge against Linda for years and convinced herself that her one chance at happiness lay with the man Linda had stolen from her. She really had stepped a long way from reality."

"How sad that she never got any kind of help," Loralee said. "So much misery, including her own, might have been avoided."

"People with problems of that sort," a nearby nurse said, "don't always realize they need help. They can twist things around so gradually that what starts as a defensive alibi becomes rationalization, then finally — to them — the absolute truth. And they often manage to put up a good front of normalcy so that others don't see what's churning inside them. Until, that is, something happens to break through that thin covering."

"Running into Linda started the break for

Meg," Dulcie said.

"What will happen to her now?" Loralee asked.

Everyone turned to Russ, who said, "She'll be charged, of course, and have to face those charges. It'll be up to the courts to decide what her state of mind was at the time of her crimes. The best scenario — for her — would be commitment to a mental hospital. This is still incarceration, but she would receive psychiatric treatment."

"As long as she's unable to hurt anyone else," Ina Mae said.

"Amen," several others in the crowd agreed.

The commanding voice of a nurse suddenly rose above the others. "Everyone," she said, "I'm going to have to ask you all to leave, now. Lieutenant Morgan is still recovering from surgery, remember, and needs to get some rest."

General murmurs of acknowledgment sounded, and final congratulations and good-nights were called out as people began to shuffle out.

"Harry will be pleased as punch," Javonne said to Jo on her way out, "to know that photo of his made such a difference. Someone had to stay with the boys, or he'd be here too."

"Tell Harry," Jo said, "that I owe him a terrific dinner out. Maybe at his cousin Delroy's restaurant."

"Oh," Javonne said, "and remember Harry's Uncle Ralph who lives not too far from that barn? Harry called him once he got the word about what was going on, and Uncle Ralph went out to the road to meet the police and make sure they found the way to it."

Jo grinned. "Bring Uncle Ralph to the dinner too! And Aunt Eulie. Heck, bring the whole darn family."

"Good night, Jo," Loralee said, waving as she and Dulcie were carried along by the crowd toward the door. "Get a good rest yourself, now."

"She'll need it," Ina Mae said, "to handle all the customers that will be flowing back to the store, full of apologies, once word of all this gets out."

"Knowing the Abbotsville grapevine," Jo said, grinning, "it's already out and gone around twice."

"Jo, can we drive you home?" Carrie asked as she and Dan waited for the bottleneck at the doorway to thin.

"I'll see she has an escort home," Russ said, gripping the hand Jo had slipped into his more firmly.

"We can drop you off, no trouble, Aunt Jo," Charlie piped up. "Dad, you have to swing over that way anyway to get Amanda, and —" Charlie broke off as Dan clapped him on the back and pushed him soundly toward the door.

" 'Night, you two," Dan said.

"Good night," Russ said, grinning.

The nurse who had started the whole exodus saw the last of the crowd out, then pulled the door behind herself, saying to Jo and Russ, "I'll be back with your medication, Lieutenant, but it may be a while. Things are pretty busy on the floor tonight, so I could be a very long time."

She pulled the door shut with a smile, and Jo felt Russ squeeze her hand. She turned and saw him gazing at her warmly. She smiled, swallowing the lump that had formed in her throat, aware they had both been equally relieved to find each other unharmed.

Suddenly all the worries Jo had struggled with in the past seemed miniscule. What mattered most was how much she and Russ cared for each other, feelings that had only deepened as old baggage and secrets were swept away and false barriers broken down.

Jo listened as the voices of the last of the banished visitors faded away into elevators and stairwells, then leaned toward this man who was so wonderful, so intelligent and understanding.

"Now," she asked softly, thinking of that earlier embrace that had been cut much too short, "where were we?"

DECORATED GIFT BOX

See decorated box samples on the
author's website
www.maryellenhughes.com.

Materials

Any size paper board gift box, round,
square, or oblong
Scrapbooking paper in two coordinating
colors
Scrapbooking stickers
Decoupage glue
Sponge brush
Craft knife or scissors

1. Place upper lid section of box on scrapbooking paper and measure a single piece
of paper to cover top, outer sides, and inner sides, extending about half an inch on
inside flat portion of lid. Mark with a

pencil and cut.

2. Spread decoupage glue with a sponge brush over those surfaces. Carefully fit the cut paper over lid, pressing and smoothing into place, overlapping the edge and a small amount of the flat, inner lid. Let dry.

3. Cut contrasting paper for flat, inside section of lid. Brush decoupage glue on that area and press paper in place, covering the edges of the first paper. Let dry.

4. Measure and cut one piece of paper to cover outer sides of the lower half of your box, the inner sides, and a half inch of the flat, inner bottom. Brush those sections of the box with decoupage glue and press paper into place. Let dry.

5. Cut contrasting paper for the inside bottom of the box and glue into place, overlapping the edge of the paper already glued in place.

6. Choose a scrapbooking sticker to glue onto the inside of your gift box lid. (Some come with tiny batteries to light up!) Whoever opens your beautiful box will get

a nice surprise!

Designed by Karlene Hicks, Annapolis,
Maryland

PAPER-CRAFT TIPS

1. To add a spectacular effect to your tissue paper flowers, dip the petal edges in white glue, then in glitter.

2. Add texture and interest to your picture collage with objects such as beads, plant materials, or whatever strikes your fancy.

3. If your collage arrangement is elaborate, lay it out before gluing until you're satisfied, then snap a picture before disassembling.

4. Jo started off her group with simple origami, using regular origami paper. Heavier weight papers can be used for wet folding, and foil-backed paper is recommended for more complex projects. You might also want to try "moneygami," origami using paper money!

LORALEE'S PASTA SALAD WITH SHRIMP AND SNOW PEAS

1 1/2 pounds unpeeled, medium-size fresh shrimp
16-ounce package linguine
6-ounce package frozen snow peas, thawed and drained
6 green onions, chopped
4 medium tomatoes, peeled, chopped, and drained

Dressing
3/4 cup olive oil
1/4 cup chopped fresh parsley
1/3 cup red wine vinegar
1 teaspoon dried whole oregano
1 1/2 teaspoons dried whole basil
1/2 teaspoon garlic salt
1/2 teaspoon coarsely ground black pepper

1. Cook shrimp in boiling water for 3 to 5 minutes. Drain well and rinse with cold

water. Chill. Peel and devein.

2. Cook linguine according to package directions and drain. Rinse with cold water.

3. Combine shrimp, linguine, and vegetables.

4. Mix dressing ingredients together in a small jar, cover, and shake well, then pour over shrimp mixture, tossing gently.

5. Cover and chill at least 2 hours.

Serves 10.

ABOUT THE AUTHOR

Mary Ellen Hughes is the author of *Wreath of Deception* and *String of Lies,* the first two Craft Corner Mysteries, as well as two other mystery novels and several short stories. A member of Mystery Writers of America and the Chesapeake Chapter of Sisters in Crime, she has long been fascinated with both mysteries and crafts and enjoys being able to combine them. A native Milwaukeean, she presently lives in Maryland with her husband, Terry. You can visit her website at www.maryellenhughes .com.

The employees of Thorndike Press hope you have enjoyed this Large Print book. All our Thorndike and Wheeler Large Print titles are designed for easy reading, and all our books are made to last. Other Thorndike Press Large Print books are available at your library, through selected bookstores, or directly from us.

For information about titles, please call:
    (800) 223-1244

or visit our Web site at:
    http://gale.cengage.com/thorndike

To share your comments, please write:
    Publisher
    Thorndike Press
    295 Kennedy Memorial Drive
    Waterville, ME 04901